To
Priscilla,
I always look forward
to seeing you at bookclub.
Carol
12-10-17

MW01535662

TEACHING MYSTERIES 201:

THE STRIKE

A NOVEL BY:
CARYL DIERKSEN

Copyright © 2017 by Caryl Dierksen
ISBN-10: 1977744621
ISBN-13: 978-1977744623

All rights reserved. No part of this book may be reproduced or transmitted in any
form or by any means, electronic or mechanical, including photocopying, recording,
or by any information storage and retrieval system, without permission in writing
from the copyright owner.

This is a work of fiction. Names, characters, places and incidents either are the
product of the author's imagination or are used fictitiously, and any resemblance to
any actual persons, living or dead, events, or locales is entirely coincidental.

This book is dedicated to my biggest fan

and most loving supporter, my mother,

Marjorie Hahn Dierksen

(1920—2016)

PROLOGUE
September 8, 1972

Dying is a wild night and a new road.
　　　　　　　　—Emily Dickinson

The dying time comes on a wild night.

Who can say when the murderous impulse begins? Who can say when the act becomes inevitable?

There is a murderer and a victim. The victim—defined by new-found strength, purity of heart. The murderer—defined by desperation, blindness to any option but violence.

Traveling separate ways, both veer off course onto a new road, the same road, and that changes everything. One strike, and they will be forever connected.

I have no choice. I have to do this, the victim says.

I have no choice. I have to do this, the murderer says.

The murderer whispers a name. The victim hears it, turns too late. A weapon looms. The victim looks death in the eye. An arm is raised; the weapon strikes, landing hard.

The physical pain lasts but a moment. Then a body tumbles through the air, down and down and down.

A soul rises, up and up and up.

CHAPTER 1
August 31, 1972

"Hey, when are you teachers going on strike?"

The question, lobbed from the back of my classroom, was one I had been ducking all day. Finally, I had made it to the last class of the longest first day of school in my three-year teaching career. I was hot, tired, and cranky; my juniors were too.

As much as I wanted to, I couldn't ignore the strike question. I gathered the remnants of my patience and parroted what the faculty had been instructed to say. "My purpose today is to get the year off to a good start. I will be discussing only academics and classroom expectations."

A boy in the front row wasn't willing to let go of the question that easily. "Come on, Miss Jackson. That's exactly what my history teacher said last period. Did they brainwash you guys or something?"

I took a closer look at him. He was wearing—honestly—a *Re-elect Nixon in '72* button on his white shirt, a skinny black tie, and black dress slacks. His one and only concession to the late-August heat was a pair of scuffed Jesus sandals. Surrounded by classmates of both sexes clad in floor-dusting bell-bottoms and T-shirts, he looked like the social outcast he most likely would turn out to be.

"Good one, Gordo," said a snickering boy sitting by the windows. "By-the-by, love your shoes." I watched the guys sitting near him perk up, looking hopeful. Probably for something entertaining to happen. I did a double take. Identical twins? Great.

"The name's Gordon. As you know, Cliffie," said the first guy.

I glanced at my seating chart, hoping the antagonists would be split up by alphabetical order. With two years of teaching under my belt—and enjoying my newly awarded tenured status—I was confident I could spot a problem early enough to head it off.

That eighth-hour class should have been a snap because it was my second time through American Literature Survey. The other section, which met first hour, had gone smoothly enough, but all bets are off during the periods after lunch. I could already see that this was going to be *the* class.

With each hour of the day, the heat and humidity in the school had risen a notch. My room's ancient, cement-block walls, high ceiling, and tall windows thrown wide open were not doing much to keep us cool. It didn't help that the class filled every single desk in the room. The kids' sweaty bodies were literally elbow to elbow.

I handed out my syllabus and list of classroom rules; then I braced myself. "So this class is called ALS?" asked a girl staring at the name on the handout. A girl the seating chart told me was named Candy said, "That's dumb—just three letters." I watched her chomp on the wad of gum in her mouth, reminding myself to check that it didn't end up under her desktop.

Before I could say anything, a thin, mousy-looking girl with Coke-bottle glasses interrupted. "Excuse me, but Miss Jackson just explained why it is called ALS. The A and the L are for American literature. The S stands for survey, which is a type of English class that is structured chronologically and includes representative samplings from the literature of the various time periods and movements."

All heads swiveled toward her, most with their mouths open, as I'm sure mine was. "Who the heck are you anyway?" the boy by the windows—Cliff—asked.

"Shut up. She's new." I was pleasantly surprised when the gum-chewer stuck up for the new girl. But then Candy ruined the effect by blowing a bubble so large it popped all over her nose. I shot her the teacher stare, and the gum went back in her mouth.

"Well, I can see that she's new," Cliff said. "I've never run into a talking encyclopedia before."

"I'm Lois," the new girl said in a near whisper. "Lois Mohn from Toledo."

That set off Cliff and the twins again. Gradually, silence returned as I calmly—at least that was the look I was going for—stared down the boys.

Cliff refused to make eye contact with me, turning toward the window. With the light hitting his face from that angle, I noticed a shadow on his left cheek. Could it have been a fading bruise?

I handed out textbooks and assignment sheets and then sailed into my introduction to the class. But when I began talking about Puritanism, the first unit of the course, I could see their attention waning. I looked up from my notes to find most of them using my syllabus to fan themselves. I quit talking and gave them the last few minutes of the period to begin reading the next day's assignment, an essay about Puritan beliefs.

ALS was not an easy course to teach. The readings came in chronological order, with the older ones, those the kids had the most trouble relating to, stacked at the beginning. Later on, the reward for our perseverance would be delving into Hemingway, Fitzgerald, and Faulkner. The course content was presented to me, and I was not free to alter it. Having tenure made no difference when it came to school-board approved curriculum.

Most of the kids opened their books lazily, some yawning as they glanced at the first page. Cliff, though, didn't even go through the motions. He put his head down on his desk and, moments later, was snoring. I walked over, startling him awake. Yes, he definitely had a bruise on his cheek. He had probably shot off his mouth to the wrong person. Then I looked down and frowned at a sweat-smeared spot on the desk where his face had been resting.

The bell rang, and he sprang from his seat and flew toward the door. "Hold on a minute, Cliff," I said, not catching him until he was halfway out of the room. "I want to talk to you."

He turned in place and scowled at me. I opened my mouth to speak, but he beat me to it. "I gotta go catch my bus. Besides, don't you know who my dad is? Haven't you heard about how he got my brother's grade from old lady Sadie changed?" And he was gone.

Who his father is? He got a grade changed? I shook my head. I would deal with Mr. Cliff Pendling the next day. I found my bottle of Smut Off and wiped his desk clean for the timid girl who would have to use it the next morning.

I kicked off my heels and limped over to the nearest window, hoping to catch a breath of air. My sleeveless linen dress was the coolest one I owned that had a mid-knee hem length, a requirement of the dress code for women teachers. I lifted my long brown hair off my neck, fanned myself with a leftover worksheet, and ran a finger under the chain of my peace symbol necklace.

Though the Age of Aquarius had technically ended by 1972, change came more slowly to conservative little Hancock, Illinois. The '60s still held a strong grip on everything from our style of clothing to our music to our language. The peace movement was still hanging on, but then so was the war in Vietnam.

———

It was only the first day of school, but I was already missing Chrissie. I shook my head, remembering all the times I had run down the hall to her room, anxious to share news both good and bad, laughter and tears, with my best friend.

From the beginning, Chrissie had had a harder time mastering the challenges of teaching than I had. She had struggled with discipline, especially with immature boys in the required classes that she taught. It didn't help that she was pretty, petite, and soft-spoken.

So when the home economics teacher announced her retirement the previous spring, Chrissie applied for a transfer. With her minor in the subject, she got the job. Unfortunately, the home ec room was way across the building.

Bud Nolan stuck his head in my door and said, "Hey, Andrea. Ready for our traditional first-day caffeine fix with Chrissie?"

I smiled and nodded happily. "I'll be right behind you. I just have to grab some work and lock up. How about The Grounds in twenty minutes?"

"Right on. You seen Chrissie today? She's going, isn't she?"

"Sure. She'll be there."

Whistling, Bud continued down the hall. What a change. It was hard to believe that two years earlier, Bud—then also a first-year English teacher—had nearly lost his job when his substance abuse problem came to light. But his God-given talent for relating to teenagers and faithful attendance at twelve-step meetings had put his problems in the past. By all appearances, he had turned his life around.

On my way to the office, I walked by Chrissie's former room, now Jennifer Sweeney's. It was already dark. Our principal, George North, had decided to save money by replacing Chrissie with a part-time teacher. Jennifer taught only three classes during the middle of the day, so I didn't expect to see much of her.

I ducked into the office to check my mailbox, where I found an avalanche of pink schedule-change forms. "Let me guess," said Bud behind me. "More students added to your classes than dropped."

"No," I said, pausing to check the last one. "Worse. All adds, no drops at all."

"Yeah, looks like bigger classes again this year, that's for sure. I'd ask the janitor for more desks—if we had a janitor."

———

The Grounds, a coffee shop on Hancock's town square, was the teachers' unofficial hangout. In the early '60s, the original owners, so the story went, had named it Grounds for Matrimony, hoping to attract a following of young singles. But since Hancock was a far cry from a hotbed of swinging singles, it ended up with a shortened name, The Grounds, and an expanded clientele including coffee lovers of all ages and marital states.

As usual, the coffee house was doing a brisk late-afternoon business. It took me a minute to spot Chrissie in a booth at the back of the room. Seated across the table from her, their backs to me, were two curly gray heads, one with tight ringlets, the other with looser sausage curls. That could only be Sadie and Sarah, the two most senior teachers in the English department.

My first year, I had wondered if these close friends were also a couple. As I got to know them, I learned they were just very close friends. If anything, they both appeared married to their jobs.

They had shocked the entire school in June when they announced that they would retire after this year. Not that they weren't old enough. Both had to be well over the official retirement age of sixty-five. I halfway assumed they had opened the school in the 1920s, and I couldn't imagine it without them.

"Hi, ladies. How was the first day of your last year of teaching?" The minute the words were out of my mouth, I wanted to take them back. Both became teary-eyed at my question.

"Well, it was bittersweet, I guess you could say," Sadie said, and Sarah nodded. I had always considered them remarkably sturdy, though older, women. But that day they looked tired and somehow slighter than I had noticed before.

Sadie gestured for me to come closer, and I stooped down beside her. "Dear, do you have a student named Cliff Pendling in ALS?" she whispered.

"Yeah, I sure do. Unfortunately."

"Watch out for his—"

We were interrupted when Bud walked up. Sarah and Sadie slipped out of the booth to make room for him. "I think we'll be off," Sarah said. "We don't want to intrude on you young people."

"Don't be silly," Chrissie said. "You don't have to run off. Why don't we get a bigger table so you can join us?"

"Wait, Sadie—" I said, but she had already moved out of earshot. What had she started to tell me about Cliff?

"No, no," Sarah said. "We'll be on our way and let you enjoy yourselves."

I sighed as I kicked off my shoes under the table and settled back into the cushy leather seat. "It almost looks like they're bummed to be retiring," Bud said. "If I ever get to that point, I'm gonna be hooting and hollering when the rest of the world goes back to school without me."

"Yeah, but what else do they have in their lives?" Chrissie asked. "Teaching has been everything to them for so many years. What will they do?"

"I have no idea," I answered. "Maybe sub? But, Chrissie, how was home ec?"

"So much better than English—I can't believe it," she said with a wide grin. "My girls were good, and most of them actually seem interested in cooking and sewing. It was a fab first day. I just hope it continues."

Bud didn't look as happy as Chrissie. "I don't know about you two, but the kids asked me if we were going on strike every damn period."

"I know. Me too," I sighed. "It would have been a decent day except for that. Well, that and my last class. Man, I wish I still had prep the last period of the day. I didn't realize how good I had it our first year."

"What?" Bud said with a grin. "Yeah, that year was a real piece of cake for you. You didn't have a care in the world."

Bud was known for his dry, sarcastic sense of humor. My

nightmarish first year actually had included the attempted murder of a student, a class that endangered my job by trying to investigate the crime, and a violent man holding the class and me hostage. Somehow, I managed to survive it and end up stronger, with my love of teaching intact. But I wished I could have made it through all of that without becoming the Nancy Drew of Hancock High.

After a pause, Bud said softly, "I screwed up a lot more than you did."

"But it all turned out fine," I said. "Especially you, Bud. Who would ever think you used to have an addiction problem?"

He held up a hand before I had finished the sentence. "There's no such thing as *used to have* an addiction problem. It's a lifelong battle."

"We know, Bud," Chrissie chimed in. "But you've completely turned things around. Now you're such a teaching pro that Susan is having her student teacher work with you."

"Nah…" he said as a pink flush rose from his collar. "Julie will just be with me for one class. She's really Susan's student teacher."

"You know," I said, "It's almost like there's a rule that difficult school years have to alternate with easier ones. Last year was the exact opposite of our first one, as peaceful and uneventful as I could ask for. And I'm sure glad it was because this one looks like it's going to be another doozy. What do you think? Is there really a chance of a strike?"

"I sure hope not," Chrissie said. "I would feel so guilty if we went on strike, like we were walking out on the kids. I can't believe all the older teachers are in favor of it."

"Just what I was thinking," I said. "I don't know how I could sleep nights. And you know what else? Tom says it's against the law for teachers to strike. And because it's illegal, tenure might not protect our jobs. Of course, he's a cop, not a lawyer. We should check with someone else. I mean, in case it comes down to a strike vote at the union meeting next week."

Chrissie looked shocked. "Oh, dear, I didn't know any of that." She paused and, with her eyes lowered, said, "I don't like being so selfish, but I'd hate to have a strike interfere with my new life. Starting a marriage and teaching a new subject are plenty for me to handle right now. Not to mention losing our total income since we both teach in the district. I just wish Rob was on tenure too. And he would be if he hadn't been drafted and gone to Vietnam. This is really not a good time to be a first-year teacher."

"I have mixed feelings too," Bud said. "I mean, I'd probably be willing to strike if that's what it takes to keep that asinine morals clause from ending up in the new contract. You know how I am. No one better tell me how to live my life unless it directly affects my teaching. And that includes the school board."

"I totally agree, Bud." I said. "I mean, don't they know there's a sexual revolution going on out in the real world?

There's something wrong if a wholesome farmer's daughter like me could lose my job over my relationship with Tom."

"Yeah, I always felt like Rob and I were being watched," Chrissie said. "But it all goes away once you're married. So when are you going to get respectable like me and tie the knot?"

The question took me off guard. "Uh, who knows? It takes two to make that decision, and I'm not sure…"

Bud saved the awkward moment. "Well, of course I wouldn't want a strike to drag on so long that we missed a paycheck or anything. Okay, plenty of time to think about that later. What have you chicks got planned for tonight?"

"I want to get home and get dinner started," she said. "Tom comes home from football practice famished, and I'd like to surprise him with one of his favorites, my spaghetti and Italian meatballs."

"Lucky dog," Bud said. "Looks like a Big Mac on the way to a meeting for me."

"I see a frozen dinner in my immediate future," I said.

"Way to go, Snoopy Andie," Bud said. "Always the gourmet cook."

"Bud, you are such a pain, using both of those awful nicknames back to back. You know that Dad called me Snoopy because I loved Charlie Brown's dog when I was a kid. And now that I'm all grown up, I'm trying to leave the nickname *Andie* behind me too."

"Aw, c'mon. One of many reasons you love me." He flashed

me the megawatt Bud smile. "Okay then, see you fellow rooks tomorrow. And lighten up, for Pete's sake. Peace out!"

Bud had called us *rooks* during our first year. Hearing it again brought a smile to my face. Despite its challenges, dangers even, our first year of teaching now seemed like a long-ago, simpler time.

CHAPTER 2
August 31

As I walked up to the back door of my little cottage, I heard a thud from inside. I opened the door and stepped in, held out my arms, and braced myself. A large orange ball of fur launched off the kitchen table and hurtled toward me. "Marmalade!" I said, catching and hugging my tomcat. "I missed you today, boy. How's my best guy?"

The past spring, I had moved from my tiny upstairs apartment to this four-room Victorian cottage a couple of blocks from the square. It wasn't very big, just a living room, kitchen, one bedroom, and an old-fashioned bathroom. None of the rooms was large, but they were cozy. I had often walked by the place and had coveted it for months. The day I saw a moving van in the driveway, I asked the departing tenant for the landlord's name and number.

Within days, I had convinced him to let me have a pet and signed a lease. The Iowa farm girl in me could no longer exist without an animal companion. The next day Marmalade and I had chosen each other at the local animal shelter.

My stomach's growling must have tipped Marm off that it was time to eat, and we both headed to the kitchen. I served his dinner before peering into the fridge in search of my own. Finding nothing of interest but a bottle of Chablis, I reached for a well-worn takeout menu from my favorite Chinese restaurant.

The line was busy when I tried to call in my order, so I sat back, took a long sip of the chilled wine, and felt myself begin to unwind. Starting the school year with chicken chop suey and white wine was a tradition for Chrissie and me, dating back to our momentous first day of teaching. We were already well on our way to a lifelong friendship, and it was nights like that one that sealed the deal.

I knew I should try again to call in my order, but I didn't reach for the phone. The food would be delicious, as it always was, but eating it without Chrissie wasn't going to be nearly as much fun. I sighed. Time had moved on, and now she was a married lady while I was…what?

Not married, not engaged, but going on two years of dating a man who suited me perfectly. Tom and I had met the fall of my first year when he investigated an attack on one of my students at Hancock High. Outside of official business, our first talks were about books. I was attracted by the idea of a policeman who read as much as my English-major friends and I did. Our discussions about books and ideas taught me a lot about him. And I liked what I learned—a lot.

I hadn't dated too much before Tom, so I enjoyed that phase of our relationship. In the beginning, neither of us was in a hurry to make things more formal.

But lately, every time I saw Chrissie's wedding picture on her desk, I felt a twinge of envy. "Your time will come," she had told me more than once. "Rob and I made it to the altar first, but that doesn't mean that you won't get there too."

A tap on my back door interrupted my thoughts. Tom was the only one who tapped that way, but he was on duty. I hurried to the door and there he was, tall and wonderful and sweet and handsome in his dark blue uniform. He leaned down to kiss me while transferring two bags from his arms to mine.

"What a nice surprise, Tommy! I was just thinking about you. What are you doing here? What's in these bags? What—"

"Hey." His deep blue eyes twinkled as he laughed. "Slow down, Andie. I'm taking an early dinner and thought you might be available to share it with me. Do you, by any chance, like chicken chop suey and eggs rolls? Hey, you haven't already called in your order, have you?"

"Nope. I hadn't gotten around to that." I set the bags on my kitchen table and gave him my biggest hug. "Tommy, you are the best, most thoughtful man I've ever known." He flashed the smile I had loved from the beginning.

"I was thinking you might be missing Chrissie about now, and I hope you'll settle for my company instead, Andie."

Andie. Hearing the nickname reminded me of the name game we had made up when we first met. Thomas Jefferson and Andie Jackson, a match for the history books, he always said.

The smell of the food made my stomach growl. "Let's eat. I'm starved."

It was fabulous—good food, good company, good conversation. Finally, all that was left was the fortune cookies. "You go first," he said. I broke the cookie open and picked out the slip of paper.

"'You are facing a new beginning. Make wise choices and you will succeed.' New beginning? I already know it's the start of a new school year. Big deal. I hope yours is better."

He fished out his fortune, skimmed it, and laid it down.

"Well…?"

"Yeah, mine's nothing special either."

"Come on. Read it to me."

He picked it up, cleared his throat, and read in a monotone, "Don't let your dreams slip away. Follow your heart."

"Oh, Tommy, I think that's sweet. And it's good advice— for both of us."

When I didn't get a response, I said, "Don't you think it's time to talk about our future? I'm ready to, if you are."

An awkward silence followed. Clearly, he was searching for words. "Andrea…I don't want you to take this the wrong way. I love you. I do. This has been the best two years of my life."

"But…?"

"But I'm not quite ready to have this conversation. I will be…in the future. But for now, can't we just go on like we have been? I'm happy. Aren't you?"

I hesitated, trying not to let my disappointment show. "Yes, I'm happy. But I'd be happier if I knew where we were heading. If anywhere."

"It's just that this feels kind of rushed. We both have so much going on with our careers. I haven't had a promotion yet. That worries me. I'm still waiting for the right case to come along, one where I can prove myself. And, when it does, I have to go all out. So, please, be patient a little longer. Just a little."

"Okay, Tommy."

"Andie, this is terrible timing, but my break is over, and I have to get back on duty. Are we still okay?"

"We are."

After we kissed goodbye and he left, I allowed myself one deep, heartfelt sigh. He loves me, I told myself. He still wants to date me. He can picture us together in the future. He's just not ready to think about marriage yet. I could live with that if I had to. For now.

Then I settled down to prepare for the next day. I skimmed the first chapter in *Of Mice and Men* for Freshman English. It would be fun hearing my kids' first impressions of George and Lennie. I loved it when one of my favorite books turned out to be one of theirs too.

I yawned and was thinking of heading to bed when the phone rang. "Mrs. Jackson?" a man's voice barked.

"This is Miss Jackson," I said, all politeness. "How can I help you?"

"I believe you are my son's English teacher. Cliff Pendling? According to his schedule, he is in your eighth-period class. Oh, yeah, this is Wayne Pending of course."

"Yes, he is, Mr. Pendling." Why was he was calling me on the first day of school, and at home no less?

"I want to nip any possible problems in the bud. This afternoon I had a call from one of Cliff's other teachers complaining about his behavior in her class today, and I didn't appreciate it. If the woman can't manage her class on the first day, she must be a very poor disciplinarian."

I hated it when parents complained to me about my colleagues, even when I suspected the criticism might be justified. "I don't want to be rude," I said calmly, "but what does that have to do with me?"

"Well," he huffed, "I don't want any more surprises. If Cliff needs to be corrected, my wife and I want to be involved from the beginning. Do you understand my point?"

Honestly, I didn't. Isn't that what the other teacher had done? Notified him of a problem right away? Besides, Cliff's behavior and attitude had been the worst of any of my kids that day.

"I'm finished with this now. I will expect your cooperation on this. And—oh, my wife wants to say something. I'm putting her on now."

Without giving me a chance to respond, he was replaced by a whiny female voice on the line.

"This is Natalie Pendling." I heard a door close in the background as she said, "I agree with everything my husband just told you…but sometimes he can be a little abrupt. He has so much responsibility at work. So many people depend on him and respect him that it can be difficult."

I wondered exactly what he did for a living but didn't want to extend the conversation any longer than necessary.

"Anyway, I want you to know that, of course, we support our schools," she continued. "But we have to put our sons first. How is Cliff doing in your class?"

"Well, since you ask, Cliff might be heading toward a problem in my class. For one thing, he fell asleep near the end of the period. Does he sometimes have trouble adjusting to the school routine in the fall?"

"But it's just the first day of school. Don't you teachers give the kids a few days to get back on schedule?" Her whining was testing my patience.

"I don't think expecting my students to stay awake is unreasonable, even on the first day." *Listen to me,* I thought. *I would never have been brave enough to say that to a parent my first year.*

I didn't want to get into a full-blown argument, so I told her I would call her right away if Cliff showed any more signs of problems.

"That will be fine." She ended the call without a word of thanks.

"Yikes! Some people…" I said to Marmalade. He opened one eye and then returned to his nap. Still shaking my head, I tried to picture the woman who would go along with that voice. But I couldn't do it.

CHAPTER 3

September 1

The memo I had been dreading landed in my mailbox a couple of days later. An update on negotiations, it was too detailed and too serious to read in the office. I almost missed a second memo lying beneath it. A new custodian had been hired, and he was someone I knew and liked, a former student named Billy Gannet. At least that was good news.

I stuffed the papers in my book bag and headed to my room. It wasn't until lunch that I had time to concentrate on the negotiations update. Once I had finished reading it, there was no need to walk to the cafeteria. My stomach was tied in knots.

Union president Harvey Linck reported that negotiations with the school board had come to an impasse. There had been no progress on the crucial issues of salary, class size, and a morals clause in the contract. Their salary offer was a two percent raise. But to lower class sizes, more teachers would have to be hired, and the board would take the two percent raise away from us to cover their salaries. As for the morals clause, the board demanded language that would allow it to discipline or dismiss any teacher considered morally unfit.

I was shaking my head and muttering under my breath as I read. This was truly unacceptable, but what could we do about it? The next paragraph answered my question. Harve, as his friends called him, wanted us to show up at the following Tuesday's board meeting to demonstrate support for our team and its efforts to win a better agreement.

Harve had been president of the union for as long as I had been at Hancock, but our paths rarely crossed. All I knew about him was that he taught wood shop and that several years earlier he had coached the boys' swim team to a sectional championship. I hoped that he was competent enough to lead us through such dangerous times.

On my way out of the building after school, I came upon a group talking with Harve in the hall. Susan was asking, "Is the next step a strike vote, then?"

"No. We aren't to that point yet," Harve said. There were audible sighs of relief at his words. "We'll see if they respond to our presence at the meeting. They may not realize how much support we have from the faculty."

"Okay, what if that doesn't work?"

"Then we meet to decide our next move," Harve said. "Let's take it one step at a time."

———

Tom had the day off, so I wasn't surprised to find his Jeep in my driveway. He was stretched out on my couch, sound asleep, with Marmalade curled up on his stomach. I doubted that either was watching the Cubs game on the TV. I went over and turned down the volume.

"Hey, it's Marm One," Tom said in a sleepy voice as he stirred. "Marm Two has been keeping me company while I waited for you."

Shortly after I adopted Marmalade, Tom had come up with the nicknames. "It's perfect," he said when I told him what I had named my cat. "The schoolmarm and the orange tomcat. Hey, did I say tomcat? I just noticed my name even works into the deal."

"Come over here and sit with me," he said, patting the couch. "I need to know that we're okay."

"We're okay," I said, squeezing between him and Marm. It was the first peaceful moment I had had all day.

"How was your day? Anything new with negotiations?" he asked.

Sometimes I was sure the man could read my mind. "Um, yeah."

"Oh, no. Please tell me you're not going on strike."

"No, nothing that serious yet. We are going to the school board meeting Tuesday night, and then the negotiating team is going to give it another try after that."

"Sounds like I won't have to be arresting you or Chrissie or any of your rabble-rousing friends for a while, then."

"Now, Tom…" I felt my peaceful mood slipping away.

"Just kidding, Andie. Just kidding."

I wasn't so sure about that. Immediately, I changed the subject. "Hey, I had a surprise today. I met our new custodian."

"Glad to hear they got one. Is it anyone I know?"

"Yes, it's Billy. You know, Billy Gannet, from my Mystery Stories class my first year?"

"Sure, I remember him. Lonely kid who lived at the children's home, right? You really made a difference in his life."

"Thanks for saying that. I hope it's true. Anyway, I'm happy I'll be seeing him again. He'll probably be a good custodian. I've never had a student more eager to please his teachers."

———

A few minutes after Tom left, the phone rang. "Hi, Andrea," Chrissie said. "Is Tom there? Am I interrupting anything?"

"No, he just left. I'm glad you called, though. There's something I need to talk to you about. But, hey, did we win the game?"

"Sure did. By a landslide. Rob and his head coach are ecstatic. But, to tell you the truth, I'm kind of worried."

"About the memo on negotiations?"

"Yeah, that definitely. But I called because of Bud. Have you noticed anything unusual about him?" Chrissie asked.

"Well, now that you mention it, yesterday I overheard two of my girls talking about him being late to their class. If it were anyone else, I wouldn't think much of it, but with him..."

"Yeah, he was late this morning too. I'd hate to think he was backsliding."

I thought for a moment. "You don't think it's pre-strike stress, do you? But he didn't seem particularly upset the last time we talked about it."

"No, he didn't. But remember, there's usually a lot going on under the surface that Bud doesn't show. Oh, Andrea, I just wish the contract would get settled and we could have a normal school year. Now what did you want to ask me?"

"I had another run-in with Cliff today, and I wanted to get

your take on a couple of things. First off, do you happen to know what Wayne Pendling does for a living?"

"Well, yeah," she said, "I thought you knew. He owns Hancock Die Cast. It's the biggest factory in town."

"Ah, that explains why his wife and son make it sound like he's the biggest hotshot in town. Then here's my other question. Today Cliff said something I could hardly believe. Did you hear anything last spring about Sadie having a kid's parents try to get a failing grade overturned? Supposedly, North changed her F to a D-."

"Wow, I don't think so. Can North even do that? I thought our final grades went onto the kid's permanent record and that was that."

"Me too. But not according to Cliff. He claimed his older brother was the kid in question, and their dad got North to change the grade so Wayne Jr. could graduate with his class."

"Wait, Andrea. I *do* remember hearing something about Sadie having trouble with a belligerent parent at spring conferences. But that was a couple months before final grades. I think it ended up in North's office, though. I bet it was the same family. You don't remember that?"

"No, I must have been so booked up with appointments that I missed the whole thing. Man, that's awful. Poor Sadie. Gosh, I sure hope I don't become the next Pendling family target."

CHAPTER 4

September 5

The parking lot was already packed half an hour before the school board meeting was to start. I was lucky to find one small space for my Beetle.

I hurried to the library, where a large crowd filled most of the chairs. I didn't see Chrissie, Rob, or Bud, so I went to the front of the room, the only place I could find four empty seats together.

It looked like most of the faculty was there, as well as some parents and a few students. I spotted Cliff sitting between a tall, thin red-headed woman and a bald man with a small frame covered in marshmallowy flab. So that had to be Cliff's parents, I thought, the ones who had called me at home to complain.

Harve and the rest of the negotiating team were in the front row, almost directly ahead of me. He certainly did not look like a union leader, at least not my idea of one. He was a couple of inches shorter than my five ten and had a wiry build. His brown hair was beginning to thin on top, and he wore those half glasses for reading. If it was possible to combine nerdiness with cockiness, that was Harve.

Chrissie and Rob slipped into two of the seats I had saved. "Where have you been?" I asked. "Bud's not here either."

"We were watching the news. Didn't you hear?" she asked. "The trouble at the Olympics in Munich?"

"No. What's going on?"

"A Palestinian group, Black September, has taken some Israeli athletes hostage. They're demanding that their prisoners in Israeli jails be released or…else."

Shocked, I was about to ask Chrissie another question when an expectant hush fell over the room. All eyes shifted to the table in the front where the school board and superintendent were seated. The only board member I recognized was Mrs. Jenkins. I had talked with her a couple of times my first year of teaching when her daughter, Peggy, was in my Mystery Stories class.

A small man, identified by a nameplate in front of him as Ray Dalby, president of the board, cleared his throat. He winced as he leaned forward in his chair to speak into the microphone in front of him. "I hereby call the meeting to order."

The board quickly approved the minutes of the previous meeting. Then Mr. Dalby said, "Next up is communications from the floor. If anyone would like to address the board, step up to the podium, speak into the microphone, and state your name and your business." He glared at the large crowd, almost daring anyone to take him up on the offer.

After a long pause, a man walked up, gripped the podium, and said, with visible anger, "Our son is a senior and a varsity football player. It's early, but the team is undefeated so far. This is the best team we've had in years. So my question is this: Is it true that games scheduled during a strike can't be made up? That they'll be forfeited? And that there won't even be any practices?"

Chrissie and I both turned toward Rob, who nodded so slightly that no one else would have noticed.

Dalby glared at Harve, who apparently stared back, neither willing to deliver the unpopular truth. There would be no extracurricular activities if classes were canceled due to a strike.

It looked as though no one else was going to speak when finally Harve walked to the podium. "I'm Harvey Linck, president of the teachers union and head of the negotiating team." I wanted to turn around to see how the crowd was reacting, but I didn't.

"The teachers have been patient," Harve said. "That's the first thing you need to know. We came to the negotiating table with a fair and reasonable proposal in May, with plenty of time to settle things before the school year started. And what did the board and their lawyer do? Stalled us, nitpicked our proposals, took a month-long break for their vacations. They acted like there was all the time in the world. And that's how we ended up here, in the second week of the school year without a contract.

"And there's more. The board is ignoring our pleas for smaller classes, something that would directly benefit our students. They are trying to cram a morals clause down our throats, something no one else in this town has to obey to keep their jobs. They refuse to give us a fair raise, one that they have all but admitted they can afford to pay. Why? That's the question, isn't it? Why?"

He sat down, and everyone in the room waited to see what the other side would say. Harve's points were good ones. They were making me a bit more comfortable with the idea of striking. I glanced around the room, finding other thoughtful faces.

Dalby pushed himself to his feet and limped to the podium. His face glowed a bright red, whether from anger or high blood pressure, I didn't know.

"What a bunch of poppycock!" Dalby spat out the words one at a time. "The board is more than willing to give our

employees a fair wage for an honest day's work. But these…
teachers…are asking for the sun, the moon, and the stars."
Then he turned to the reporters in the second row. "I wish I
could give you the numbers, but I can't while negotiations are
ongoing. But you—all of you—will be thunderstruck when
you eventually hear what they're demanding—"

"Bull!" Harve shouted from his seat. "We're not asking for
more than the inflation rate, and the money is there. Both
sides have seen the figures."

"Wait your turn," Dalby said.

"Don't be feeding them any more of your crap, and I
will." The men scowled at each other, neither speaking for a
moment.

"I'm done for now," Dalby muttered. He made his way
back to his chair and sank down, still scowling.

Harve stood by his chair, not bothering to walk to the
podium, turned to the audience, and raised his voice. "All
your teachers are asking for is fair treatment in terms of
compensation. You know as well as I do that a paycheck has
lost some of its purchasing power due to inflation this year.
What you may not know is that we have three teachers whose
families qualify for food stamps." When he saw surprised
expressions, he pressed the point.

"That's right. A teacher with less than four years of
experience who is supporting a family of five qualifies for food

stamps. So far, all three have been too proud to apply, but I will continue to encourage them to. They're entitled."

Dalby sat shaking his head; the rest of the board just sat, their expressions unreadable. How could they not see the sympathy of many in the audience shifting to the teachers?

"The hell!" Dalby exploded. "Let them get a second job if they're so poor. Or not. They can eat dog food for all I care."

The crowd gasped. Harve turned to the negotiators sitting near him and mouthed the words, *That's it!*

Without another word, Harve and the team rose to their feet. I watched—the entire room watched—as they walked toward the door in silence. Then, as one, we teachers rose and followed them. I stared straight ahead on the long walk up the aisle until I was out the door.

———

Emergency union meeting. Later that evening, I had gotten the call from Lizzie saying we would meet before school. Her ominous words kept me awake much of the night.

In a matter of hours, I would come to a crossroads in my life. It was time to decide once and for all how I would vote. On the one hand, I loved my job and my new life in Hancock. How would it feel to lose it all? Equally important was my obligation to my students and the guilt I would feel if I walked out on them. Could I live with that?

Yet Dalby's words kept replaying in my mind. He honestly didn't care about us, and that made my blood boil. *These teachers are asking for the sun, the moon, and the stars. They can eat dog food, for all I care.*

No, no, we weren't demanding everything in the world. We were asking only for fair treatment. That's what was so infuriating.

Most of all, there was Tom. He loved his job as much I loved mine. If I were to break the law by going on strike, I would put him in an awkward position. How would he react?

Still struggling with my decision, still needing to get some sleep, I took my frustration out on my pillow. I punched it, over and over. But all I did was scare Marm off the bed.

CHAPTER 5
September 6

My situation still looked grim the next morning, as did the world news. The standoff in Munich was worse, with West German police preparing to use force to rescue the hostages.

A dark silence hung over the school library. I took the last empty chair at a table with most of the English department. A member of the negotiating team walked by and set a stack of campaign-style buttons in the center of our table. On the top half of the button, white letters on a green background read *I do not want to strike*. On the bottom half, green letters on a white background completed the thought. *But I will.*

Susan pushed a button toward each of us. I fingered mine nervously. I wasn't sure I was ready to wear it in public. And what about in the classroom? No, definitely not there. Susan and Bud pinned theirs on immediately. Chrissie and I both slipped ours in our purses. One table over, I saw Sadie and Sarah exchanging worried glances.

Harve walked to the front of the room.

"Thanks for coming out so early. This is an important vote. One way or the other, it's going to be the decisive one."

I caught myself sliding my peace symbol back and forth on its chain. I put my trembling hands under the table.

Harve said, "Let me start by explaining why we're here. After the fiasco last night, I got a call from the board's chief negotiator. There aren't going to be any more offers from their side."

"Oh, no," Chrissie whispered, her face pale.

"They refuse to budge on the crucial issues, not even one of them." He paused, waiting for a response that didn't come. "So what are we willing to do about this?"

After an unbearable silence that went on forever, someone finally asked, "What does the team suggest?"

Harve's answer was immediate. "We see only one choice if we don't want to accept the board's offer and live on dog food. We recommend calling a strike vote right here and now. I think we all agree that the status quo is intolerable, right?"

"Right!" people responded.

Sadie began to cough. She tried to control it, but it was one of those tickles that won't be ignored. With a red face and still coughing, she gathered her belongings and hurried out. I wasn't surprised to see Sarah follow her.

Harve continued, "Before we call for a vote, are there any questions?"

"Is striking legal?" asked a worried voice in the back of the room. "Are we going to be arrested?"

"I don't think you need to worry about that," Harve said. "There isn't enough room in the Hancock jail for all of us." I guess he was trying to make a joke, but no one laughed.

"What I mean to say is, if anyone is arrested, it would be those of us on the negotiating team. They may try to make an example out of us to scare the rest of you back into the building, but don't let them do it. We have an attorney from the state union, and he'll be looking out for us."

"When would the strike begin?" someone else asked.

"I would expect it to be within the next couple of days, possibly tomorrow, assuming we receive that directive in the voting."

The thoughtful silence that followed was broken when Harve nodded at the members of the team who began circulating to hand out ballots. "Your only two choices are yes or no, strike or settle for the offer on the table."

Many marked their ballots quickly. Other faces, though, reflected my mixed feelings. I kept coming back to one thing: I was twenty-four years old, old enough to make my own decisions and to live with the consequences. I knew what I had to do. Taking a deep breath, I checked the "yes" box.

I looked around for Sadie and Sarah, but they hadn't returned. Their strike buttons lay unclaimed on the table, their ballots unmarked.

Counting the votes went on forever. Finally, Harve took the slip of paper handed to him and stepped to the microphone. "Eight no votes, three blank ballots, and seventy-three votes for a strike."

His face relaxed just a little. "People, we have approved a strike against the board of education. The team will meet to strategize, and you will get a call tonight at the latest. Now go teach and fulfill all of your duties as usual. But I would recommend that, when you leave at the end of day, you take your personal items with you for safekeeping."

My stomach was churning as we walked out of the library. Billy met us at the door. "You heard the news?" When we shook our heads, he said, "It's bad—real bad."

My heart sank. "Oh, no. What's happened?"

"They're dead. At the Olympics. Eleven wrestlers and some coaches. All dead."

Billy's words, *all dead*, kept echoing in my mind. The utter senselessness of it haunted me as I walked toward my classroom. If people couldn't be safe in a place like the Olympics, could they be safe anywhere in the world? Even in Hancock?

———

The warning bell was ringing when I arrived at my door. I let the kids in and tried to compose myself. Then I spent the day pretending everything was normal, but my performance wouldn't have won any awards.

Every class asked about a strike. Each time, I gave the same noncommittal answer and tried to fake interest in what I was doing. The truth is, more than anything I felt numb.

When the final bell of the day rang, I took my time packing up my things. What do you take when you're going on strike, when you may, in fact, never be back?

Bud was whistling when he walked in my room. "Hey, Andrea, ready to go?"

"Nooo." By then I was fighting back tears.

"Aw, c'mon." He put an arm around my shoulders. "Try to think of this as an adventure. How many people ever have a chance like this to make a big move against the establishment? Damn it, I say let Dalby eat Alpo himself."

"You're right, Bud. I know you are. I'm just so sad…"

"I know. Come on, get your stuff together and we'll walk out to our cars together."

I nodded gratefully, grabbed my pictures of Tom and Marm and the books I was teaching. Then, swallowing a lump in my throat that nearly choked me, I turned off my lights and left.

There was a small group gathered around Lizzie at the door to the parking lot. "Strike plans," she said, handing me a sheet of paper. "We're going out tomorrow morning.

Picketing will start at seven. You'll find all the directions here. Oh, and Harve's number is at the bottom in case you have any questions."

"Thanks." That one simple word was all I could manage to get out.

————

I reached into my bag for my car keys and yelped in pain when something stuck my pinkie. More cautiously, I tried again and pulled out the strike button. I sighed as I pinned it on my jacket.

I wanted to get home and call Tom before he heard about the strike from someone else. But first I had to make one quick stop to pick up cat food. I was out of Marm's favorite, and I couldn't let my guy down no matter what else was going on.

It was too early for the A&P to be very busy. Within ten minutes, I had the cat food as well as several other things I needed. I joined the shorter of the two checkout lines, standing behind a man whose cart was overflowing.

Turning from the magazine rack, he smiled and said, "I can't believe anyone takes this alien-invasion crap serious—" He looked at me again and stepped back.

"Yeah, it's pretty far-fetched…"

"Sorry," he mumbled. "Never mind. Just…never mind."

"What?" I felt my cheeks getting red.

"That." He pointed to my button. "I don't want to say anything I'll regret." He kept his back to me while he unloaded his cart and paid for his groceries.

My face still felt warm when I caught the cashier staring at my button too. My fingers fumbled as I tried to turn my lapel over it. In the safety of my car, I reminded myself to take the button off when I was out in public.

"No. I am not going to do that," I said out loud, my embarrassment turning to anger. "I shouldn't have to hide this." I tapped the button, and as I withdrew my hand it brushed the chain of my peace symbol necklace.

I loved that necklace and everything it stood for. I had worn it continuously since I first put it on during my junior year of college. It was a symbol of my values, a sign of peace and love, and a reminder of some of the biggest days of my life. I had worn it the day I graduated from college, with my maid-of-honor dress in my roommate's wedding, the day I learned I had been hired at Hancock.

When I started teaching, I kept it under my clothing more often than on top of it, worrying about the reaction to it in the conservative atmosphere of Hancock. But I always had it on. The chain was beginning to wear thin after five years, and I was planning to replace it. But I had no intention of taking it off one minute before that war was completely over. Not while a hundred thousand people

were showing up for anti-war demonstrations. Not until
the last American soldier was home. And not until Tricky
Dick Nixon was out of the White House.

The strike button was a different kind of symbol, though.
I would wear it, but with mixed feelings.

———

Tom's squad car was in my driveway when I got home. Good. I
could tell him face to face. I conveyed the strike news as briefly and
unemotionally as I could. He stood up, took a few deep breaths,
walked around, and said nothing for a long time.

"Jeez, Andie—"

"Don't be mad, Tommy. This is something I honestly feel I have
to do. Please say that you support me."

"Andie…" His voice was gentle. Maybe everything would be all
right after all.

"Of course, I support you. I thought you knew that. What I
don't support is teachers going on strike. Knowingly breaking the
law. This puts me in a really awkward position. I'm supposed to be
enforcing the law."

"I know. And I'm sorry."

We both paused for a moment to collect our emotions, to
choose our next words carefully.

Tom spoke first. "Look, I'm worried about you. I think our
department should have someone there in the morning."

"Do you really think that's necessary?"

"Yes, I do. The people of Hancock are not used to seeing their teachers on a picket line. And unless I miss my guess, a lot of them are not going to be happy. A few will probably be pretty riled up."

"Well, yeah, I know they aren't going to like it, but nothing dangerous is going to happen…is it?"

"I don't know if you've heard. Last night there was an incident down on the square. The Grounds was vandalized sometime after it closed."

"What do you mean *vandalized*?"

"Rocks thrown through the windows. Spray paint on the door. Nothing taken, not even cash."

"Oh, dear. Were there any words? On the door?"

"Yep. ON STRIKE in big capital letters with a huge red X crossing it out." His fingers slashed the air as he drew an X.

Why did he sound angry? None of this was my doing.

He headed for the door. "Please, Tommy. You can't go when things are like this."

"I have to get to the station."

"But Tom…" His lips brushed mine, and he was gone.

———

Tom was no more than out the door when my phone rang. "Andrea? This is Sarah."

"Oh, good. Sarah, I've been wanting to talk to you. Are you

and Sadie both all right? I was worried when you didn't come back to the meeting after she had that coughing fit."

"Well, she does still have a nasty cold. But we're so upset with everything that's going on. Andrea, please don't think poorly of us," she said with a tremor in her voice.

"Of course I don't think poorly of you. Is it the strike that has you upset?"

"Yes. It's so unprofessional and undignified that we can't bring ourselves to do it. How can we walk out on our responsibilities to our students? But we don't want the other teachers to think we're disloyal. This may be our last year, but we still care about their future."

"I haven't heard any talk like that at all. There was so much going on today that no one except me may even remember that you left the meeting."

"Oh, it was noticed all right. About an hour ago, I got a call from Harvey Linck, and he was most unpleasant. 'We have to project unity,' he said. 'You have to stand up for the good of all of the faculty.' Well, I didn't promise anything except that I would think about it again. He didn't like that, but it was the best I could do."

How dare Harve try to browbeat those two? I urged her to find Chrissie and me in the morning and to stay with us during the picketing. It wasn't much, but it was all I could think of to help them.

CHAPTER 6
September 7

My heart started pounding the instant my alarm jolted me awake at five. I hadn't felt that kind of sheer terror since my first day of teaching, if even then. With a sense of dread, I showered and got dressed, not really sure what one wore on a picket line. I stepped into a pair of flats that I hoped would see me through a long day. I gulped down half a cup of coffee and was on my way out the door when the phone rang. I went back and answered it.

"Andie—"

"Mom, I'm on my way out. Can I call you later?"

"No, I need to talk to you now, before it's too late. Honey, I know you've explained this strike to us before, but your father and I have been talking. We're afraid you're making a big mistake. You love your job. Why are you going to risk it? For a little more money each month? If you lose this job, don't you think it will be hard to find another one when they hear you were fired for striking?"

"Mom, I have been over all of the pros and cons so many times that I've lost count. This is something I have to do. I'm sorry about worrying you and Dad. I really am. Please try to understand. I'll be fine, and I'll call you back when I have more time to talk, but right now I have to go."

Her exasperated sigh came through the line loud and clear. "Be careful, honey. Don't do something you'll end up regretting."

"I won't, Mom. I love you. Dad too. Please tell him."

Again I headed for my back door, and again the phone began ringing. I closed the door firmly behind me and kept going. But I could still hear it. What if it were Sarah or Sadie? I went back in and answered it.

"Andrea —" Tom was using my real name. This was going to be serious. "You know there's still time to step back and reevaluate, right?"

"No, Tom, it's too late for that. I love you very, very much, but I have to leave right now." Ever so gently, I replaced the receiver in its cradle.

I was ready to strike. Dalby and Alpo, the morals clause, teachers on food stamps, Sadie and Sarah and Harve—all of that and more. I wasn't sure what the final straw had been, nor did I care.

Yes, I felt guilty, and yes, I was scared. But my time on the sidelines was over. *Dammit*, I whispered. Then, louder, *Damn. It*. It felt good to swear. It absolutely felt wonderful.

———

On the drive over to school, for some reason, Huck Finn popped into my head. I guess in a way I identified with him. I kept thinking about how he struggles with a decision of conscience, as I just had.

Huck's world tells him that it is wrong not to turn in a runaway slave. But when he remembers all of the ways Jim has been there for him, he can't do it. He tears up the letter he has written to Jim's owner and says, "All right, then, I'll *go* to hell."

It was my favorite passage from one of my favorite novels, and one that I was scheduled to teach later in the year. I hoped I would still be teaching at HHS when it came up in the curriculum.

———

As I was getting out of my car, Chrissie pulled into the parking space beside mine. "Man, I'm glad you're here," she said. I hooked my arm through hers, and we walked to the back of the building where a crowd had formed outside the door to the woodshop.

Lizzie checked off our names and gave us each a sign. They were smaller and lighter in weight than I had expected, a white piece of poster board with the word *Settle* written in blue letters.

"School colors," Bud said, as he came up behind us. Soon the rest of the department joined us—that is, everyone but Sarah and Sadie. A strike captain walked over to pair us up for picketing.

Sarah arrived as we were about to begin walking. I looked around for Sadie but didn't see her. Susan sized up the situation and said, "Dan, why don't you let Andrea walk with Sarah?" He nodded and stepped aside.

Sarah and I didn't speak at first. We just walked, one foot in front of the other. Cars passing by slowed, their occupants staring at us. Several horns blared. One guy shook his fist at us; another gave us the finger. Only one shouted, "Good luck. Go get 'em."

I tried to stay deep within myself, not exactly ashamed to be there but far from proud of it. I stared straight ahead, avoiding eye contact with everyone—people in the cars, my students, their parents, everyone.

When Sarah and I reached the end of the sidewalk, we

turned back and I saw the line stretching more than a block behind us. Everyone looked scared, but then I probably did too.

"Are you okay?" I asked Sarah as we began our second lap. She was shivering in her heavy coat despite the pleasant fall weather.

"No, I'm afraid I'm not. But I will be."

"Where's Sadie? Is she coming?"

"No, I don't think she is."

Her tone made it clear that she didn't want to discuss it. But I had to try. "What's going on, Sarah?"

She sighed deeply. "After you and I talked last night, I spent a long time trying to convince her this was the right thing to do. But I couldn't get anywhere. It was so frustrating. But, in a way, understandable."

Sarah's face softened and her voice became wistful. "Did you know that Sadie almost became a nun when she was eighteen?"

"Gosh, no, I had no idea. Why did she change her mind?"

"Something about the mother superior saying she might not be well suited to it, I believe. But what's important is that Sadie ended up changing directions and making teaching her calling. She has always treated it like her God-given vocation. Certainly, we are all committed to our students, but Sadie is on a different plane. Her conscience, her whole makeup, won't let her turn her back on her students and her obligation to teach them. She says she feels bad about letting down her colleagues, but we are a distant second to the kids."

With that, Sarah's mood shifted again. Her features hardened and she shook her head. "After all these years, you'd think I'd know how bullheaded that woman can be. Andrea, I'm afraid she's going to turn her back on us and go in today. And I don't even care anymore."

Sarah's red eyes said otherwise. Theirs was a thirty-plus-year friendship. I couldn't bear the thought of it ending. I didn't know what to say.

Finally, she broke the silence. "Darn it! I'm furious with her. I'd like to just shake some sense into her."

A piercing whistle brought the picket line to an abrupt stop. "Can you see what's going on?" I shouted over my shoulder to Bud.

"No, I can't see much, but the whistle means a scab crossed the line to go in. I can't imagine who would do that."

I glanced toward Sarah to see if she had heard Bud. She had. She bit her lip and nodded at me.

The line lurched ahead again, and all eyes turned toward the front of the school. When I got a clear line of vision, I saw a slight woman with tight gray ringlets walking toward the main entrance. She did not acknowledge the shouts of "scab" raining down on her. Shoulders slumping, she walked in the front door of the building.

"Oh, Sadie, what have you done?" I whispered, fighting back tears.

"Stupid old woman." A single tear trickled down Sarah's left cheek as she moaned, "Stupid, stubborn, old…scab."

———

Things got more chaotic as the start of the school day approached. Traffic on East Street was bumper to bumper. Were people driving out of their way to take in the spectacle?

Most of the student body was milling around on the lawn, staying just out of our way. "Hey, Jackson," a voice called to me. I glanced to the side and saw Cliff Pendling smirking at me.

"You! Watch it!" Bud shouted at him. "She's *Miss* Jackson to you, and you should be—" the warning bell interrupted him.

Ignoring Bud, Cliff kept pace with us and yelled directly at me, "I hope they fire you. I hope they fire all of you."

The first-hour bell rang, and, trying to control my temper, I said, "Go to class, Cliff."

"You've got to be kidding. You think I'm going to school today?"

"Then why are you here if you're not going to classes?"

"I wanna be here when they haul your asses off to jail." The picket line kept moving, and, thankfully, I lost sight of him.

I felt a tug on my sleeve and turned to see Lois Mohn. "What should I do, Miss Jackson? Is it okay if I go to class now? The other kids said I shouldn't." Tears filled her eyes.

I stepped out of line and gave her a quick hug. I was nearly in tears myself. "Lois, go to class. You're a good student. That's where you belong. It's what I honestly want you to do."

But who would be teaching them? Sadie was apparently the only teacher who had crossed the line. It wouldn't have been easy to find enough subs to fill all the classrooms.

I caught up with Sarah in line, but Bud was no longer behind us. I spotted him standing with the student teacher. Her eyes were red, and she brushed away a tear. "You're not being disloyal, Julie. This isn't your fight," I heard him tell her as he moved back into the line, and she walked toward the school.

There still had to be more kids outside the school than inside it. I watched North confront a trio of guys who looked ready to take off. I couldn't believe my eyes when he grabbed one by the jacket and tried to push him toward the door.

The boy jerked free and motioned to his friends to follow him. On their way off the school grounds, they cut through the picket line just ahead of us.

"They can't do nothin' to us," he was saying to the others.

"I hope none of the kids gets in trouble today," I said to Sarah. She nodded but appeared lost in thought.

After some time, she moved a step closer to me. "This

is just between you and me," she said quietly. "But I've remembered something. Sadie changed when it started looking like the strike might actually happen. She wouldn't really talk to me anymore. Finally, I cornered her and asked what was troubling her. And what she said was strange. She said it was time to set things straight. With the strike ruining her life anyway, she was going to do the right thing. At the time, I thought she was threatening to cross the line because she felt striking was wrong. But now I wonder if it was more than that."

"What else could it be?" I asked. "Wait, do you think it had anything to do with the Pendlings?"

"It's possible. That man! I haven't been able to abide him ever since…"

"Since he caused trouble for Sadie?"

"Well, yes. She doesn't want us talking about it, but she isn't here. Obviously. And I'm mad as all get-out at her, but still, she didn't deserve the ruckus he caused her last spring."

"With her grade being changed by North?"

She nodded but said nothing.

"Is there more to it?" I asked.

"Why would you ask that?"

Before I could answer, a red-faced Harve came toward us, nearly running, and stopped when he got to Susan and Bud. "I need you. Take some of these people and get behind the building. A bus is pulling up, and it's not kids getting off. We think there's scabs coming in."

Susan and Bud moved down the line, pulling out pairs to take with them. When they came to us and saw Sarah's face, Bud said, "You two stay and hold our place in line here."

"No," I said. "I'm coming with you."

"Sarah needs you worse than we do, Andrea," Susan whispered to me. She was right. I stayed with Sarah.

———

When Harve gave us an hour's break for lunch, Susan encouraged Sarah to take the afternoon off to rest. I assumed she did. I didn't see her again that day.

For the rest of us, it was back to picketing after lunch. Chrissie and I walked together, not really saying much for a long time. "I feel like we've dug a trench in this sidewalk," she finally said. "All we do is plod along."

"Yeah, my feet will never be the same. I wonder what's going on in the building."

"I wonder how good the subs are at academics. I bet this is a lost day for any learning."

"I'm sure. One thing they better be good at is crowd control."

"Yeah. How's it going with Tom?"

"Ouch! Not too well. He called just as I was leaving this morning, and I kind of hung up on him."

"What? Why?"

"He called to try to talk me out of striking—again. Mom had just done that too, and I couldn't go over it all with him again. And I was running late, so I told him I loved him and set the phone down. It's not like I did it in anger, really. And, of course, I haven't been able to talk to him during the day, so I'm not sure how things are going, to be honest."

She murmured something encouraging, and I changed the subject. "How is Rob doing?"

"I ran home at lunch to check on him. He's grumpy, but I can understand that. As bad as this is, I'd rather be here than hiding out at home, like he and other the nontenured teachers have to do."

When the final bell rang, a smattering of kids left the building, some getting onto buses and the rest walking off campus. Nearly empty buses crossed our line on their way out.

The picket line dispersed when the team motioned us to gather on the lawn. A voice from the back of the group shouted, "Harve, have we accomplished anything at all?"

"Yeah, definitely," he said. "We are sending a very clear signal to the board and the community that we are standing our ground in a unified manner. I know we have their attention. And that's why I have an important announcement. The board has called an emergency meeting for tonight."

"Could it be a new contract offer?" Susan asked.

"Well, I would expect that to made formally to the negotiating team, not in a public meeting. But I plan to be there to see what's going on, and I encourage you to be too."

As we walked to our cars, Chrissie said, "I'm sure going to that meeting. You too?"

"Oh, yeah, I'll be there. I hope I'm wrong, but I have a bad feeling about it."

CHAPTER 7
September 7

The faculty and their families filled the chairs on the left side of the library. On the right was the non-striking contingent that included parents, townspeople, school administrators, and a handful of students. I spotted Gordon near the front and, farther back, Cliff and his father. Apparently, his mother had not come. Out of the corner of my eye, I saw Cliff nudge his father and point at me.

I took an empty chair next to Susan. Chrissie and Rob were three rows ahead of me, and Bud was just behind them. Harve and the negotiating team were back in the front row.

It was a special emergency meeting so the board skipped the preliminaries. When Dalby stood to address the crowd, I heard a quiet "woof" coming from our side of the room.

I managed to keep a straight face, but I was amused and impressed by the pluck of whoever had barked. Dalby frowned and kept talking, ignoring it.

I sensed movement behind me and turned to see Sarah searching for an empty chair. I caught her eye and motioned to the one on my left. "Thank you," she whispered. The poor woman did not look well.

"Is Sadie coming?" I whispered.

She gave a curt shake of her head. "I haven't seen her or heard from her."

Dalby moved away from the microphone and whispered with the board's attorney. An uneasy quiet settled on the crowd as we waited.

I heard the door open and close again and turned around to see Natalie Pendling enter. There was no room for her to sit with her husband and son, so she took one of the few empty chairs in the last row near the door.

Finally, Dalby cleared his throat and slowly, awkwardly, rose to speak. "Acting upon advice of counsel," he said in a booming voice, "the board is taking the following action."

Harve glared at Dalby, his face set. Whatever was coming, he appeared to be expecting it. Still, he braced himself ever so slightly.

"Due to his pursuit of illegal strike activity against the Hancock School District, I move for the immediate termination of Harvey Linck," Dalby said. "All in favor, signify by saying 'aye.'"

The other six board members responded with quiet "ayes." There were gasps throughout the room. Harve's face had turned bright red.

"How awful," I whispered to Susan.

"And I don't think we've seen the worst of it yet," she whispered back.

Dalby was just getting warmed up. He repeated the same statement eight more times, firing every member of our negotiating team. Each time, the rest of the board gave its unanimous approval.

Lizzie looked straight ahead as her name was called. I couldn't see her face from where I sat, but her shoulders slumped when it was over, and Dalby moved on to the next person.

At last, he finished and sat down. The crowd broke into a buzz. A couple more woofs came from behind me. Dalby slammed his gavel on the table. A loud crack echoed around the room as its handle split. He held the pieces together and kept pounding.

"That SOB enjoyed firing them way too much." Susan spat out her words, as angry as I had ever seen her. "And the others, they couldn't even look the teacher in the eye. They just fired more than two centuries of teaching experience."

"Lizzie's a single mother, Susan," I said. "How's she going to take care of her kids without a job?" There was no answer.

I saw Bud and Chrissie talking intently and wished I were close enough to join in. Bud looked furious and Chrissie more scared than anything.

Again, Dalby rose to his feet and spoke slowly and emphatically. "Due to her pursuit of illegal strike activity against the Hancock School District, I move for the immediate termination of Rose Anderson. All in favor, signify by saying 'aye.'"

The board members' collective "aye" was drowned out by the startled reaction of the crowd. "Oh my God," Sarah moaned, while Dalby kept pounding his gavel.

Why pick on Rose? She was an ordinary teacher, like us. Then the truth hit me. They weren't just making an example of our leaders. They were going to fire the entire faculty.

I was right. Proceeding in alphabetical order, Dalby moved for the termination of every single teacher, one by one, with the board granting their approval each time. As he worked his way through the g's and h's, I was afraid my racing heart would burst from my chest. I vowed I would not let him make me cry.

"Due to her pursuit of illegal strike activity against Hancock School District, I move for the immediate termination of Andrea Jackson." I fought to hold back my tears. If even one escaped, it would be all over. "All in favor, signify by saying 'aye.'"

There would be no miracle to save me. Mrs. Jenkins, though, must have remembered the close relationship her daughter and I had shared two years earlier. Her eyes shone with tears as she said "aye" in a shaky, nearly inaudible voice.

Chrissie came a little later, and Bud was right after her. Sadie Malcolm would have fallen between them in alphabetical order. But she had not gone on strike, and she was not fired.

Sarah had to wait until the very end. I cried during her firing, tears of sorrow and tears of red-hot anger. I reached for her hand as Dalby repeated the formal phrase that would end her life's calling. The moment I touched her cold skin, though, she shifted her hand away from mine. She sat ramrod straight, almost paralyzed, until it was over. Then she rose to her feet, carefully stepped over the legs of those between her and the aisle, and walked out of the room, head held high all the way.

Everyone in the crowd watched her leave in silence, people on both sides of the aisle shaking their heads in dismay. Harve noticed too and motioned for us to stay in our seats. I wasn't sure what he had in mind, but he wanted us there so we sat obediently and waited until the meeting ended fifteen minutes later.

I was one of the last out of the room. When I turned to

see if Chrissie and Rob were behind me, I spotted Dalby conferring with the superintendent and North. "Maybe they're planning how to hold classes tomorrow with their entire staff fired," Bud said as he came up behind me. I nodded and turned away, not in the mood to talk. Billy was emptying trash containers in the hall, but I didn't talk to him either.

I wanted only one person. I wanted Tommy.

Somehow I made it home. I scooped up Marmalade and squeezed him until he meowed his protest. "If I could turn back the clock, boy, I sure would," I whispered into his velvety ear.

I loved my job. I wanted it back. And, most of all, I wanted to see Tom. But he didn't call, and I knew better than to call him while he was on duty. Maybe he had heard the news and was too angry to call. I'll figure out how to make things right with him in the morning, I promised myself. But before I could, life only got a lot more complicated.

CHAPTER 8
September 8

My phone ringing at 2:15 was the most beautiful sound I had heard in a long time. Tom was calling. He wasn't mad. He wanted to talk to me.

But it wasn't his voice that spoke my name when I answered. "Miss J., I need help." The voice was so full of terror I wasn't sure I recognized it.

"Who is this? Billy?"

"Yeah, it's me, Billy Gannet."

"Billy, it's two in the morning. What's wrong? Why are you calling?"

"I don't know what to do. It's so awful. I don't know what to do. There's been this accident…"

"What accident? Where are you?"

"At school. I mean at work. And it's so awful…"

"Calm down, Billy. Tell me about the accident." I was wide awake, unnerved by the pounding of my heart. "Are you okay? Is anyone hurt?"

"Yeah." My god, he was sobbing. "It's bad, real bad. It's Miss Malcolm. She fell, and she's hurt real bad. And I'm afraid she could be…"

"Have you called for help? Billy, I want you to hang up right now and call 9-1-1. Do it now. Then call me back. No, wait, first call 9-1-1, then call your boss. Call Davis Hayes and tell him. Do whatever he tells you to do. Billy, did you hear me? Can you do that?"

"Yeah, Miss J. I'll do that now. But can you come over here?"

"I'm on my way. But, Billy, this is important. Make the call now. You have to get help for Sadie right away."

"Yeah, okay. I will."

I grabbed something from my closet, threw it on, and headed for school. Sadie had to be all right. She just had to be.

When I drove up the East Street hill, I saw flashing blue and red lights. Good. Help had arrived. Two squad cars and an ambulance were blocking the circle drive, so I pulled into Mr. North's reserved parking space at the side door.

I was running full out as soon as I got in the door and skidded a little turning the corner to the main hallway. I spotted them just down from the principal's office. Four or five uniformed men surrounded what I assumed was Sadie lying on the floor. I couldn't be sure. Billy stood off to the side, literally wringing his hands. He saw me and walked over, moving slowly and stiffly like an old man. When he got closer, I saw the still-wet streaks of tears on his face.

"Miss J.," he whimpered. "I couldn't help it. It was already too late when I found her."

"What do you mean too late?" I could hear my voice rising with panic. "You don't mean—"

"I'm sorry. I'm just so sorry that I couldn't do anything." Frantic, I hurried toward the group around Sadie. "Don't come any closer, miss," said a man whom I recognized as Tom's sergeant. "Stand clear. Better yet, go home." He turned, then recognized me, and said, "Hey, aren't you Jefferson's girlfriend? Andrea, right? I'm sorry. But please stay out of the way. The paramedics are going to move her to the ambulance."

"Sure. I'm sorry." I knew better than to get too close, but Billy's words had scared me to death. They sounded so final. If the paramedics were taking Sadie to the hospital, though, that had to be a good sign. She was alive.

The group around her parted to let two men with a gurney approach, and finally I caught a glimpse of Sadie. Her petite body looked even smaller under the blanket they had thrown over her. One of her legs was sticking out, the foot still clad in a rubber-soled oxford. The knee bent at an unnatural angle. I gasped when I saw the sticky, red streaks in a gray curl poking out from the top of the blanket. As they lifted her, the blanket slipped and I shuddered at what I saw.

I backed out of the way, stumbling into Billy. "What happened to her?" I asked him as the paramedics wheeled out the gurney.

"I don't know, Miss J. I was on my way up to the second floor, and I found her laying here. It looked like she maybe fell down the stairs. Or fell over the railing up there." He pointed up the stairwell that rose two stories to the third floor. "I tried to wake her up, but she never opened her eyes."

"Was she breathing?"

"I don't know. I didn't want to, you know, touch her. And there was the blood on the floor under her head. I cleaned it up as good as I could without moving her." It was then that I noticed the smears of blood on the sleeve of his shirt.

He shouldn't have touched that blood or cleaned it up, I knew, but I didn't tell him so. He felt badly enough the way it was.

"What was she doing in the school at this time of night anyway?" I asked. Billy shrugged his shoulders and squeezed his eyes in a futile attempt to prevent more tears from spilling.

Suddenly Tom was there. "Andie, what are you doing here?" Rather than answer his question, I ran toward him. He held me in a quick, awkward hug and then released me and backed away. I knew he had to act professional, but the rebuff still stung. "How did you find out so fast? You shouldn't be here."

"Sadie. Is she going to be all right?" I searched his face for a clue.

He looked an inch above my eyes and said, "I don't know yet. But what about you? At the moment, you're the one I'm worried about. What are you doing here?"

"Billy called me. Where did he go? He was just here."

"I don't know, but I'm going to find out. I'm supposed to get him to the station for questioning right away." He pointed to red smudges leading down the hall. "It's not going to be hard to find him."

"Tommy, please be gentle with him. He's so upset about this. He's heartsick. And, to answer your question, I'm here because he called me."

"Why you? He should have called us."

"I know. He just panicked, and I guess he felt more comfortable with me than the police. I told him the same thing, to call you and the head custodian."

"Andie, this is serious," he said as we followed the footprints down the hall. "I'll be as easy on him as I can, you know that, but I have a job to do. I need to talk to him. He has blood on his clothing. He's the one who found the victim—"

"She has a name, Tom. That victim is Sadie."

He exhaled. "Of course, you're right. I'm sorry, honey. But I still have to talk to Billy. We need information right away."

"Yeah, I know. It's just that I'm so sure he's not involved. Anyway, why are you assuming this was anything but a horrible accident? I have no idea why Sadie would have fallen down the stairs, but if she came all the way down from the third floor, that would explain the blood, wouldn't it?"

"It could, but remember there's a landing at the second floor, so it's unlikely she would have fallen all the way down if she had stumbled over something or slipped. I think it looks more like she went over the top of the railing. Where's her classroom?"

"It's out in the new wing, on the first floor out there."

"Then why would she be on the third floor here? Isn't it just classrooms?"

"Yeah, mostly. Well, there is a women teachers lounge on the floor, but I don't understand why she'd be in the building at all. Oh, no. You do know she crossed the picket line and came in to work this morning, right? I mean, yesterday morning."

"No, I didn't know. And that's the kind of information we need. It opens up more possibilities, that's for sure."

The faint footprints ended at the janitor's closet. Tom gently steered me away from the door. He opened it and there, in the back corner, sat Billy, his head resting on his knees, his slight form shuddering. Tom walked in, took him by the arm, and carefully helped him to his feet.

Billy's eyes never left the floor as Tom spoke. "I need you to come to the station with me, Billy. You were most likely the first person on the scene. We need you to help us figure out what happened. Why your teacher got hurt."

"I don't know nothing," he mumbled. "By the time I found her, she was the way you just saw. I couldn't help her, not with her like that."

"I understand. But you may have information that you don't even realize you have. I need you to come with me."

"Am I in trouble, Miss J.?"

"No, Billy. You're not in trouble." I hoped I was right.

"Tom…I mean, Detective Jefferson. Will you call me when you get an update on Sadie's condition?"

"I'll do that, Miss Jackson." He gave me a quick hug. "Now go on home and stay put."

———

It was after three when I got home. I was beyond exhausted, both physically and emotionally, but I had little hope of sleeping. I collapsed on my couch, kicked off my shoes, and settled down with Marm.

It seemed moments later that I heard my back door open. I was startled, but when Marm didn't react, I knew it was Tom.

He slowly lowered himself onto the couch with Marm and me. It was a long time before he spoke. "I'm so very sorry, Andie. She didn't make it."

"You mean…Sadie's…?" I couldn't bring myself to put it into words. If it wasn't spoken, then it hadn't happened. "Are you sure?"

"I'm afraid there's no doubt." His voice was gentle. "She died in the ambulance."

I swallowed several times before I could speak.

"*Because I could not stop for Death/He kindly stopped for me.*"

"What's that from?"

"An Emily Dickinson poem. She was Sadie's favorite poet. Dickinson wrote about death a lot, but she didn't get it right this time. There was nothing kind about the way Sadie left this life."

I couldn't shake the image of her small, limp, broken body on the hard tile floor. I took a shaky breath and, suddenly cold, reached for the afghan draped over the couch. "Oh, Tommy."

"I know, honey. I know."

He held me so tightly I could scarcely breathe. But it wasn't long enough. All too soon, he began to let go.

"Wait…"

"I'm really sorry, but I can't stay. I'm still on duty. In fact, I shouldn't even be here, but I just couldn't tell you on the phone. And I wanted to be the one to tell you."

"I'm glad you were. Thank you, Tommy."

"Are you going to be okay?"

"Yes. I will." I wished I was as confident about that as my words sounded. The moment he was out the door, I began sobbing. I cried until I had no tears left. I checked my bookshelf for a collection of Dickinson poems, but I didn't have one. That started my tears again. I might have found some comfort in reading poetry.

I knew I should be making phone calls. At the very least, Susan and Sarah had to be told right away. But it was four in the morning. Why not let them sleep a little longer?

I moved from the couch to my bed and stretched out without bothering to pull back the covers. Why get in bed at all when there was less than two hours until I had to get up? But would we even be picketing in light of Sadie's death?

With that thought, anger temporarily replaced my grief and tore through my fatigue. This stupid, wrong, hateful strike. It had ruined Sadie's last year of teaching, and in the end it had taken her life. And whose fault was that?

Dalby and the school board. Their callous, unreasonable actions had backed the teachers into a corner. They were the ones who had made the strike inevitable. Because of them, we had lost Sadie.

Was I oversimplifying the situation? I didn't think so. Without the strike, would Sadie have gone careening down the stairs? If not for the strike, would she have even been in the school so late at night?

I was left with not only my anger, but haunting, unanswered questions. Why hadn't I tried harder to talk her into honoring the picket line? Her last interaction with the faculty, if you could even call it an interaction, had been angry, shouted insults. Why hadn't I stepped forward to support her? I could have walked her to the door if that was what she really felt she had to do. Just my companionship might have eased some of the pain of that long, lonely trek.

I dissolved into tears again, with my sobs bringing Marmalade to my side. He gently butted his head against my cheek, not seeming to mind that his fur was getting wet. He purred as loudly as he could while he sat watch over me. If only I had treated Sadie as tenderly as my cat was treating me. Remorse over lost opportunities threatened to overwhelm me.

Finally, I dragged myself off of the bed and into the kitchen, where I put on a pot of coffee. Then I reached for the phone to call…who? Susan first, or Sarah?

But before I could dial, the phone rang, startling Marm and me. "Andrea," Susan's voice said quietly. "It's Susan."

"You've heard?" Really, the question was unnecessary. Her tone of voice was all I needed to hear.

"Yes. Harve is calling the department chairmen to activate the phone tree. But you already know. How…? Oh, Tom?"

"Well, I was over at school right after they found Sadie."

For some reason, I didn't tell her about Billy's call. Word would soon spread that he was the one who found her body, but why not protect him as long as I could?

"Oh, Susan, it was awful." I was close to tears again. "I don't even know how to put it into words."

"And I don't want to hear the details. Since you already know, I need to make the rest of my calls. The others will be hard enough, but I dread having to calling Sarah."

"I'll call her." I regretted the words as soon as they left my mouth. "But Susan, what about picketing today? Will that be called off?"

"I have no idea. I'm going to show up unless I hear otherwise."

"Well…" I began and then realized Susan had hung up.

I had a little time before I had to decide whether I would go to picketing duty, so I decided to get the phone call to Sarah out of the way. I looked up her number and then looked for excuses to put off dialing it. I fed Marm, took a shower. Finally, I knew I had to do it.

After seven rings without an answer, I wondered if Sarah was there. I let it go up to twelve before I hung up, both relieved and worried.

Where could she be? Why wasn't she answering? Surely, nothing had happened to her too, I wondered.

I waited five minutes and then tried again. Still no answer. While I debated whether I should drive over to her apartment, my phone rang. Sarah, in a tentative voice, asked if I had called her.

"Yes, and I was worried when you didn't answer. Where were you?"

"Oh, I'm still not answering my phone, Andrea, in case it's Harve calling again. There's no one I feel like talking to anyway, and it's simpler this way." Was it possible that she hadn't heard about Sadie? My heart sank. I was going to have to be the one to tell her. I could only hope that the right words would come to me.

"Sarah, there's some bad news." I swallowed a sob and then tried again. "Some really horrible news that I have to tell you. This is going to come as a shock to you; I know it did to me. Would you like me to come over there and tell you in person?"

"No, dear, that's not necessary. What could be so bad? Is it about the strike?"

"No. Well, maybe. I don't know. Sarah, we lost Sadie this morning. And I'm just so, so sorry."

"What do you mean, lost her? She's going to cross the line again this morning? She left town?"

"No, no. She passed away. Sarah, she died this morning, at school."

"Oh."

It seemed an eternity before Sarah spoke again. I wanted

to fill the unbearable silence, but I couldn't think of anything more to say.

After a long pause, she asked, "Why was Sadie at school?"

"I don't know."

There was another long pause. Then, in a voice so weak that I could barely hear her, Sarah asked, "How?"

"I'm not sure." I took a deep breath and said, "Billy found her outside the office at the bottom of the stairs. Apparently she fell all the way down from the third floor. The rescue squad came and took her to the hospital, but it was too late. She passed in the ambulance. I'm just so sorry. I know that you two have been so close for so long, almost like sisters."

"Yes, she is...*was* more a sister to me than my own sister."

"We will all miss her terribly. I'm sorry. I don't know what else to say. Of course, I'd like to know how and why it happened, but those questions can wait. Are you okay?"

I could hear quiet sobs as Sarah said, "I'm so sorry, Andrea. This is all my fault. I killed her. It was me."

"What? What are you saying? You weren't—"

A quiet click told me she had hung up. Immediately, I redialed her number. It rang and rang, and she wouldn't answer. I tried again. Still no answer. What in the world had she meant? Sarah hadn't even been there. How could she be responsible? It's not like she had tripped her or, heaven forbid, pushed her.

Frantically, I dialed one more time, but she didn't answer.

What could I do? Should I drive over to her apartment? But would she even let me in? I looked at the clock. If I were going to picketing duty, it was time to leave. I hadn't heard that it was canceled, so I decided to head over to school. The one thing I did know for sure was that I didn't want to be alone.

CHAPTER 9
September 8

Chrissie was hugging me before I was completely out of my car. "I saw you pull in and waited for you," she said and then burst into tears. "Sadie...I just can't believe it. I don't want to believe it. Do you have any idea what happened?"

"No. I mean, I saw her right before..."

"What? You were there?"

"No, not when it happened. I got there just before the paramedics took her away. Billy called me when he found her and I made a mad dash over there."

"Was she still...?"

"I don't even know. There were paramedics, cops, people I don't know standing around her, and I only got a glimpse of her from several feet away. Even that was so terrible. The blanket slipped off her body when they raised up the gurney. Chrissie, she looked broken, just broken all over."

"Well, then her body was like her spirits. The poor, poor woman. Oh, no, what about Sarah?"

"I called her about an hour ago, and, Chrissie, she didn't know. I had to tell her. It was the hardest conversation I've ever had. And that wasn't even the worst part."

"Then what was?"

"She started talking crazy, saying she was responsible. Her exact words were, 'I killed her. It was me.'"

Chrissie's face went white. "What did she mean? That she felt guilty, like she wished she could have prevented it, right? Not that..."

"Before I could ask her anything, she hung up. So I don't know. Maybe she was feeling guilty about their falling out over the strike. That has to be what she meant. I was hoping to find her here. I have to talk to her and now she won't answer her phone. She can't go around saying stuff like that. Someone could take it the wrong way."

"Hoping to find who? Take what the wrong way?" Susan asked as she came up behind us. "Have you seen Sarah? Is she here?"

Chrissie and I both shook our heads. "Susan, she didn't take it well when I told her. Of course, she wouldn't. But she said something crazy that really upset me." I repeated what I had just told Chrissie.

"Oh my God. I'm sure she didn't mean that the way it sounds. But we have to be sure she doesn't repeat it, or she could end up being questioned in her best friend's death."

"Yeah, that's what I'm afraid of."

"Okay, first we need to see if she's shown up here. Let's circulate through the crowd and try to spot her."

We each grabbed a picket sign and a cup of the coffee that the team was distributing and then headed out. People were much more subdued than the previous morning. Obviously, everyone had been called about Sadie. As I wandered around the parking lot, several folks tried to stop me to ask about her death. But I kept moving, scanning the crowd for Sarah's gray head.

Somehow, out of the confusion, a picket line formed and pairs of teachers began walking. I hadn't spotted Sarah when I met up with Chrissie and Susan. "Nothing," Susan said. "No one's seen her."

"Maybe we should drive over to her—" I said.

"Wait. Look," she said, pointing to the front entrance of the school. There was Sarah, squinting into the sun as she walked unsteadily out the door carrying three boxes stacked so high she could barely see over them. We all hurried over.

"Here," I said. "Let me help you. What's in these?"

"Things from Sadie's desk and her awards. I couldn't bear the thought of someone else handling her things. They mean a lot to her, you know."

We nodded. I took two of the boxes from her, Susan took the other, and Chrissie put an arm around her shoulders to steady her. As we slowly made our way across the lawn, I felt every eye on us.

By the time we reached Sarah's car, Bud, Dan, and Dee Dee had joined us. Each in turn hugged Sarah, who shook with sobs.

While we were huddled around Sarah, two police cars quietly pulled up. My first thought was that they had come to arrest our strike leaders. But the cars had driven right by the picket line and pulled into the parking lot, near where we were standing.

Tom got out of one of the cars and walked over to us. An officer I didn't recognize got out of the other car and followed Tom. "Miss Wittingham," Tom said, immediately going over to Sarah, "I'm very sorry."

"Thank you, Tom." She looked like she wanted to say more; her lips twitched, but no words came out. Frustrated, she began crying again. Dan and Dee Dee hurried to her and, one on each side supporting her, walked her a distance away from the rest of us.

"We're going to need to talk to you—all of you," Tom said, avoiding my eyes. "This is Officer Bertrand, by the way. I believe you people knew Miss Malcolm better than anyone else. Perhaps if we can put together what you know about her thoughts and actions the past few days, it may help us find an explanation for what happened."

"But, Tom," I said, "Sadie has avoided all of us since the strike vote. Even Sarah. I don't know how we could possibly be much help."

"That may be, but, as I said, if anyone knows anything, it's most likely someone in your department. Billy has been doing his best to cooperate with our questioning, but he hasn't been much help."

"Probably because he really doesn't know anything," I said and then bit my lip. Tom shot me a warning look that all of my friends undoubtedly caught. I felt my face redden.

"Now we're going to talk to you each individually. We'll be using the conference room in the office."

"Wait," Susan interrupted. "We're on strike. We aren't going to cross the picket line and enter the building. Can we do this somewhere else?"

"Yeah," Tom said after a pause. "If you guarantee you'll be here when we need you." We all nodded our agreement.

"Okay, then, we'll take you to the station if you'll feel more comfortable there. I'm going to start with Susan and Sarah, and, Officer Bertrand, why don't you take the Dixons? When we're finished, we'll bring them back and get the others. Oh, and just to make this very clear, my colleague here will be questioning Andrea. I'm counting on finding the rest of you right here when we return." Again, we nodded.

A shrill whistle from the front lawn startled all of us. Immediately, several more joined it. "What's that?" Tom asked.

"Someone's crossing the picket line," Bud said. "I have to get over there." Without waiting for Tom's permission, Bud hurried around the building. Tom frowned as he helped Susan and Sarah into his squad car.

"Let's go," Chrissie said to me as soon as his car left. We caught up with Bud just as a school bus pulled into the circle drive. A dozen of us positioned ourselves between the bus and the school entrance. We waited in tense silence for the door of the bus to open.

The moment the first man set a foot on the ground, the group burst into whistles and catcalls. "Scabs!" Outraged cries spread from our smaller group to the picket line. "Go back where you came from, scabs."

I couldn't bring myself to shout "scab," but I didn't back away. Bud and I positioned ourselves so that everyone getting off the bus had to look directly at us.

To a person, they avoided making eye contact. In fact, they appeared as unhappy to see us as we were to see them. "Someone said they're from Schaumburg," Bud said. I was sure they were from out of town. I didn't recognize anyone until the bus was nearly empty.

As the last two people stepped off, I drew in a breath. I had seen them before. The man and the woman with him had been at the board meeting, sitting with Cliff. I was sure it was Mr. and Mrs. Pendling.

"Look at how he's strutting around," Chrissie said in disgust.

"And there, right behind him, that's his wife," I said.

"Hey, isn't that the Pendlings?" Bud shouted loudly enough for them to hear.

The look Mr. Pendling shot at Bud was pure venom.

"Scabs." I aimed the word at their retreating backs. They gave no indication they had heard me. So I shouted it. "Scabs."

Anger burned through the numbness of my grief and sleeplessness. Well, better to be mad than sad. I picked up a sign and, along with Chrissie, joined the picket line.

"Chrissie," I said a few moments later. "Have you thought how much things have changed in just one day?"

"I don't want to think about it. It's overwhelming. I just can't…"

"Yeah, I know. Last night I didn't think anything could be more horrible than losing our jobs. And now we've lost Sadie too…"

A black car roared into the driveway. "Hey, he should slow down and be careful," I said to Chrissie. And as we watched, the car came dangerously close to hitting Harve, who grabbed his upper arm.

"Oh, no, I think the car hit him. Look, it must have gotten his arm." People gasped as they realized what had happened. Holding his left elbow, Harve waved to us with his right hand.

"I'm okay," he shouted. "This jerk's rearview mirror just grazed me on the way by. I'm okay." But I noticed he was still holding his arm.

"Who the heck is that driver?" Chrissie asked. "Did you get a look at him?"

The buzz got louder as the name *Dalby* sped up and down the line. *Ray Dalby hit Harve.*

Chrissie reached over, tugged on my sleeve, and pointed. A police car pulled into the drive and stopped. "Good. Maybe they're going to arrest him," I said. I watched as Tom got out, opened the door to the backseat, and stood aside while Dan, Dee Dee, and Susan emerged. As they began walking our way, Bud motioned for us to leave the picket line.

"Oh, no," I said. "Where's Sarah? Why didn't she come back with the others?" Their faces looked grim; Dee Dee had red eyes. I wanted so badly to ask about Sarah. Tom nodded to Bud, Chrissie, and me and walked us toward the car.

"Can I just ask one question?" I said.

"You can ask, but I doubt if I can answer it," Tom said, but his tone was regretful.

"Where's Sarah? Is she okay?"

"She's all right. She's still at the station. I'm sorry. That's all I can say."

Officer Bertrand pulled up, got out of his car, opened the rear door, and motioned for me to get in. My question about

Dalby flew out of my mind. "Please, officer, can you tell me anything about Sarah Wittingham? I'm very worried about her."

"No." And so we rode the three blocks to the police station in total silence. As he walked me to a conference room, I peered in every open door, hoping to catch a glimpse of Sarah. But there was no sign of her.

Officer Bertrand led me to a conference room and got right down to business. I had a fleeting memory of Tom questioning me during the investigation two years earlier. His professional yet gentle manner had marked the beginning of my falling in love with him. The happy memory brought a slight smile to my lips. The officer seemed to take it as permission to begin.

"What was the last time that you saw Miss Malcolm previous to her fall?"

I had to stop and think. "Well, it would have been that morning when she, um, crossed the picket line to go into the building."

"Yes, I heard that she had done that. Did anyone else cross the line too?"

I shook my head no.

"She had to have ticked off a lot of people." He made a note on the pad of paper in front of him.

"Well, yeah, it did. But not to the point where—"

"Did you talk to her that morning? Wednesday, I think it would have been?"

"No. Yes. I mean, no, I didn't speak to her and yes, it was Wednesday, the first day of the strike."

"Then when was the last time you actually spoke with her?"

"Oh, it seems so incredibly long ago now. Let me think. I saw her at the union meeting early in the week. Was it Monday or Tuesday? I can't even remember."

He scribbled another note. "Did you speak to her at the meeting?"

"No. She wasn't feeling well and left before the meeting was over. So if you want to know the last time I had a real conversation with her, it would have been the previous week, the day she called in sick. That was very unusual for her, and I was worried."

"And how was she the last time you spoke?"

"She was pretty shaky emotionally, I guess you'd say."

"Mm-hm." He was writing again. "Now let's move ahead to the night of Miss Malcolm's death. Did she attend the school board meeting that night?"

"Not that I'm aware of. I looked around the room but didn't see her. But it was so crowded in there that I could have missed her. Did anyone else see her?"

"I can't answer that, Miss Jackson. When did you leave the meeting?"

"I'm not sure what time it was. I stayed until the end, though. It seemed very late, but it was probably around nine or nine thirty. It took a while to fire all of us." I wasn't really expecting any sympathy for my last statement, and I didn't get any.

"When you left the school, who was still there?"

"How would I know that? The building is so spread out."

"Let me rephrase that. Who was still in the library when you left that room?"

"I was one of the last out, but I did notice that Dr. French was still at the front table talking with Ray Dalby and Wayne Pendling. Oh, and Mr. North. I think the others were leaving right behind us."

"And did you see anyone in the halls on your way out?"

"I don't remember anyone. Well, yes, I do. Billy, the custodian. I didn't talk with him, but I did see him cleaning in the hall."

Again he jotted something down.

Fifteen minutes later, I had answered all of his questions to the best of my ability. I couldn't believe I had been much help. When he closed his notebook, I tried again. "Will Sarah be riding back to school with us?"

"No."

"Has she already gone back?"

"I don't know."

"Well, is she all right? I'd feel better if one of her friends were with her."

"She's not alone."

"Oh, good. Who's with her?"

"Her lawyer."

CHAPTER 10
September 8

When I got back to the school, Bud and Chrissie were already picketing with the rest of the department. They saw me, and everyone shifted. I ended up with Bud, leaving Susan walking alone. Minutes later, Harve came over and fell into step with her. He was still holding his arm a bit stiffly.

"How was it?" Bud asked me.

"The questions? I guess about what I expected. It was what I learned afterward."

"What was that?"

"Sarah was still there, and that's not the worst part. There is a lawyer with her."

"Damn, then they think she had something to do with it?"

I shrugged my shoulders. "Bud, it was an accident. I'm sure of that, aren't you? What am I saying? Of course, you are."

"Well…I didn't want to say this to you, not this soon afterward, but…" he hesitated.

"But what? You don't think…"

"That she was pushed? No, I don't know if there was anything criminal about it. But we all do know how upset Sadie was about the strike, and it started a long time before yesterday. And then crossing the picket line. That had to be the hardest thing she ever did. I guess I didn't even want to admit it to myself, but isn't it possible that she fell halfway on purpose?"

"Oh, no." I heard myself moaning at the unthinkable. "Oh, no, Bud. She never would…"

"Andrea." His voice was all gentleness. "Who's to say what anyone would do given the right, or I guess I should say the wrong, circumstances? The last time I saw her, she looked and sounded like a broken woman. God, I'm sorry. That's too close to the truth, but you know what I mean."

"Yeah, I do."

"But that wouldn't explain why Sarah is still there and needs a lawyer."

"Oh, Bud, I think I might know how that happened." And I told him about her alarming statement to me that morning. Could it really have been only hours earlier?

We both walked in silence, considering one unacceptable possibility after another, until Susan interrupted our thoughts.

"Let's shift again, people." After years of following Susan's orders, we automatically did what she said. I ended up with Dee Dee, who looked even more tired and stressed than I probably did.

"Are you okay?" I asked.

"Andrea, I hate to sound like someone's mom, but leave your peace symbol necklace alone. If you keep tugging on it like that, you're going to break the chain."

"I wasn't even aware I was doing it. Thanks, I'd hate to lose it. But how are you?"

She shook her head. "Just when I thought things couldn't get worse, they did. Dan told me that he quit his part-time job last night. Andrea, I don't know how we'll get by without that extra income. Things are really tight the way it is. I don't even want to think what will happen if this strike drags on for any amount of time."

"Then why did Dan quit?"

"He says it's a matter of principle. Not North, the other kind of principle." She giggled with a touch of hysteria. "You know he works for Dalby at the hardware store, right?"

"I know he works at Turner's, but what does that have to do with Dalby?"

"Why, he owns it."

"I assumed it was owned by someone named Turner. So Dalby owns that store and the Die Cast?"

"Yeah, plus more. Anyway, last night they got into a

discussion about the strike that ended up being a shouting match. Dan said he quit rather than getting fired. I mean, I can see why he doesn't want to work for that man, let alone in two jobs. It's just that I'm scared for my family."

"I don't blame you." Before I could think of something reassuring to say, Susan called out again, "Shift, people."

"Why's she doing that today?" I asked.

Dee Dee shrugged her shoulders. "I have no idea. Maybe she's trying to break up the boredom of walking the same route over and over."

Dee Dee thanked me for listening before stepping ahead in line. I returned to walking with Bud.

"Have you noticed how quiet it is around the building today?" he asked.

"Honestly, I haven't. I've been worried about too many other things. But you're right. Yesterday there were quite a few kids milling around outside, but not today."

"While you were at the station, I heard that most of the kids cut today. There are only five or six in some classes."

"Who told you that?"

"Julie."

"Julie? Why is she here?"

"Since she's not an actual teacher, she's not on strike and she has to go in. And she's afraid that if she doesn't show up, she'll have to repeat student teaching next semester. For her sake, I hope this ends soon."

"I hope so too. Poor Julie."

"Anyway, she said a lot of the parents didn't even want their kids to come. They knew they wouldn't be learning anything anyway. So I passed that along to Harve, and he said that's a good thing. If parents aren't comfortable sending their kids to school, that has to put a lot of pressure on the board."

"I know you're right, Bud, but still, it's so sad. For parents to feel their kids are better off out of school. So where do you think they are? At home watching the boob tube?"

"Julie said a lot of them are heading down to the square. Wonder how the storeowners feel about that? Too many kids with nothing but time on their hands doesn't sound good to me. I hope all hell breaks loose down there."

"Yeah, me too, but I hope no one gets hurt."

"Well, Julie told me something else. Andrea, you'll love this. Your favorite student, Cliff, is in there lording it up like he's boss of the place. He's doing whatever he wants, only dropping into a class when he feels like it, making an ass of himself."

"Like usual," I murmured.

"Right on! Now that's more like the old Andrea we all know and love." I had to admit, Bud could always make me smile.

And just then, Cliff—or someone—struck again. The fire alarm blared, and students began streaming out of the building. Normally, during a drill, they would be fairly quiet and orderly. But under the circumstances they were rowdy, laughing and pushing each other, treating it like more entertainment provided by the strike.

I don't think any of us considered the possibility of a real fire. This had the look and feel of a prank. Trailing behind them were the so-called teachers, who were greeted with a loud round of boos and cries of "scabs." Many, I noticed, headed for the parking lot, having had enough of "teaching" for the day.

Last in the procession were North and Wayne Pendling. They gave it a token effort, but they couldn't corral the kids who were darting through the picket line and playing a game of keep-away with the administrators.

Gordon appeared at my side. "Hello, Miss Jackson. How's it going?"

"I guess okay. How have things been inside today? Is everyone all right?"

"I guess. You should see some of the lame excuses they have for teachers. Those scabs aren't even trying to teach anything, just busting heads."

"But you said no one had gotten hurt?"

"Oh, sure. I didn't mean busting heads in the usual way. They're just doing stuff like handing out detentions that we all know we won't have to serve. And for a while they put everyone who got kicked out of class in the cafeteria for detention. And you'll never guess who was guarding them. Cliff's old man and old lady. Well, I'll be going now, Miss J."

As soon as he was out of earshot, I turned to Bud. "Did you hear that?"

"Mm-hm. Interesting. Sounds like chaos in there. Maybe they'll actually start to miss us soon—hey, look at that!"

I followed his gaze to the front entrance of the school, where North, Pendling, and Dalby were huddled. It was Dalby who appeared to be doing most of the talking. When they dispersed a couple of minutes later, Dalby gestured to Harve to join him. They spoke briefly and then Harve returned to the picket line. Once Dalby's back was turned, Harve broke into a huge grin and gave us a thumbs-up.

He motioned for us to gather. "Score one for the good guys. They've given up on holding classes."

"For the rest of the day?" someone in the crowd asked.

"For the rest of the strike. They've been forced to admit that they can't maintain a safe atmosphere in there, so they really didn't have any choice. Dalby wouldn't say it, but I think he's been getting complaints from parents who are worried about their kids. It's another good sign, folks. That's the kind of support that we need.

"But this isn't the time to let up. We have to stick together. There's a long way to go. So we'll keep to our regular picketing schedule. I don't care if we're marching in front of an empty school. This is where we send our message to the town. They need to see us out here in force. They need to see we're not backing down."

———

There were a lot of people on the picket line, so I went home to rest a bit. I had just stretched out on the couch when I heard my back door open. "Good. I was hoping to catch you at home," Tom said as he came in. He stooped to scratch Marm's ears but kept his gaze on my face.

"How you holding up, Andie?"

"I'm all right, I guess, considering. How about you? Shouldn't you be home sleeping?"

"Yeah, that's where I'm headed, but there's something I need to tell you, and I wanted to do it in person." He came over, put an arm around my shoulders, and gently steered me to the couch, where we sat side by side.

"Please, tell me it's not more bad news. Is it Sarah?"

"No, it's not Sarah, honey. She has gone home. I can't tell you much more than that, though. No, this is about Sadie."

"What? Do you have a cause of death yet? Any information at all?"

"Well, the coroner is still working on his report, but he has given us some preliminary findings. It looks like Sadie did fall over the railing. She doesn't have the type of injuries you would expect if she had bumped all the way down the stairs.

And, as we already said, it would be likely that the landing would have stopped her fall."

"So what does that mean? If she didn't trip walking down… and I know she was wearing her rubber-sole shoes, so I doubt if she did—you aren't thinking she jumped, are you? Oh, no. Did the strike cause her to…?" I could feel the tears start and was grateful when he wrapped his strong arms tightly around me.

"Honestly, honey, I don't know at this time." He paused and then sighed. "I shouldn't even be telling you this much, but it's going to be released to the press, so I don't see how it can hurt. Also, I can tell you that her body has been released to her family so they can make funeral arrangements."

"Family? What does she have in the way of relatives? I don't think I've ever heard her mention anyone."

"A nephew from New York state is the one we've been in contact with."

"Well, I hope he plans to have the funeral here where her friends are."

"I hope so too. I know it would make you feel better to be able to say goodbye to her."

———

When I got back to school, the line was still in motion. Everyone was paired up, and all of the smaller picket signs had been snagged from the truck. I was left with a larger, heavier one, and hoisted it to my shoulder. I walked alone. Soon I was so lost in thought that I didn't notice the line slowing until I nearly ran up on the heels of Mary ahead of me.

"Sorry," I said. "I wasn't paying attention. What's going on?"

"It looks like someone handing out cookies and coffee. How nice."

"Oh my gosh, it's some of my kids. I mean my former students," I said, spotting Rachel and Peggy.

"Weren't they in that class…from your first year?" Mary asked over her shoulder.

"Hey, thanks so much," I said to the girls, stepping out of line. "This is a nice surprise. And it's good to see you. How are you doing this year? What are you doing?"

"Miss J.," Peggy said. "Have you heard? Me and Gus got engaged."

"Why, congratulations! That's just great."

"And it never would of happened except for your class. Will you come to our wedding?"

"You just try to keep me away. But, Peggy, does your mother know that you're doing this? For the teachers, I mean?"

"Yeah. She's cool with it as long as I don't let anyone think it was her idea."

"I wish I could talk longer, but I really shouldn't. I'm glad I got to see both of you. This gesture means a lot to your former teachers. Thank you."

I finished my cookie and lifted my sign back to my shoulder, sipping coffee as I walked along. But my good spirits faded quickly.

Chrissie was a newlywed. Nearly all of my college friends were either married or planning their weddings. Even my students were getting engaged. And then there was me. One thing was for sure. As long as this strike was coming between us, Tom and I would not be going anywhere with our relationship. I just hoped we still had one when it finally ended.

"Anything wrong?" Chrissie asked as she fell into step with me.

"It's more like is there anything *not* wrong?"

"Then you're not going to want to hear this right now, but you're going to in a few minutes anyway, so I'm going to just get it over with. Sadie's funeral won't be in Hancock. Bud just told me that her nephew is planning to have it in New York."

I broke down in tears, not even caring who saw me. I must have been a sight as I trudged along, sobbing and hiccupping and blowing my nose. And if that wasn't enough, a cold, driving rain began falling. I could not remember being more miserable in my entire twenty-four years.

Finally, mercifully, enough time had passed that Harve dismissed us for the day. He must have sensed that morale had slipped because he said to us, "I know this is tough right now. I wouldn't ask you to do this if I still didn't think it would be worth it all in the end. Maybe you're too close to the situation to feel public opinion turning in our favor, but it is. Really.

"Look at it this way: We've always had the backing of the majority of our students, and now their parents are getting tired of the whole thing. And they're blaming the board more than us. Dalby in particular. They want their kids back in classes. Tomorrow's Friday. We're going to do this whole thing again and then take the weekend off from picketing. Now go home, dry off, and warm up. Maybe even raise a couple. And just wait till this is all over. We are going to have the party to end all parties."

———

I went home, but I didn't follow Harve's suggestion of raising a couple. Not even one. I did take a hot shower and change into warm, dry clothes. I fed Marm and myself and tried to get interested in TV, but all three channels were showing the news. I had been hoping for less reality, not more. I wouldn't exactly say I missed planning lessons and grading papers, but the comfort of the usual routine would have been welcome.

I checked the stack of books waiting for me on my nightstand. *The Stepford Wives, The Odessa File, All Creatures*

Great and Small—recent bestsellers that had been gifts from
a college friend who worked for a publishing company. *All
Creatures* turned out to be the perfect choice. It was warm,
funny, and perfect for a stressed-out animal lover like me. I
read for quite a while, until Herriot's words soothed me to
sleep on the couch.

When I awoke, it was with a head full of questions. Sitting
up, I said, "Marm, I can't wrap my mind around the idea
that Sadie climbed up on the railing on the third floor and
jumped. Even if she were disturbed enough to take her own
life, would she do it at school? And why was she there anyway?
If she was going to cross the line again in the morning,
why…?"

"Unless she couldn't face walking through a line of her friends
and colleagues a second time. Maybe she had planned to stay
in the school overnight so she wouldn't have to. There's a couch
in the third-floor teachers lounge, and the bathroom is right off
the room. Could that be what she had in mind? I wish I could
find out if she had an overnight bag with her. Tom might know,
right?"

"Mmm-row."

"Do you think I'm on to something here, boy?"

"Mmm-row."

I was tempted to call Tom at work but held off. Instead, I
stared at my phone, willing it to ring. It took over an hour, but
finally it did. And it was Tom.

I knew from his first words that he was upset. It was a mistake to ignore his tone of voice, but I plowed ahead anyway. As soon as we had exchanged the usual how-are-yous, I said, "Tommy, I have a question. I just thought of something about Sadie's... about Sadie. Did you happen to find an overnight bag at the school? Maybe in the teachers lounge on the third floor?"

There was a long silence. "Why do you ask that?"

"I'm just curious, that's all. It might help explain what happened. Why won't you answer my question?"

"Andie, we've been over this before. I'm not answering because I can't. I can't discuss an ongoing investigation with you. You know that." He sounded very tired.

"But—"

"There are no 'buts' about this. It's police procedure."

"She was my friend, Tom. I'm trying to make sense of her death. That's all."

"Andie, she's gone. What difference does it really make if she had a bag in her room?"

"Then she did? Don't you see? It could make a big difference. If she had taken things to stay overnight, that means she expected to be alive the next morning."

"How do you figure that?"

"Well, I was just thinking...maybe she planned to sleep at school so she wouldn't have to cross the picket line again. She could have gone in the building when it was open for the board meeting and hidden out in her classroom. Don't you see? That would make it so unlikely that she took her own life. Don't you see?"

"Yeah, I see where you're going, Andie, but—you're doing it again. Don't let your curiosity drag you into our investigation. And, for the record, I never said that an overnight bag was found."

I couldn't help sighing, and that was not a good idea. He kind of snorted in frustration, said he had to get back to work, and ended the call. He was right. He hadn't answered my question about an overnight bag. At least, he hadn't answered it with words. But as I gently returned the receiver to its cradle, I said to Marm, "I just bet I'm right, boy."

Of course, Tom also had been right about something. Whatever the reason for her death, Sadie was gone and nothing would bring her back. I'm not sure why I thought learning she hadn't taken her own life would make it easier to bear, but it would.

CHAPTER 11
September 9

As strange as it sounds, striking was beginning to settle into a routine. It was almost like picketing had become my job in place of teaching. I shook my head impatiently, trying to toss that idea out of my brain. Teaching was the job I loved and the one that I missed very much. Striking was…temporary.

The third day of the strike, a Friday, opened with sunny, warmer weather—along with another reason for optimism. A larger crowd than usual had gathered on the front lawn. There was a contingent of parents and former students ready to join us with signs that read SUPPORT OUR TEACHERS. We greeted them with a cheer, shouts of *thank you*, handshakes, and hugs.

Harve motioned the teachers over. Though he was still favoring his left arm, it hung in a nearly normal position.

Before he could speak, a question came from the crowd. "Harve, are you okay today? Any trouble with that arm?"

"Naw. Just a couple bruises. I'll live."

His face grew solemn as he continued. "As you probably know, Sadie Malcolm's funeral will be held out of state. Since we won't have a chance to formally pay our respects to her, let's have a moment of silence in her honor at this time. And, before we do that, let me say, on a personal note, that no one was more, uh, vexed with her actions in regard to this strike than I was. But I will continue trying to understand and forgive her even as we honor her. She had a long and unselfish career that deserves the respect of all of the community."

Something about his words—as nice as they were—seemed a little off to me. I caught Bud's attention and saw him raise an eyebrow and frown slightly. Harve had been livid with Sadie what seemed like just hours earlier. Had he really forgiven her so quickly?

But if Harve was acting, he was doing a fine job of it. He bowed his head, and we all followed his lead. Chrissie and I reached for each other's hands. Susan came up behind us and put an arm on each of our shoulders. It was, after all, only a moment of silence, but I was pleased that we were doing anything at all in Sadie's honor.

Harve cleared his throat, raised his head, and began lining us up. He had the teachers intermingle with the parents and former students. Their presence, along with the sunshine, lightened the mood for all of us.

The next hopeful sign was something that didn't happen. Eight o'clock came and went without a single school bus pulling up to unload either students or scabs. School was officially canceled.

The only people I saw enter the building were a handful of administrators and school board members. I nudged Chrissie and pointed to Dalby and Mrs. Jenkins as they walked in. "Maybe something's going on," she said. I crossed my fingers and smiled for the first time in days.

Whistles began blowing as a towel company delivery truck pulled into the driveway. Harve rushed over and motioned for the driver to lower his window. The driver nodded, waved his arm toward us, and, of all things, broke into a grin that I could see from the sidewalk. Taillights lit up as he shifted the truck into reverse and slowly backed out of the driveway. Harve gave us a thumbs-up as he said, "The driver didn't realize this is an AFL-CIO strike. Be sure to tell anyone else who comes along if I don't notice. All of the union guys will honor our picket line."

Applause spread up and down the line. It wasn't a huge thing, but it was another small victory. I felt some spring return to my step as Chrissie and I began another lap.

While we walked, I told her what Tom had said about Sadie's injuries and watched her expression as she realized the implications. "So…then Sadie must have fallen over the railing at the top of the stairs, but I don't see how that could've happened unless—you don't think someone pushed her over, do you?"

"I don't know what to think. I can't believe that's what happened. But I can't believe she would have committed suicide at school either. I just don't know, but I do think I'd feel better if I knew what really happened. Not that it would bring her back, of course. And not that I still wouldn't blame the strike for taking her from us."

We walked slowly, both lost in our thoughts. After what seemed like a long while, Chrissie asked about my weekend plans. "Well, I hope I'm still on with Tom for our Friday night movie date. He wasn't at all happy with me the last time we talked—"

"Oh, I'm sure he won't want to miss your date. No matter what, he's crazy about you, Andrea. Anyone can see that."

"Hope so. What are you and Rob doing?"

"I'm not sure. It feels just plain wrong to have a Friday night without a football game. He hasn't said a lot, but I know it's eating on him. It was going to be a sure win too, so to have it turn into a forfeit isn't going over well with the players or their parents. I just wish this whole thing would end."

"I've been thinking about that. Would you be willing to make more concessions to have the strike over? I might be getting to that point."

"Yeah, that's gone through my mind too."

"Well, put it out of your minds right now, girls." Bud had come up behind us and jumped into the conversation. "Don't you see that we can't back down now? Not when the townspeople, at least more of them, are coming over to our side. And what would you give up? A raise that isn't one, barely enough to keep up with inflation? Compromise on the asinine morals clause? God, tell me you wouldn't."

Before either of us could answer, Harve motioned us over again. "I have news, people. The board has requested that we return to the table and resume negotiations. I don't know what they have in mind, but as a sign of good faith we are calling off picketing for the rest of the day. And we won't resume it as long as both sides continue talking.

"But let me caution you. This does not necessarily mean we're close to a settlement. We won't know until we see what happens this afternoon. Anyway, you can go on home. If there are any developments, we'll let you know."

———

Six hours later—six painfully long, frustrating hours—my phone had not rung. There was no word on developments in the strike, no word from Tom. Therefore, no Friday night date with Tom.

I felt at loose ends. I tried watching TV and checked out

my choices of programs on the three networks—*Temperature's Rising*, *Maude*, and *Bonanza*. None of them appealed to me.

So I decided to read for a while, picking up the shortest book from the stack beside my bed. I made it through about twenty pages of *Jonathan Livingston Seagull* before putting it down. Chrissie had loved it, but I didn't. I knew it was a fable, but still, it was too saccharine for me. At least for my mood that night.

I wondered if I were getting jaded. Maybe the events of the past few months had knocked some of the idealism and optimism out of me. Or maybe I was just growing up. Well, adulthood certainly wasn't all it was cracked up to be.

CHAPTER 12

September 10

My grandmother used to say that no matter how bad you think you have it, there is always someone worse off. I thought of her when Sarah showed up at my door early the next morning. Her light knock barely broke into my restless sleep, but Marmalade wouldn't let me be until I had shuffled over to the door and opened it a crack.

It took me a moment to recognize Sarah, who appeared to have aged a decade overnight. Red eyes ringed with wrinkles dominated her thin, drawn face. Her stooped shoulders looked like they were sagging under the weight of the world.

"I'm sorry to bother you on Saturday morning, dear," she said, barely above a whisper. "May I come in?"

"Of course. Forgive me for being rude."

"I hardly know where to begin," she murmured as we settled onto my couch. "I've been up all night, and I'm afraid I'm far from my best."

"Sarah, what kept you up all night? The one thing you really need right now is your rest."

"I know, but I was at the police station again last night. And when I got home I couldn't get any sleep. I just feel so... lost, I guess. Everything has turned upside down in the past week, and now things will never be right again, I'm afraid."

"Why were you at the station?"

"Oh, Andrea, it just keeps getting worse. They think I was the one who...hurt Sadie."

"What? No. Why?"

"All they would say was that new information had come to light, and they had more questions for me. They insisted I bring my lawyer."

Had the coroner's report come in? Well, I would think about that later. At that moment, Sarah and I both needed sustenance so I went about making us a simple breakfast. I put on a pot of coffee, scrambled some eggs, and made toast.

Though Sarah had insisted she couldn't eat a thing, we both dug in and finished it to the last crumb of toast. As we sat sipping our second cups of coffee, I turned the conversation back to the previous night.

"Sarah, were you arrested? Did they charge you?"

"No. At least, I don't think so. They let me go home, but

they said they would have more questions today or tomorrow. I'm afraid that means I still could be in trouble, and my lawyer seems to think so too. Oh, dear…" She appeared to be near tears as she looked me in the eyes and said, "Andrea, I hate to do this, but I have to ask you a favor—a rather large one, I'm afraid."

"Anything, Sarah, you know that."

"I'm so glad to hear you say that. What I need is for you to look into this whole thing for me. How Sadie died, why the police seem to think I was involved, what I should do…"

My heart sank. "Oh, Sarah, I don't think I can do that. You know I would do anything in my power to help you, but that…"

"But, dear, you did such a commendable job when you solved that crime two years ago. I just thought you could do a little poking into this too. You don't seem to realize it, but you're quite good at this kind of thing."

"Oh, no, I'm not that good at it. I just got lucky with the Joe incident, and, even with a lot of luck on my side, I still almost managed to get some of my kids and myself hurt. I couldn't do that again. Besides, Tom has clearly told me to stay out of this. And he means it."

Sarah's lips trembled, her eyes filled, and her face slowly crumpled. "Oh, no," I said. "Please don't cry. I can't bear it, Sarah. Please don't."

"At least say you'll think about it. Don't get yourself in any trouble. I don't want that. But if you could just think about it…" Her plea was so compelling. What could I do?

Very reluctantly, I nodded. "I'll think about it, but that's all I can promise. I don't see why it should be necessary for anyone to investigate anyway. No one who knows you believes you could be capable of hurting Sadie, not after all the years you've been friends."

"Well, the police don't seem to care a whit about that. Not a whit." She stood. "I can't begin to thank you for our talk, dear, and for breakfast. I really didn't know who to turn to… with Sadie gone."

I hugged her and walked her to the door. Once it closed behind her, Marm gave me a disapproving look.

"I know, Marm. I may have misled Sarah when I told her I'd think about it." Oh, man, I thought, talking to the cat like he's a human. But I kept right on doing it. "I can't get involved in her problems without risking some major hassles of my own. First and foremost, there's Tom. Our relationship is strained as it is, and if he found out that I was looking into Sadie's death, that could be the end of any future we might have. I know I'm being selfish, and I feel terrible about it. But I just couldn't risk losing Tom to help Sarah clear herself. I'll have to tell her the next time I see her."

I swear that my cat gave me a little nod and then toddled over to his empty food bowl.

CHAPTER 13

September 11

The next day, a Sunday, was the first good day I had had in ages. First off, Chrissie invited me over for coffee. She had wanted to include Tom too, but he had to work again. That was all right, though, because Rob wasn't there either. It would be just the two of us girls.

The weather was so nice that I decided to walk over to her place. I left a little early and took the long way through the square to see if The Grounds had reopened. And it had. The windows had been replaced, the graffiti removed from the door, and the shop was bustling with customers.

Chrissie saw me coming up her walk and flew out the door to meet me. "I think something's up!"

"Really? What?"

"I think we might be close to a settlement."

"Why? What did you hear?"

"Rob's head coach called him to a meeting to make plans for the team to practice tomorrow morning."

"Wow! I like the sound of that."

"Me too! So before I pour the coffee, we're going to have something special to celebrate. Wait here. I'll be right back." While she was in the kitchen, I looked around the cozy home she shared with Rob. It was filled with touches of Chrissie's style—macramé plant hangers and wall hangings, artful groupings of photos, Impressionist prints. I could have had a million dollars to spend and not ended up with a home as lovely as theirs.

Chrissie returned with a bottle of champagne and two glasses.

"Oh, wow! What beautiful crystal!"

"These flutes were wedding gifts. First time I'm using them, and I can't think of a better occasion to break them in. Well, *break* is a poor choice of words," she said with a giggle.

Wedding gifts. Lovely things that people give you when you get married...I shoved the thought of weddings firmly out of my mind. Why let my envy of Chrissie drag down my spirits?

After we toasted the possible good news, I said, "But Chrissie, why would the head coach know something the rest of the teachers don't?"

"Because school is first and foremost all about football, silly! Seriously, though, don't you think it sounds hopeful?"

"Yes. I do. The football team wouldn't be practicing if we were still on strike. But hold on. They wouldn't practice on a Monday morning if we were having school, would they?"

"No, you're right. But still…"

"I agree that it's a good sign. It's the best news I've had in so long. Which reminds me: there's something I need to tell you. I hate to bring this up right now, but I'm afraid it could be important."

"What's up?"

I told her about Sarah's visit and, without meaning to or wanting to, sent her good spirits plunging. "Oh, no, what could they be thinking? Sarah would never…"

"I know. I tried to tell Tom that when they first questioned her. You know what it is, right? The way she said she was responsible for Sadie's death. Why can't the police see that she didn't mean it literally, that it was just her huge sense of guilt?"

"You know that, and I know that. But she really did—does—feel responsible, just not in the way they are taking it. It probably makes her look guilty as hell."

"Yeah, and here's the worst part: She begged me to look into it and help clear her. She thinks that I have these amazing abilities to investigate based on what happened two years ago.

I couldn't get her to see that I'm not the brilliant detective she thinks I am."

"No, Andrea. You cannot let her talk you into that. You know how that would go over with Tom." I nodded grimly. "And maybe she doesn't remember how much danger you ended up in. You have to tell her no. And stick to it."

"I know, I know. But I just couldn't do it yesterday. You should have seen her. She looked so terribly lost and alone. I didn't have the heart to turn her down cold."

"I understand, and I feel a ton of sympathy for her. But I don't want anything bad to happen to you either."

———

When I walked in my back door a few minutes later, the phone was ringing.

"Andrea, this is Lizzie. And I'm calling with good news. We have a settlement."

"Oh, thank you, Lizzie. That's wonderful! When do we go back to work?"

"Wait, we're not quite that far yet. First, both sides have to ratify the tentative agreement."

"Oh, of course."

"So here's the plan. Tomorrow afternoon at one, we'll have a union meeting to go over the terms of the contract and vote on it. Of course, it won't be official until the board also ratifies it, and that won't happen until tomorrow night. We are sure the faculty will approve it, and everyone seems confident that the board will too."

"But, Lizzie, are we still the faculty? They fired us."

"Yes, we're still the faculty. As part of the settlement, the board agreed to rescind our terminations as the first order of business at their emergency meeting tomorrow. But I also have to tell you that we didn't get everything we wanted. I guess you never do. But we got a lot of it. It's a two-year contract with a 2.5 percent raise this year and 3.5 next year. Then, next year, the board will add five teaching positions to get class size down a bit. And there is no morals clause in the contract."

"Okay, but what's the catch? Are we really getting all that?"

"There is no catch. Well, not in the contract. Our pay will be docked for the three days of the strike, but we knew that would happen. It's normal procedure. And we will eventually get that money back, plus more, with our raise."

"That's terrific! Then when's the party that Harve promised us? The party to end all parties?"

"Well, there's a problem with that. So far we haven't been able to find a place we can hold it. We wanted The Outpost, but the owner turned us down. He said he would lose too much business if his anti-union customers found out we were there celebrating. We'll try a couple other venues, but we may not have any luck."

"Well, that's disappointing. So there are no classes tomorrow?"

"That's right. It will be called an emergency day, not a strike day, so we won't be docked for it. We'll go back to work on Tuesday morning. Now I have to get on with my calls, but I'll see you tomorrow at the meeting."

"Thank you, Lizzie," I said again. "Thank you so much."

I had expected to feel relief when the strike finally ended. And I guess I did, to some degree. But the price of the contract was so much higher than I could have imagined. First and foremost, we had lost Sadie. Plus, how long would it take to regain the trust of the community? And then there were the kids. Would there be behavior issues that had developed as a result of the strike?

Still, it was with a lighter heart that I retrieved the book bag I had brought home before the walkout. I pulled out my ALS textbook and syllabus to see where we had left off.

"Hmmm. How appropriate," I said to Marm. "Looks like our first new assignment will be 'Rip Van Winkle.' That's a guy I can identify with. I know it's only been a few days, but I feel like I've been asleep a long time and just woke up in a different world."

CHAPTER 14

September 13

Brushing away tears, I walked back into the school and the career I could have lost forever. I took a shaky breath and headed to the office to pick up my mail, carefully avoiding the spot where Sadie's broken body had lain. Everything looked the same, but nothing was. What should have felt like a triumphal return dimmed under the pall of her death.

There was a line to get to the mailboxes; there was a line in the copy room. But I got everything ready and still had plenty of time before first hour. So I grabbed the chrysanthemums I had brought from home and headed out to the new wing.

I told myself I was checking in on Sarah, but, to be honest, it was Sadie's room that was drawing me like a magnet. Before I even turned the corner, I caught the aroma of fresh flowers.

Several bouquets leaned along the wall outside her door. As I approached, a girl who looked to be a junior or senior added another small bunch to the growing memorial.

I set my flowers down gently and whispered, "I miss you so much, Sadie."

Then a hand touched my left shoulder. I jumped, turned, and came face to face with a stranger. "Excuse me," he said. "I don't want to disturb you, but I need to get to the door. I'm Johnny Antag, and I'll be filling in for Miss Malcolm until they hire a permanent replacement."

"I'm Andrea Jackson. Welcome. Um, you do realize the circumstances, right?"

"Oh, yeah. It's not going to be easy. I know that. But I think once the staff and kids get used to the idea, they'll like having a younger, energetic guy like me around."

"I'm sorry. I don't recognize you. Have you subbed here before?"

"Um, well, yeah, last week…"

A scab? How could North have done that?

"I have to get to my room," I said, and left.

But I made a detour on the way back. I threw open Susan's door, startling her as I stormed in. "How dare he?"

There was a long pause. "I assume you've met Johnny."

"North couldn't have chosen a worse sub for Sadie if he had deliberately set out to sabotage her. A scab? Give me a break."

"Yes, I agree completely. I argued this one till I was blue in the face, and it made no difference. I told him we have several regular subs who've earned the position, but he just tuned me out. He mumbled about wanting to reward someone who had shown loyalty during the strike."

"Didn't he even look guilty?"

"No, I wouldn't say that he did. But George definitely does not look happy today. I would have thought he'd be relieved to have the strike over, but he seems just as cranky as he did before the walkout. I wonder what it would be like to have a principal who actually supported us."

"I wouldn't know, since he's the only one I've ever had. And you know how well that worked out my first year. If it hadn't been for you, I would have been totally on my own. But back to today. Is anything going to be said or done to acknowledge Sadie's death? Shouldn't North say something to the kids?"

She shrugged her shoulders. "I agree that something should be said, but I'm not sure he's the one to do it. He doesn't have a sensitive bone in his body, and his idea of communication is a memo stuffed in a mailbox. Speaking of which, did you get his memo telling us to check for vandalism?"

"I did," Bud said, holding it as he walked in. "And I can't say I liked the tone of it. Is it just me, or did it sound like he was blaming us for the damage? Like it happened because we weren't in our rooms?"

"That was how I read it too," Susan said. "Anyway, did you notice anything wrong in either of your classrooms?"

"Not me," Bud said.

"Me either."

"Nor have I," Susan said. "It sounds like it's all in the back wing, concentrated in the shop and art rooms. I wonder if it's a coincidence that Harve and Lizzie were both leaders of the strike and it's their rooms that were targeted."

"Gosh, Susan, now that you say that, it really is kind of suspicious," I said. "I haven't been down there. What kind of stuff happened?"

"Harve said some of his students' projects were damaged, and several tools had been thrown around the shop. It was about the same thing in art, random damage to some of the kids' work, paint spilled on the floor. Looks like North has his hands full. No wonder he's in such a foul mood."

"I don't care what his problems are," Bud said as he left for his room. "He's a jerk and he always will be."

I opened my mouth to reply and then stopped, surprised to find myself wiping away tears.

"Andrea," Susan said gently. "I understand. I do. I'm still adjusting to the loss of Sadie too. That reminds me. Have you seen Sarah this morning? If we're having this much trouble, I'm sure it must be worse for her."

"No, I haven't seen her. I meant to stop in her room, but after I ran into Antag, I took off. I'm almost sure her door was still closed when I was down there."

"I believe I'll go take a look. And I should probably pay a

visit to Mr. Antag while I'm there. I don't want him here any more than you do, but I'm going to try to keep the needs of our students first in my mind."

I walked back to my room wondering what, if anything, I should tell the kids about Sadie's death. It didn't feel right not to acknowledge it, and it looked like the administration wasn't going to do it. But I wasn't sure I could talk about her and keep my composure. I wished I had asked Susan and Bud how they planned to handle it before our conversation got sidetracked.

———

To say it was a difficult day in the classroom would be a gross understatement. In many ways, it was like starting the school year all over again. I had to restate and reinforce my rules with every class. A lot of the kids had trouble settling back into the routine; many hadn't even bothered to bring their books to class. Since no assignments had carried over, I ended up lecturing, and when that got old quickly, all kinds of annoying disruptions broke out. By eighth hour, I was wondering why I had missed teaching so much.

For a change, Cliff was one of the first into the room. He tried to hide his face as he passed my desk, but still I noticed his black left eye. The next thing I knew, he was huddled with Rick-Jack by the windows.

I walked over to use the pencil sharpener near them, and their voices dropped so I couldn't eavesdrop. I heard Cliff start to say something about his dad and the strike, but Jack noticed me and shushed him.

Then the bell rang, and I opened my mouth to begin my lesson.

"Hey, teach," Cliff interrupted me.

"As you will remember, it's Miss Jackson, Cliff. It's still common courtesy."

"I don't see why I have to show you respect when you didn't respect your duties to us. You walked out on us, teach."

A chorus of voices responded with a loud "yeah."

"I didn't walk out on you…"

"That's not how it looked. My old man was right. They should of fired all of you. Oh, yeah, that's right. They did. Well, they should of left you fired, if you ask me. Get us some new teachers who want to teach."

Like you want to learn. I wanted to say it but held my tongue.

Then Cliff's next comments pushed me over the edge. "I'm gonna try and get into a different ALS class. That new teacher, Mr. Antag, the one who took over for Old Lady Sadie, he sounds pretty cool. Doesn't he teach ALS too?"

"Her name is Miss Malcom, and—"

"Miss Malcolm," he practically spat out the name, "was too old and mean to be teaching anyway. I already told you what she tried to do to my brother. And my dad, well, he said that someone needed to make an example of one of you teachers, and it might as well be an old bird like her. Except he didn't say 'bird' but the real b-word."

There was an audible gasp in the room, followed by complete silence. Even Rick and Jack looked shocked. Once it was too late, Cliff appeared to realize he had gone too far.

When I found my voice, it shook with fury. "Cliff, you will never, ever again say anything in the slightest way disrespectful about Miss Malcolm. Am I making myself clear?"

He sank into a resentful silence but did not break eye contact with me.

"As for your desire to change to a different ALS section, that is certainly your right. And to make it easier for you, I'm going to write you a pass to go down to see your counselor about a schedule change."

"Right now?" he asked, a little abashed.

"Yes, right now." My hand trembled as I reached for my pad of passes and a pen. I knew I might regret it later, but it felt so good to get him out of there.

As soon as the door closed behind Cliff, it was my class again, and a cooperative one at that. I let the silence drag on a few moments while I breathed deeply, trying to steady myself. Then I began my lecture introducing the Romanticism unit. Jotting the main points on the board, I glanced over my shoulder and saw the kids taking notes. When I finished, I handed out the syllabus for the unit and offered them the last few minutes to begin reading "Rip Van Winkle."

But no one moved to open the book. It wasn't a refusal as much as a reluctance to get to work. It appeared they weren't quite ready to move on.

Finally, Candy raised her hand, pushed her hair behind her ears, said, "Miss Jackson, I just wanted to say that my brother had Miss Malcolm for ALS two years ago, and he thought she was a good teacher. I mean, old-fashioned and all, but smart and fair. He had to read *Huck Finn* again in college, and he said his professor noticed how much he already knew about the book. I guess it's like they say: two sides to every story."

I had to make a conscious effort to keep my jaw from dropping open. Had I misjudged Candy as a self-centered snob, or had she matured over the past few days?

"Yeah, consider the source, Miss Jackson," Gordon said. "Cliff's whole family hates Miss Malcolm. Everyone knows that." Many of his classmates nodded.

After the ice was broken, others talked about their shock and sadness over Sadie's death. They didn't put it into words, but it was clear that at least some of them disagreed with Cliff's opinion of her.

"Have you walked by Miss Malcolm's room today?" Lois asked me.

"Not since before school. Why?"

"There are a lot of flowers outside her door and little notes and some pictures from old yearbooks. You should go see it."

"I think I will, right after school." And with that, the bell rang. For the first time all year, I was a little sorry to see the class end. What a difference the absence of just one key student could make. I crossed my fingers, hoping his counselor would make the change permanent.

On their way out of the room, I heard Rick say to Jack, "I wish I could change classes too. This one isn't going to be near as much fun without Cliff."

Alone at last, I sat at my desk. How had one teenage boy managed to crush my happiness when I had been so excited to return to school? Bud and Chrissie walked in then, and I said, "Boy, am I glad to see you two."

"Long day, right?" Bud said. "Kind of like the first day all over again."

"Maybe even worse."

"Hey, were either of you in the faculty lounge today?" Chrissie asked. Bud and I both shook our heads no. "Well, the pop machine was turned off, and the phone we always use was gone. No one knew what was going on, and North was in such a foul mood that no one wanted to ask him."

"Sounds like revenge on the part of our fearless leader," Bud said.

"Do you think he'd be that petty?" she asked.

"Yes," Bud and I said at the same time. "That's exactly the

kind of thing he'd do," Bud added. "Well, hey, I'm ready to get out of here. How about you two?"

"Oh, yeah," Chrissie said.

"You guys go ahead," I said. "There's something I want to do before I leave. I'll see you tomorrow."

————

I took the long way down to Sadie's room, enjoying the solitude of the empty halls. How long would it take me to process everything that had happened? Months? Years? It was still September, but it felt like it should be Thanksgiving.

I walked toward the office, again stepping around the place where Sadie's body had lain. Then I slowly climbed two flights of stairs to the third floor, to the place from which she had fallen. When I peered over the railing, my stomach lurched and I felt dizzy.

Finally, I examined the area where I was standing, hoping to find something to explain what had happened that night. It's not that I expected to see bloody fingerprints on the railing or a shoe print on the floor. My logical side told me that the police would have already done a thorough search, and the custodial staff would have cleaned the entire area.

Finding nothing but a stronger sense of loss, I went back down one flight of stairs and poked along the second-floor hallway for a while. Gradually I made my way to the first floor and headed toward Sadie's room. I was surprised to see how large the memorial had grown during the day. No one, not even freshmen boys who would rather shove each other than walk, had disturbed a single petal of the flowers.

I didn't hear Sarah come up behind me. "It's a beautiful tribute, isn't it?"

"Yes, it is. I so wish she could have seen how much her death has affected the kids. And all of us, of course."

"Oh, yes. I'm afraid she passed thinking that she had failed in some way. She tried to put on a brave front, but that whole blowup with the Pendlings last spring shook her deeply."

"Speaking of them, Sarah, I had trouble with Cliff Pendling this afternoon. Again. This time it ended up with him going to guidance to try to transfer out of my ALS section into Sadie's—I mean, Johnny Antag's. I don't think I'll ever get used to him using Sadie's room and taking over her job."

"Miss Wittingham," Mr. North's voice boomed over the loud speaker. "If you are still in the building, report to the main office. Miss Wittingham, please come to the office."

"Oh, dear, now what can that be about?" Sarah's voice was so timid I could barely hear her.

"I don't know, but I'll walk with you. I'm headed that direction anyway."

She lapsed into a worried silence. The poor woman did not need this additional stress. When we walked in the door, we both stopped and stared. There, in uniform, was Tom. I gave him a little wave and tentative smile, but he had his official bearing about him and did not respond.

As Mr. North motioned for Sarah to enter his office, I walked over to my mailbox. I took as long as I could, reading each piece of mail slowly while trying to overhear what was going on. I hoped to catch Sarah on her way out, but she did not leave the office. Instead, she appeared to sink deeper and deeper into her chair.

When she finally emerged after about twenty minutes, Tom held her left arm and escorted her into the hall. Neither of them met my gaze. I watched them walk down the hall toward the front door, too stunned to say a word.

Mr. North appeared at my side. "Miss Jackson, do not even think about interfering in this."

"But what's going on? Is he arresting Sarah? Why?"

"What did I just say?" He sounded as if he were correcting a wayward student. I turned, put my hands on my hips, and glared at him. But I held my tongue, at least for the moment.

"Come in here," he said. "I have to talk to you about a different matter."

Confused, I walked into his office and sat in the chair Sarah had just left. "Miss Jackson, I have been informed of a request by Cliff Pendling for a schedule change."

How had he heard about it so quickly? As if he had read my mind, he said, "Cliff's counselor felt there might be more to the request than what was on the surface and forwarded it to me. I understand that you gave this student permission to withdraw from your class. Is that correct?"

"Well, yes, I did. I admit I didn't have time to think it through, and I could have just as easily sent Cliff for discipline as a schedule change. He made very disparaging remarks about Sadie. And when he mentioned switching sections of ALS, I wasn't sure it was such a bad idea."

"You weren't, were you? So once again you're overreaching your authority, Miss Jackson. I thought we had reached an understanding on that, but perhaps we haven't. A teacher does not have veto power over which students are in her classes. Can't you see the chaos that would produce, the favoritism?"

"I never thought of that."

"No, I'm sure you didn't. That's the problem. And here's my solution: Cliff Pendling will remain in your class, and you will establish a working relationship with him. I don't ask you to like the boy, but I demand that you teach him. And I don't want to receive any more complaints from his parents either."

I wanted to point out that he was siding with scabs over one of his own teachers. But I bit my tongue. He was angry enough with me already. But I did say, "Wait. What does that mean? Any *more* complaints?"

"Yes, his mother contacted me earlier in the year—"

"And you didn't inform me? Aren't you supposed to?"

He reddened, then mumbled, "Um, perhaps I forgot to.

But it is not your place to question me. And do not make me regret having given you tenure, young lady."

I had heard all that I could stand. I didn't care how rude it was. I stood up so abruptly that I nearly knocked the chair over and stormed out of his office.

I hurried into the hall and headed for the parking lot. Halfway blinded by unshed tears of rage or grief—I wasn't sure which—I nearly ran into Billy as he swept the hallway.

"Hey, Miss J., you okay?"

"No; yes. I don't know." It took all of my strength to keep from crying in front of a student. Former student.

"I'm sorry," he said timidly. "I just hoped you weren't too upset about Miss Wittingham…"

"What do you mean? What happened to her?"

"Well, I couldn't help seeing her get in the police car a little while ago. Do you think she's getting questioned again?"

"That, or worse."

"Not busted?"

"I'm not sure, but I'm afraid she might be under arrest, Billy."

"What a bummer. She didn't do anything, right?"

"Right. Of course not," I said, calming down a bit. "But, just to be sure, I'm going to go check it out. The poor woman has been through so much this past week, I don't see how she's still functioning. I'll see you tomorrow, Billy. Thanks for the talk. And it's good seeing you."

"You're welcome, Miss J. Hey, do you have one more minute, or are you in a big hurry?"

"No, I have time. It's probably too soon to see Sarah at the station anyway."

"Thank you. It's just that there's something I've been wanting to tell you, but with Miss Malcom and everything there hasn't been a chance." He paused, searching for words.

"I want you to know that I'm doing what you told us to do, Miss J. I'm taking a class at the junior college while I work. Yeah, me—a college student. I never would have thought I could do that if I hadn't been in your class. I wanted to thank you for helping me."

I almost gave him a hug, but I held off; it would have embarrassed him. "Billy, I am so proud of you. And thank you for telling me. You have made this day so much brighter for me."

He beamed at the thought of having helped me in return.

———

I wasted an hour by going to the police station. All I learned from the taciturn officer at the desk was that Sarah was still there and was unavailable to speak to me. I plunked myself down in a chair near his desk and waited. But she didn't come out, and at five o'clock he told me to leave so he could lock up the office.

I was in such a foul mood when I got home that even Marmalade could not cheer me up. I paced the floor of my little cottage, fuming. Was anything at all being done to learn more about Sadie's death? Or had the police already decided that Sarah was guilty? Should I, or could I, help her? What if I tried to and ended up losing my job, the one I had just gotten back? Or Tom. I wouldn't lose him, would I?

CHAPTER 15

September 14

The next morning I was fumbling for the key to unlock my classroom when Billy came up behind me. He reached out to hold my book bag and lunch until I had the door open.

"Thanks, Billy. Do you want to come in for a few minutes?"

"Yeah, sure, Miss J. I mean Andrea," he said softly, blushing. "Sure. You having a better day today?"

"Yeah, so far, so good. The thing is, these questions about Sadie. They keep nagging at me. Know what I mean?"

"I sure do. I been having a lot of trouble sleeping ever since it happened. Hey, are you going to work on the crime? You're good at solving stuff like that. And I could help you again. Just like that other time when I was in your class."

"Oh, no, Billy, I'm not planning to do anything like that. We were both lucky we got out of that situation safely. No, this is different. I'm just curious, and I have a couple of questions, things that probably only you would know. Do you mind?"

"Nah. I'm always happy to help. What do you want to know?"

I closed the door and we both sat in student desks. "Well, one thing is, do you know if Sadie had intended to spend the night in the school?"

"Well, now that you mention it, she might have, Miss J. I went into the third-floor teachers lounge that night to change a light bulb, and there was this tote bag in the corner. I didn't make that much of it right then, but here's the thing: after it was all over and the ambulance took her away, I went back to see if it could have been hers, and it was gone."

"Hmmm. Maybe the police found it during their search and took it."

"Why would she want to sleep at school?"

"I'm guessing that she probably didn't want to cross the picket line another time. I wonder if she got the idea of coming into the building during the meeting, when no one was picketing, and staying here overnight."

"Yeah, maybe. I guess she could of."

"Okay, here's another question, Billy. After the board

meeting ended, did anyone hang around in the hall for a while?"

"Let me think." He squinted in concentration and then slowly shook his head. "Not that I can remember. That seems like so long ago. I'm sorry—oh, wait. It was later, I don't know, maybe half an hour or so after the meeting broke up. I saw three guys come out of the library. I remember being surprised because I figured everyone would have been long gone. One was the superintendent, and I think another one was the guy running the meeting."

"Do you mean Ray Dalby? Did he walk with a limp?"

"Yeah, like he was in pain? Uh-huh."

"What about the third one? Have you ever seen him around?"

"Yeah, during the strike. He seemed like he was in charge of the sc—I mean the subs."

"Pendling. That makes sense. I remember seeing those three with their heads together right after the end of the meeting. So they stayed behind for a while and then left together?"

"No, I don't think they left together. I saw that Dalby guy go down the stairs toward the front doors, and the other two looked like they were heading for the side parking lot. But I think they all would have been gone before Miss Malcolm... fell."

"Yeah, I guess so. Unless someone waited around or came back. Did you see them actually leave the building?"

"No, I was cleaning up on the third floor and kept right on working. I was behind schedule because of the meeting tying up the library when I was supposed to be cleaning it."

"Did you see or hear anyone else in the building that night, Billy?"

"Well, there were a few people in and out of the library during the meeting. It looked like bathroom breaks. The only other one I remember seeing afterwards was Mr. Linck. He wanted to know if the gate was locked or if he could still get to his room to pick up something he forgot. I told him to go ahead. We leave the gates open later than usual when there's meetings."

"That's strange. I mean that Harve would need to get in his room. We were on strike and weren't teaching the next day, so what would he need?"

"I don't know. I didn't see him again. Like I said, I was just trying to get my work done because I was running late. I even cut my lunch short that night."

"What time did you take your lunch break?"

"It would have been around midnight."

"Where do you eat?"

"In the janitor's office."

"So if you were out there in the yellow hall, you wouldn't have heard Sadie or anyone else in the main part of the school, would you?"

"Nope. Nothing but cement blocks around you out there."

His face fell. "Oh no, Miss J. Maybe if I'd been close enough to hear she was in trouble, I could have…done something to help her."

"No, Billy," I said quickly. "I didn't mean to suggest you could have prevented her death. There's nothing you could have done to save her."

He shook his head forlornly. "But I was the only one here who maybe could have helped her."

I had lost track of time and was startled to hear the warning bell. "I have to get to work, Billy. I just hate thinking my questions made you feel worse."

"No, Miss J. I already felt bad, real bad, about Miss M."

"I know. We all do, Billy."

———

My first three classes went by in a flurry of quizzes, excuses for unfinished homework, writing assignments, and the other concerns that make up a typical school day. It wasn't until fourth-hour study hall that I had time to myself. As I watched the kids work, I began to ponder the implications of what I had learned from Billy.

I knew from teaching Mystery Stories that the key components of finding a guilty party are means, motive, and opportunity. And, as with all good mysteries, more than one person in this case had all three. Sarah, whom the police apparently suspected of the crime, fit the bill, at least in their eyes. But so did others.

According to Billy, Dalby, Pendling, and Harve had all been in the school late that night. Sarah, on the other hand, had left the meeting before it was over. Of course, she could have stayed in the building. And any one of them could have waited until the others had gone and later come back and encountered Sadie.

But the bigger question was, who would want to hurt her? I handed out the hall pass to a girl, glared at two guys whispering until they stopped, and continued my pondering.

Okay, motive is the big thing. Who would want to harm Sadie? Sarah was hurt and disappointed by her decision to cross the picket line, but that had been only a moment in their long friendship.

Harve, though, had been furious with Sadie, and despite his words during the moment of silence, I wasn't convinced that he had forgiven her. At the time of her death, I remembered, our future had looked pretty bleak. We had all just been fired, and the negotiating team expected to be arrested at any time. Not that Sadie's actions were responsible for any of that. I realized I was tugging on my peace symbol again and made a conscious effort to keep my hands on my desk.

What about the others? As for motive, Dalby hated teachers in general, though, in her favor, Sadie had refused to strike, which he should have liked. But Pendling had a personal grudge against her that went back for months. Both seemed mean enough to harm someone too.

To make matters worse, there were still so many unanswered questions surrounding Sadie's death. Did the fall kill her, or was she already injured before she went over the railing? Could natural causes have had anything to do with it? What exactly were her injuries? All of those questions, and more, would be answered in the coroner's report. Fat chance I'd ever get my hands on that, though.

Tom would have access to it, but I was positive he wouldn't reveal anything. Even when we were getting along famously before the strike, he wouldn't have discussed it with me. And he was treating everything about this case as top secret.

Besides, I reminded myself, I didn't need to see the report because I wasn't investigating anything. No, I was just trying to satisfy my curiosity. And, of course, to help Sarah, if I could do that without getting too involved. The bell rang, ending both study hall and my mental chess game.

———

My classes were slowly settling back into the routine—the classes other than my eighth hour, that is. Since my hopes of having Cliff transfer to Antag's section had been dashed by North, I wasn't sure what to expect from Cliff, who returned to high fives and applause from his supporters. He was in rare form for my lesson on Edgar Allen Poe's poetry.

The romantic poem "Annabel Lee" went fairly well, at least with the girls. It was when we got to "The Raven" that Cliff kicked his act into high gear. My first mention of the title elicited a croaked *nevermore* from him, resulting in muffled laughter around the room. From then on, my attempts at discussion were interrupted every few minutes with *nevermores*. Cliff had begun it, but other boys picked it up, and I couldn't catch anyone in the act. It was so frustrating to see another lesson that had worked flawlessly in my morning class crash and burn during eighth hour. Eventually, I was saved by the bell, but my bad mood hung on after the kids were gone.

I was almost to my car when I heard someone call my name. "Miss J., hold up."

"Billy, what is it? It's freezing out here, and you don't even have a coat on."

"I know. I tried to catch you in your room, but I missed you. I remembered something else I should have told you this morning."

"You want to go back inside? Or we could sit in my car and talk here."

"No, this'll just take a sec, but it's about Miss Malcolm's... you know."

"Yeah, I know." I didn't want to say the words *death* or *murder* either. "What is it?"

"You know how the police checked the floor outside the office for blood? Well, the next morning they were looking all over the school, and I think they must have found more blood at the top of the stairs. I saw them wiping the floor with these white pads like bandages and putting them inside plastic bags. What do you think, Miss J.?"

"I think you're right, Billy. They must have found some kind of evidence up there. And if there was blood at the top of the stairs, then she, or someone, must have been injured before she fell. You didn't happen to overhear the police say anything, did you?"

"No, I wasn't close enough. They looked so busy and serious that I stayed way back. I'm sorry..."

"Oh, don't apologize. I'm glad you thought to tell me this, Billy. Now get back inside before you freeze to death."

I got in my car, started it, and cranked up the heater. "Sadie, my friend, how exactly did you die?" I whispered. "If there was blood at the top of the stairs, I'm afraid you were hurt before you fell. Knowing you, you would have put up a good fight."

CHAPTER 16

September 22

One day the following week, study hall was just getting started when one of my kids asked a strange question. "Hey, Miss Jackson, is this teacher skip day or something?"

"What do you mean? Teachers don't skip school."

"Well, it sure looks like there's something going on. Mr. Linck wasn't in wood shop first hour, and my math teacher was gone second hour."

"Oh, yeah, and I saw a sub coming out of Miss Wittingham's room too," said another kid. What's going on?"

"I have no idea," I said with a sinking feeling. I hadn't seen Billy before school either. I wondered if there were more absences and if they were connected.

The kids settled into their homework, and I reached for

my lesson plan book to begin working on the following week. It was so quiet in the room that I heard Susan's spiked heels approaching several seconds before she appeared.

She and I stood in the open doorway so I could keep one eye on my study hall. Susan said quietly, "When you have time, could you go down and check on Sarah for me?"

"Sure. But where have she and the others been? The kids are asking if it's teacher skip day."

Sighing, she said, "They were at the police station and then the hospital. The department chairmen got a memo from North this morning saying that some staff members would be giving blood samples to the police. I guess it's a part of the investigation."

"So why them and not everyone?"

"He didn't say, but, looking at the names, I'm guessing that they may have all been among the last to leave the school board meeting the night Sadie was…"

"Right," I said quickly. "Actually, I could have been in that group because I was sitting pretty far forward at the meeting and was one of the last out of the room."

"Were you with anyone?"

"No, but when I went out to the parking lot, Bud was walking a few feet behind me, if I remember right."

"That may be why you weren't called in. North let it slip that right now the cops are looking only at people who were not seen by anyone leaving the building."

"But—"

"I know. Anyone could have come back in later."

"Yeah. Wait a minute. What about Dalby and the other board members? And the parents and even the kids who were at the meeting? Are they all being checked out too?"

"I don't know, but it would only be fair."

As we stood there, a boy walked up and asked to go to his locker.

"Yes," I said, only half listening to him. "Take the pass."

"So I can count on you to look in on Sarah?" Susan asked again. "I would do it myself, but I go right from classes to a department council meeting."

"Yes, sure, I'll pay her a visit."

———

I didn't hear any more about the teacher absences until my last class. Near the end of the period, I was handing back papers when Cliff said, loudly enough for all to hear, "Looks like the cops pulled in all of the murder suspects today. Wittingham had a sub, and Linck was gone this morning too. And there were probably more."

"How do you know that's why they were gone?" a girl sitting near him asked.

Suddenly aware that everyone, including me, was listening, he whispered something to her.

"Your dad?" the girl blurted out.

"Shut up," he muttered as his face reddened.

Before he could say more, the bell rang. "Quiz tomorrow," I reminded them as they made their way out.

"Cliff…" He looked unhappy to be called back. "Don't forget your makeup work. When do you want—"

"Yeah, I'll let you know," he said over his shoulder as he rushed into the hall.

Remembering my promise to Susan, I hurried down to Sarah's room. But when I got there, her door was locked and she was gone.

I knew Susan had a meeting, but I hoped to catch her before it began. I got to the library just as North was calling the meeting to order. She stepped out into the hall with me.

"Susan, I hustled right down to Sarah's room, but she wasn't there, which is strange because she always stays late to get things ready for the next day, and I'm kind of worried about her." I paused for a breath.

"Andrea, I'm sorry I couldn't save you a trip. Brenda just told me that Sarah left after fifth hour. She didn't give the office any warning, just announced that she was leaving. So they didn't have time to find a sub for the afternoon and had to dismiss her classes."

"I hope nothing's wrong. That doesn't sound like her at all."

"No, it doesn't. I mean, it doesn't sound like the old Sarah.

I know she's going through a rough time, so I'm not going to write her up for it. But I'll have to if she does anything like that again."

I wanted to stop Susan right there and complain. Granted, she had responsibilities as department chair, but this was really harsh in light of Sarah's situation. Yet I bit my tongue.

Susan was dealing with her own demons. In fact, it was Sarah who had told me how Susan had lost her kid brother early in the Vietnam War. After that, she had never been the same. Her unacknowledged grief had turned her brittle and angry.

I was glad I hadn't said anything when Susan continued, "I hope Sarah makes it through the year. It's such a shame we're having all of this turmoil. She and Sadie both deserved so much better after all they've given to Hancock."

CHAPTER 17
October 6

I had been looking forward to Friday all week, especially to a rare after-school coffee date with Chrissie at The Grounds. I could feel myself relax as we settled into our booth with the afternoon sun streaming in the newly replaced windows. The place was busier than ever, but our camaraderie with the townspeople had not been repaired as easily as the windows. It was as if an invisible line divided the coffee shop in half, with the two groups sitting on opposite sides.

Chrissie leaned across the table and said, "We haven't had much of a chance to talk lately. How are things going with Tom?"

"Oh, Chrissie, I don't even know. I wish I could read his mind over the phone because he's working so much that I hardly ever see him anymore. And when I do…I tell you, I'm tired of being on pins and needles all the time. If only we could go back to the way things were be—"

My seat bounced slightly when someone sat down in the booth directly behind me. Whoever it was had one of those voices that carries.

"What's wrong?" Chrissie asked.

"Shhhh. Can you see the people behind me? Try to find who's there without being obvious about it."

"Looks like a guy and a girl, both pretty young. His back is to me, but I can see her. She looks fascinated with him and whatever he's saying. I think it might be a first date."

"Okay, let me listen for a sec." I paused and then hissed, "He's talking about a murder, Chrissie—or actually a murder *weapon*."

"Oh, dear. It seems like everyone in town is gossiping about Sadie's—"

"Shhhh. He just said the murder weapon is a heavy but small-diameter object on the order of a hammerhead. He has to be talking about Sadie's case. How many murder weapons are there in Hancock right now? But how would he know that?"

"I don't know, unless he's a cop. And, if he is, he sure shouldn't be telling her that, and especially not in public."

"I can't make out her end of the conversation, but he just clearly said it hasn't been found, and the police really need it. I have to try to find out who he is," I whispered. "Wait. I have an idea."

I took out my wallet and dumped the loose change on the floor. And I lucked out. A couple of pennies rolled all the way to his feet. I fell to my hands and knees and started gathering them up. "'Scuse me," I said as I crawled partway under their table. "I dropped some money down here."

I didn't know the face frowning down at me, but I recognized the ID hanging around his neck. Being careful that my long hair hid my face, I retreated as quickly as I could.

I got back to my seat, brushed off my skirt, and grinned at Chrissie, giving her a slight, affirmative nod. "He's a reporter," I said under my breath.

"Then he might have learned that from the police. Maybe it's true."

"Yes, but what could the weapon be? Something heavy and blunt, possibly a hammer?"

"Or something hammer-like," she added. "What's hammer-like?"

"Right. Well, it could be several things. And hammers are not exactly uncommon items. I mean, the custodians and maintenance guys all have them. They're used in the shop classes. Anyone could have brought one from home. And we're not even sure it was a hammer—"

"Maybe a gavel?" she asked.

"Hmmm. How many people have we seen with a gavel lately?"

"Only one that I can think of. Oh, look at the time. I'm sorry to interrupt, Andrea, but I have to run. Rob is home for such a short time on game nights, and I want to be there to make him a bite to eat."

"You go on ahead. I'll be right behind you," I said.

But I didn't leave immediately. I waited to see if the couple behind me would say anything else about the case. And they did—at least the girl did.

"Wouldn't it be cool if you solved the crime before the police did? Not that there's much to solve. Everyone is saying that teacher, Sarah what's-her-name, did it."

———

It ended up being an off-kilter Friday night. When Tom didn't call at his usual time, I suspected the worst. He was still so angry he didn't even want to talk to me. He didn't think our relationship could be saved. Or he thought our relationship could be saved, but it would take more effort than he was willing to give.

When he finally did call, we were both on edge. In a tired, stressed voice, he said, "I'm sorry to be calling so late. It's crazy here. I haven't been able to take a break until now."

"I understand," I said. But I wasn't sure I completely believed him. Had he stalled until it was too late to go out?

"Listen, you're not going to like this, but I'm going to get it over with and tell you. I don't even know when my next day off will be. The mayor is pressuring our chief to make faster progress on the case. So he's canceling all of our days off for a while."

"Can they even do that? Give you guys no breaks until who knows when? Isn't anyone going to complain?"

"I don't know, but I'm sure not going to. This case is the break I've been waiting for. How often does a murder come along in a town like Hancock?" Immediately he said, "God, Andie, I'm so sorry. I know how cold that sounded. It's a very personal crime for you and for a lot of people in town. But don't you see? That's why it's even more important that we solve it. And if I can contribute to that, it would be very, very good for my career. But…I'm sorry…"

"Oh, Tommy, I know you and what a kind heart you have. And I know you didn't mean that the way it sounded. And if there's anything I can do to help—"

"Well," he said slowly, "actually there is something you could do. Look, everyone in the department knows that you and I are dating. And everyone knows that you taught with Sadie and were very close to her. I'm trying my hardest to act professional and to show the brass that my personal life will have no effect on my work. So far, I think I'm doing that."

I had never thought of that. "Oh, Tommy, I don't want to put you in a difficult position at work. I would hate myself if I let that happen. I will be very, very careful. I promise."

"Thanks, Andie. I know you will be. The best way for you to help is to stay out of the investigation entirely. That's really important. And there's one more thing. If there ever comes a time when I have to hold you at arm's length to appear professional—"

"Like when I tried to give you a hug at the school the night Sadie died and you kind of pushed me away?"

"Yeah, like that. I hated doing it, but I had to. Anyway, if that happens again, don't read anything into it. Okay?"

"Yeah, I'll try not to. I'm glad you explained that so I'll know what's going on."

"Okay. Good. Now I have to get back to work. I'll be in touch as often as I can. That you can count on."

After our phone call, I didn't know what to do with myself. I thought about going to the football game, but it was probably already halftime and there wouldn't have been a parking space within blocks of the field.

I tried to find something on TV, gave up on that and put on some music. Without looking to see what records I had left on the stereo, I turned it on and lifted up the stack of 45s to play. "Here Comes the Sun," "Eleanor Rigby," "The Long and Winding Road…" Even the Beatles couldn't cheer me up.

Finally, I admitted that only one thing would restore my good spirits—a more satisfying talk with Tom. I was reaching for the phone when it rang. And it was Tom.

"Listen, Andie, I don't care if I have to work overtime every single day for the rest of my natural life, I want to spend some time with you as soon as possible. We need to—"

"Oh, I feel the same way, Tommy." And just like that the dark cloud over me began to lift. "I'm so glad you called back."

"What do you say we go out for breakfast tomorrow? I don't

have to go in until noon, so I'll take a nap when I get off and then swing by and pick you up around eight. I was thinking of May's Country Cupboard, okay?"

"That's great. I think I'll walk over and meet you there, but could you give me a ride home afterward?"

"Sure. See you in the morning."

It had been a short conversation, but that was all right. Everything was all right. We would talk more the next day, and before I knew it we'd be right back where we were before the strike.

I scooped up Marm and gave him such a tight hug that he meowed in protest. Carefully, I set him down and apologized. "Didn't mean to startle you, boy. I'm just so happy right now." He smiled, rubbed against my legs, and gave me his loudest, most rumbling purr. Tom had forgiven me for striking, and he wanted things to work out between us. Everything was going to be the way it had been. No, it was going to be better.

I got my best sleep in weeks, and sometime during the night I made a decision. I would help Tom with his career by sharing what I had learned from Billy about people's comings and goings the night of Sadie's death. Our relationship was all about supporting each other, right? Well, that's what I would do at breakfast. Support him.

CHAPTER 18
October 7

Tom was sitting in a booth by a window at May's when I walked in. His grin was wide and warm as he stood to kiss me. I thought about squeezing past him to sit on the same bench in the booth, but I didn't let myself. It seemed kind of flirty, and in our professional roles we were under scrutiny whenever we were in public. Instead, I slid onto the seat across from him and brushed his knee with mine.

"God, I've missed you," he said softly.

"Oh, me too. You don't know how much."

We were still gazing into each other's eyes when a waitress appeared with the coffee pot. I thought she looked familiar, and, sure enough, she greeted me as Miss Jackson.

Normally, I enjoyed catching up with former students, but

I wasn't in the mood to hear about Lucy's classes at the junior college. And I was even less in the mood to admire her shiny new engagement ring. I told her we were ready to order, which we did, and she left us alone.

We were still chatting about trivial matters when Lucy brought our omelets. It was after we finished eating that I ruined everything.

"Please don't take this wrong, Tommy. I'm not interfering in your case—"

"Good. Let's keep it that way." If his words hadn't warned me to stop there, the muscle twitching in his left cheek should have. But my curiosity, as usual, got the better of me.

"I know that Harve, Sarah, and Billy all had to give blood samples yesterday—"

"Well, you're not supposed to know that. Jeez, Andrea, do you have to stick your nose in everything?"

"No, I don't have to. I only want to protect my friends. If it was supposed to be a secret, you shouldn't have taken them out of school. Don't you think the kids notice things like that and gossip about them?" I should have stopped before I made matters worse. But I didn't.

"Tom, that's not the main point anyway. I just wanted to be sure that you didn't leave any suspects out. Were Ray Dalby and Wayne Pendling blood-typed too? If not, they should be. Both of them were at the school that night, and both of them had motives to hurt Sadie. And Pendling, he's had a big grudge against her, and really more than that. He has been furious, since…"

At that point, I realized I'd crossed the line. Or, to be more accurate, stomped on the line on my way over it. But it was too late to turn back. "And when you hear my reasoning, I'm sure you'll agree."

"Well, we'll never know if I would have agreed because this conversation is over. I just asked you last night, warned you, not to interfere in the police investigation. But here you are, already doing that. Come on, Andrea. Mind your own damn business."

Was this the same man I had talked to the night before? Tom was not one to swear unless provoked. But I was getting angry too. I had important information, and he wouldn't even listen to it. But I would not cry.

"Oh, no," I moaned, as tears that I couldn't hold back began to trickle down my cheeks.

"Um, Miss Jackson," Lucy said hesitantly. "I'm sorry to bother you, but…is anything wrong?"

"No," I sniffed. "Everything's fine, Lucy."

There was no way she could have believed me, but she read the situation well enough to leave us alone.

"I have to get out of here," I said, heading for the door. Of course, I had forgotten my car wasn't there.

I sat in Tom's car and tried to pull myself together while he paid the bill. Then he got in and started the engine without ever looking at me. We drove to my place in total silence. Once there, I made one last attempt.

"I was only trying—"

"Don't say any more. Just let it go." It was his tone, more than his words, that stung.

I got out, closed the car door softly, and went inside. Once there, I leaned against the door and began sobbing in earnest. Marm tried his cat best to comfort me, and he paced in distress when his usual ministrations didn't work. It was all of nine thirty on Saturday morning, with nothing but a long, lonely weekend stretching ahead of me.

———

I spent a lot of time the next two days thinking about our disastrous breakfast date. It carried a double sting, and I wasn't sure which part hurt more. Not only had we argued, but it had started because I wanted to share valuable information with Tom. Rather than thanking me for suggesting two viable suspects, he had nearly bitten my head off.

How could he not consider Ray Dalby and Wayne Pendling as possible suspects? Didn't he know that Pendling had had it in for Sadie since their dispute over his son's grade last spring? That made me pause. Tom might very well not know about it. It hadn't even been common knowledge among the faculty. All the more reason he should have listened to me.

And Dalby? Why, he was a known teacher-hater and a mean, cruel man. That certainly should put him under suspicion.

I didn't know how I would ever be able to discuss this with Tom. He wouldn't listen to me, and I was too upset to try to reason with him anyway.

Then my phone rang, and my heart soared—until I answered. It was Mom making her usual Saturday check-in. Then my college roommate called to chat. And Chrissie called to see if I had a good book she could borrow. There was even a wrong-number call, but not a peep out of Tom.

At last, as I was getting ready for bed Sunday night, the phone rang again and I heard Tom's subdued voice.

"Uh, Andie. Listen, I'm on break and can't talk long, but I don't want to leave things between us the way they were yesterday. I don't know about you, but this has been a very long weekend for me."

"It's been horribly long for me too, Tom. I don't want things to stay like this either. Can we get together and try to talk it out?"

"Let's do that. I'm still working pretty much all the time, but I have a break for dinner tomorrow. It's early, at five, but would that be okay with you?"

"Oh, more than okay, Tommy."

"Good. Look, to save time, could you meet me here at the

station? We can go someplace close by so we have as much time together as possible, all right?"

"That would be perfect. I'm collecting essays from four classes tomorrow—"

He whistled.

"Yeah, I know—poor planning on my part. I'll have to work on them all evening, so an early dinner is good. I'll be there at five. And, Tommy, thank you so much for calling."

"You bet, Andie. Get a good night's sleep."

Right then I made a decision, one that I hoped I wouldn't regret. My number-one priority would be fixing Tom's and my relationship. That had to come before anything else, even helping Sarah, which I had never definitely decided to do anyway. During our dinner date, I would not so much as breathe a word about the crime or the suspects or their motives. The police would have to investigate it without my help. I would control my curiosity and set things right with Tom.

I smiled as my head hit the pillow and Marm curled into his favorite sleeping place on my left arm. But, crazy as it sounds, I was too happy to sleep. I couldn't settle down and, after an hour or so, turned the light back on. Marm gave me a baleful look and jumped off the bed.

As long as I couldn't sleep, I thought I might as well work on my ALS lesson plan for the next day. My classes would be discussing Emerson's essay on self-reliance, and the plan I had used the previous year hadn't worked all that well. Maybe I could do better.

The problem with Emerson wasn't his ideas but the prose he used to present them. As one of my students had complained, Emerson had a knack for taking an interesting idea and making it boring. Last year's class had related best to his concept of nonconformity, so I would start there. It was, after all, at the heart of the hippie movement that still dominated lifestyles in 1972—at least in Hancock.

I turned on my portable electric typewriter, rolled a two-ply ditto into the carriage, carefully keeping my fingers off the purple bottom sheet, and began to type. *Explain these quotes in your own words.* As I typed, I ran into one passage that seemed more familiar than the others: *To be great is to be misunderstood.*

I was almost sure I had seen it on a poster in Bud's room. I made a mental note to check before school to see if I could borrow his poster for the day. With that settled, I got back in bed and fell asleep.

CHAPTER 19

October 8

"Yeah, I think it's still around here somewhere," Bud said when I asked about the Emerson poster. "It really spoke to me my first year here, if you know what I mean, so I probably kept it. Maybe it's in this cabinet back here."

"Ta-dah," he said with a grin as he pulled it from a jumbled pile on the top shelf and handed it to me. I realized how much I had missed that smile. I hadn't seen enough of Bud for a while.

"Yoo-hoo!" A girl's voice trilled from his doorway. Whoever it was couldn't see us behind the open door of the cabinet.

"Here we are," Bud said quickly, with a slight emphasis on the *we*.

"Oh." Julie's pink cheeks matched her peasant blouse

when she realized I was there. "I'm sorry. I hope I'm not interrupting."

"Not at all, Julie," I said. "I'm just borrowing this poster and have to put it up in my room before first hour. So I'm leaving now."

Something about that exchange made me uneasy. I couldn't help feeling there was more between Bud and Julie than the usual critic teacher-student teacher relationship. I saw her with him a lot more than with Susan, who was her actual critic teacher. It was not that she wasn't of age. I knew she was twenty-one, so there was only a three-year age difference between her and Bud. But, still, she was wearing an engagement ring. I reminded myself it was none of my business and went back to my room.

I taped the poster to my door so the kids couldn't miss seeing it as they came in. On the blackboard, I wrote three of the Emerson quotes:

"Whoso would be a man must be a nonconformist."

"What I must do is all that concerns me, not what the people think."

"Trust thyself: every heart vibrates to that iron string."

I began my lesson by asking the kids to read—I hoped reread—the quotes. "What do you think the first one means?" That had been enough to begin a fruitful discussion with my first-hour class, but things were always more difficult with the afternoon group.

When no one responded to my question, I decided to wait them out. Lois gave me a sympathetic look but didn't raise her hand. Maybe she was finally tired of stepping up to help the others out. The silence stretched to an uncomfortable length; still, I resisted the urge to answer the question for them. After an interminable wait, a hand slowly went up.

Candy put on her usual scowl and asked, "What's a non… um…conformist? If we knew that, maybe we could figure it out."

"Exactly, Candy. Can anyone help us with a definition?"

Lois raised her hand tentatively and, hearing the groans, said, "Oh, knock it off. If the rest of you would do your homework, I wouldn't have to answer all of the questions in here." At my nod, she continued, "A nonconformist is an individual who thinks for him or herself. It's a person who doesn't go along with the crowd."

"Like you," Candy said. But her tone was more admiring than critical.

"Well, yeah, I guess you might say that. And like Cliff too."

"Well, I can tell you one thing for darned sure," Cliff said. "The old fogies around here don't appreciate nonconformist-ness. Any time you do something a little different, they jump your butt. Too bad that Emerson guy isn't around to run this school."

I was sure he hadn't meant to, but Cliff had actually advanced the discussion. It was easy to steer them toward the benefits and challenges of being a nonconformist. We talked for a long time in the best discussion of the year. Finally, Lois pointed to the clock, signaling me that we were running out of time. But I knew exactly what I was doing.

"Okay, let's move on to the second quote. Who can put it in your own words?"

"Hey," Candy said, her face lighting up. "It's the same thing as the first one, isn't it?"

Heads nodded in agreement. "Then what about the last one?" I asked.

After a moment, several voices chimed in. "It's the same too."

"Right! Now why would Emerson repeat himself several times in the same essay?"

"Because it's important?" Gordon said. "Like the way you do when you're making an assignment?"

"Exactly!"

"What if I want to do what I think would be best for myself and skip the homework?" Cliff asked.

"Then you may very well learn more about how the world treats a nonconformist," I said with a smile as the bell rang. When he gave me the slightest nod in return, I felt I might finally be making progress with him.

I practically floated through the halls to Chrissie's room. I found her wiping disgusting yellow splatters from a stove. "Omelets," she said before I could ask. "I forgot to watch the clock last hour, and when the bell rang a few girls were just finishing up. I didn't want them missing their buses, so…"

"Here, let me help you." I found a sponge and scouring powder. "Other than this, how was your day?"

"Fine. How about yours?"

"Terrific!" I told her about my small breakthrough with Cliff and then said, "But here's the best part: I'm meeting Tom for an early dinner. We're going to try again to work out our differences."

"That's wonderful, Andrea. I'm sure you'll be able to. You guys are just perfect together. There's nothing that can keep you apart for long."

"From your lips to God's ears, Chrissie."

"Call me when you get home, okay?"

"I will for sure. Here's hoping I'll have good news."

———

I stopped at the front desk in the police station, as all visitors were required to do. The officer on duty was engrossed in a phone conversation and, recognizing me, waved me through the turnstile with his left hand as he took notes with his right. I made my way to the door of Tom's tiny office and tapped politely.

When there was no answer, I knocked a little louder and checked my watch. No, I wasn't early, but he obviously wasn't in there. Nor was there a note on the door. I felt slightly foolish standing outside, so I tried the doorknob. It opened, and I stuck my head in. He wasn't there.

I walked over to his desk to see if he might have left a note for me there. His usually clean desktop held several official-looking papers but nothing addressed to me. I was about to take a seat in his visitor's chair when something caught my eye. It reminded me of a page from my grade book, a list of names, each followed by a letter. That's odd, I thought.

On some level, I must have realized that what I was about to do was wrong because I went over and closed the door. Snooping in a policeman's office was foolhardy, if not downright illegal. But that didn't stop me.

I walked around the desk to his chair and sat gingerly on the edge of it. As soon as I took a closer look at the list of names, I knew what I was looking at. The letters weren't A through F, as they would be in a grade book, but each did have a plus or minus after it. They were blood types. Inhaling sharply, I realized I was looking at the report of the blood types of the suspects in Sadie's murder.

I shouldn't be doing this, I told myself. I need to stand up and walk away right now. But I couldn't keep my eyes off the list. It would just take a second to skim it.

R. Dalby: O-

B. Gannet: B+

H. Linck: O+

W. Pendling: O+

S. Wittingham: O+

After taking it in, I went back and read the paragraph above the list. As Billy and I had guessed, there had been two different blood types found at the site of Sadie's murder—A positive and O positive. Sadie, it said, had been type A positive. So, I assumed, the killer was O positive.

As I was mulling over what I had just read, Tom's door flew open. He called out, "Andie, are you here? Sorry I kept you— what are you doing?"

I froze in place. He had caught me red-handed and red-faced.

Tom closed the door. He waited a second or two before he exploded. "Damn it. What are you doing? How could you? Don't you know—"

"I'm sorry," I whispered. "I'm so very sorry, Tom. I don't know what came over me. I know it was wrong. It's just that—"

"Save the excuses." He had never actually raised his voice at me before, and it was awful. "There isn't an excuse for what you did. Don't you realize how much trouble you could cause for me?" He paused and then went ahead. "Do you know where I just was? I was with my sergeant. He's threatening to take me off the case. And can you guess why? Because he's not sure I can be impartial in the investigation, due to my personal tie to the crime. *Personal tie*, Andrea."

He shook his head. "I'm beyond words. You'd better just get on your way."

"But what about dinner?"

"No." Nothing else. I knew it was pointless to try to explain or apologize any more. Maybe later, but not then. I managed to hold my tears in check as I walked out of the station and to my car. I needed to get out of there and didn't much care where I went. Automatically, I drove back to my parking space at school. There, I turned off my car, laid my head down on the steering wheel, and sobbed until I was cried out.

———

"You did what?" Chrissie asked when I finally called her. "Oh, Andrea, tell me you didn't read the official police report on Tom's desk."

"It just happened, Chrissie. Honest. I caught a glimpse of the list of names and blood types, but I didn't even know that's what it was at first. Then one thing led to another, and once I had started I couldn't stop myself. I read the whole thing. If only he hadn't caught me—"

"But he did."

"But he did," I sighed. "And I feel awful. If I could go back and undo it, I absolutely would."

"But you can't."

"No, I can't. So what do I do now?"

Before she could speak, I answered my own question. "All I can think of is to sincerely apologize and beg for his forgiveness."

"I thought you already did that."

"Well, yeah, I did. I guess I could do it again after I've given him some time to cool off."

"Yeah," she said thoughtfully. "Probably giving him some time and space is your best option. And, whatever you do, back off the case." Through the phone line, I heard her doorbell ring.

"I have to get that. Listen, I'll talk to you soon. And don't worry. Everything will be okay eventually."

"Sure, Chrissie. Thanks."

I was heartsick, afraid I had finally pushed Tom's patience so far that I had lost him. To try to cheer myself up, I fell back on an old routine from college.

I turned off the lights and lit the vanilla-scented candles scattered around my living room. I put a 45 of "Cherish" on my stereo and set it to replay automatically, poured a glass of Chablis, and then settled back into a nest of pillows on my couch. Marm jumped up beside me and began his deep, soothing purr.

I cried until my wine glass was empty, reached for the bottle, and poured another one. I stroked Marm and cried myself out while "Cherish" played over and over.

"Okay, that's it. I'm done," I announced to Marm and to

myself. I got up, wiped my eyes, and blew my nose. Things had to get better. They could hardly get worse.

As bad as I felt about what had happened with Tom, I had to admit I was also intrigued by the information I had found. I could still close my eyes and see the page. As I mentally reviewed the list, I found that some of the questions that had been bothering me now had answers.

I had to admit I was disappointed that Dalby was not a suspect. I still blamed the strike for Sadie's death, and I still blamed Dalby for the strike. On the other hand, Billy was also cleared, which was great. I wondered if he knew yet.

Neither did I believe that Sarah could have harmed her longtime friend. But it was going to take some detective work to prove that, since her blood type did match that of the killer. To me, it seemed obvious that the best way to prove her innocence would be to find the real killer.

The way I saw it, there were only two suspects left—Wayne Pendling and Harvey Linck. Both had O-positive blood. Both had been among the last to be seen in the building the night of the murder. Both bore grudges against Sadie. And, I had to admit, I didn't trust Harve a lot more than I did Pendling.

It was frustrating. The police didn't seem as interested in finding answers as I was. Well, if they weren't going to do it, I would have to. If I were careful, Tom would never know what I was doing. He couldn't get any angrier with me than he already was, and maybe I could help Sarah after all.

CHAPTER 20

October 13

With Emerson behind us, my ALS classes had moved on to Thoreau and his essay, "On Civil Disobedience." I was curious to see how his ideas would go over with the kids. And I hoped I wouldn't be hearing from any parents accusing me of teaching revolutionary ideas.

Cliff unintentionally helped me out by announcing that anything having to do with disobedience was cool. That one comment did more to set up a successful discussion than anything I could have planned.

With my help, and an assist from Lois, my students identified most of Thoreau's themes and restated them in simpler language: that the majority is not always right; that men should let their conscience govern them and not the government; that individuals have the right to withdraw their support from a government whose policies are unjust. As we worked through the concepts, their faces reflected the "ah-ha" moments that teachers live for. The kids were making connections between Thoreau's opposition to the Mexican War in 1848 and the anti-war protests of 1972.

Then we went back to the essay to figure out how Thoreau suggests that people show their resistance. We found methods like refusing to pay taxes, boycotting, and picketing. As soon as the word *picketing* was uttered, everyone wanted to talk about the strike. I was trying to redirect their attention to the essay when there was a timid knock at my door.

Sarah's face peered through the narrow glass window. "Oh, I'm sorry to interrupt," she whispered when I walked over and opened the door. "For some reason, I thought you were free this period. I'll come back after the bell."

Her eyes were brimming with tears. I couldn't just send her away. "Wait, Sarah," I whispered back.

"Hey, who's that?" I heard a boy's voice ask from the back of the room.

"Miss Wittingham," someone answered.

"No," Sarah said. "I'm not going to pull you away from your class. I can see you have your hands full right now."

"Yeah, I always do with this group. It's almost time for the bell, so come back right after class, okay?"

She nodded and slowly backed away.

———

As soon as the kids had left, I poked my head out the door. Sarah was nowhere in sight. Bud and Julie walked by, deep in conversation. He paused to ask how my day had gone, but as soon as they were out of earshot, they immediately returned to whatever they had been discussing.

I didn't want to leave without finding out what was on Sarah's mind, so I headed down to her room. The door was open, and as I got closer I could hear her classical music coming from inside. "Hey, Sarah, why didn't you…?"

But she wasn't there. I was sure she would be coming back, so I went in to wait. Her room was not in its usual immaculate condition. The desks did not line up in perfectly straight rows, and the blackboard was only partly erased. Things were just not normal. But then how could they be when Sarah was still suspected of killing her closest friend?

I sat down in a student desk to wait but was too restless to stay in one place for long. I began wandering the room, walking up and down the rows of desks, straightening them as I went. Then I went to the board and slowly finished erasing it.

When I walked past her desk, I noticed that a picture frame had fallen over. I picked it up and saw that it didn't hold a picture but a piece of paper. Written on it was a stanza of an Emily Dickinson poem: "Hope is the thing with feathers / That perches in the soul / And sings the tunes without the words / And never stops at all." The handwriting wasn't Sarah's; it was Sadie's. I held the frame to my heart for a moment and then gently placed it back on the desk.

Next, I walked over to the shelves holding the paperbacks that Sarah checked out to students. I tidied up the rows, turning around a few books that had been replaced upside down. In doing so, I got my hands dusty. Small cleaning jobs like that were left to the teachers, rather the custodians. It looked like Sarah hadn't had a chance to dust lately.

I glanced at the top of the bookcase and saw it was dusty too. On it were the decorative paperweights that she had been awarded over her teaching career. Beginning with fifteen years of service, Hancock High recognized staff members every five years with large paperweights shaped like old-fashioned school bells. But they didn't line up right. There was too much space between two of them.

Looking closer, I found Sarah's fifteenth, twentieth, and thirtieth-year paperweights, but where was the one she would have received for twenty-five years? It hadn't been missing very long because the shape of the base of the bell was still visible in the dust. I picked one up to move it and was surprised by how heavy it was. I turned it bottom up and saw that it was solid metal, not an actual bell.

"Andrea?" Sarah's voice sounded weak and tired, but it startled me nonetheless.

"Oh, hi, Sarah. I'm glad you're back. I've been waiting for you. I expected to find you outside my door when the bell rang, but you weren't there. Do you still want to talk?"

She sighed deeply as she walked over to me. "Oh, look at that. I didn't realize how dusty things have gotten in my room. I've let so many things slide this year." She hadn't answered my question, but I let it go.

"Well, you've had a lot on your mind. But look at this, Sarah. I was just noticing one of your paperweights is missing."

"Why, you're right. My twenty-five-year one isn't there. Isn't that strange? What could have happened to it?"

I pondered in silence for a minute. "Well, there was some vandalism reported right after the strike. But that was out in the shop and art wing. Have you noticed anything else missing? Or even disturbed?"

Sarah shook her head. "Nooooo."

"Anyway," I said, "why did you come to see me eighth hour?"

"You know, I'm not sure now. I can't remember why I came. Isn't that odd?"

"Well, since I'm here, is there anything you wanted to talk about?"

"No, I don't think so."

It was looking like I had wasted my time waiting for her. For someone who had sought me out to talk earlier, she was acting evasive. I tried to cover my frustration, saying, "All right. If you change your mind, give me a call."

"Okay, I will." It was the right response, but she didn't sound like she meant it. I left her room with more questions than I had come with.

CHAPTER 21

October 27

Despite my worries about Sarah and my problems with Tom, the days and weeks kept rolling along, filled with the relentless grind of preparing, teaching, and grading. Before I knew it, we were in the ninth week of school with report-card grades coming due.

I woke up one morning that week with a ferocious headache. The timing couldn't have been worse. I really had to be in school to tie up loose ends before I could begin averaging grades. So I washed down two aspirins with a cup of strong coffee and dragged myself to work.

Sometime between second and third hours, I finally realized that my shooting pain wasn't a headache at all but a toothache. As soon as I had a free moment, I hurried to the teachers lounge to call my dentist.

His receptionist, who sounded as harried as I felt, was sympathetic but asked if I could wait until the following day for an appointment. When I said I couldn't hold out that long, she offered to try to squeeze me in at three thirty.

I hesitated. I would have to leave school immediately at the end of eighth hour. But I reluctantly agreed when she told me that was the best she could do. It meant I would not be available for makeup work after school on the last day I had said I would accept it. When I looked over my list of missing assignments, though, I was relieved. Most of the names were already crossed off, and the few who remained did not seem likely to come in at the end of the school day.

I took as many more aspirins as I thought safe and concentrated on getting through the afternoon with as little effort as possible. Usually the kids can sense when a teacher is not feeling well, and I found most of them sympathetic.

That day I was like many of my kids. I had my book bag all packed up ready to dash out the door on the final bell. I felt I should at least wait until they were all out of the room before I took off. Just as I was about to leave, Cliff shuffled up to my desk.

"Hey, Mrs. Jackson." I didn't take time to correct the *Mrs.* "I was just wondering...am I missing anything in here? I mean, with report cards coming up and all."

Was he missing anything? When was the last time he had handed in anything that had to be done outside of class? What about the three quizzes he had claimed he shouldn't have to take because he had been absent the day before? Of course, he had never bothered to make them up. I sighed. "Of course you are, Cliff."

"Well, is it anything important? What will my grade be if I don't hand them in?"

I took a quick glance at the grade book. "I haven't averaged grades yet, but it looks like you'll be right between a D and an F."

"What? You mean you're going to flunk me because I never got to make up a couple of things?" His voice rose in disbelief.

"Cliff, how many times have I reminded you? And didn't you see your name on the list I put on the board last week? The one with those missing work?"

"Yeah, I guess. Well, then I'll do it now, I guess."

"Cliff, I have to leave for an emergency dental appointment. In fact, if I don't leave this second, I'm going to be late."

"But what about my makeup work? I gotta do it, right?"

"You waited until the very last minute. And I can't stay today. I have an appointment that I really have to keep."

"Then when can I do it? I thought you said today was the last day."

"Today is the last day."

We stared at each other, both unwilling to budge. Finally, I was the one who blinked. "I'll tell you what. It's too late to take the quizzes, but if you want to hand in the missing assignments, I'll accept them up until the first-hour bell in the morning."

"But I lost the directions for how to do the paper on the Trans…whatever."

"Transcendentalists. I'm sorry, Cliff. I really have to go."

As I walked him to the door, he was saying, "I can't come early tomorrow. I don't have a ride."

"You're a junior, Cliff. You're old enough to take responsibility for your work. Now I really have to go."

He was muttering on his way out, but he left, and I was right behind him.

———

When I got home a couple of hours later, my phone was ringing. I grabbed the receiver as I nearly stumbled over Marm and winced when I held it to the left side of my face.

"Hello." It was hard talking with half of my mouth still numb.

The caller harrumphed at me and said, "Finally." Something about the voice sounded familiar.

"Who is this?"

"This is Mr. Pendling, of course. Where have you been? I've been trying to call you for over an hour."

I ignored the question and tried to be polite. I asked what he wanted, though I already knew. For someone who had such an important position, he sure kept updated on the home front. I could see he wanted to be in total control, both at work and at home.

"How dare you refuse to help my son with his makeup work?"

"Mr. Pendling, how many times has Cliff been absent so far this year?"

"Why, I think only two or three times."

"Yes, you're right. Then why is he missing seven assignments?"

He spluttered a little before saying, "Young lady, I demand that you extend the deadline an extra day since you refused to let him stay after school today. And you have not heard the end of this."

"Fine with me," I said into the dead line. He had already hung up.

Oh, I'm going to regret this, I told Marm. I walked into my bedroom and studied my face in the mirror. As a result of new fillings in two of my teeth, I looked like a chipmunk or, rather, half a chipmunk, with my left cheek swollen. But the pain was numbed and the dentist had promised I'd feel like a new woman in no time.

CHAPTER 22
October 28

Early the next morning, feeling like a new woman as promised, I stopped by to get my mail. Mr. North called from his private office, "Miss Jackson, a word with you." I knew immediately that Wayne Pendling had already gotten to him, that in fact he must have called him at home right after getting off the phone with me.

I took a breath to steady myself, walked into his office, and sat in the chair in front of his desk. He wasted no time on small talk.

"How is it that you refused to work with a student who asked for help with his work yesterday?"

I thought about explaining the situation, about my painful toothache and my need to keep the only appointment available to me, about Cliff's irresponsible approach to his work, about his father's attitude. But I had a lot to do before first hour, so I saved us both the time. "It's true that I wasn't available to help Cliff after school yesterday, but he waited until literally the last minute when he had had weeks to make up the work."

"You will extend the deadline for him until the end of the day today." Clearly, he believed that the matter was settled.

I seethed as I walked to my room. Replaying the conversation in my mind—if it could even qualify as a conversation—I was lost in thought and nearly bumped into Bud. "Sorry, Bud," I said and then noticed Julie behind him. He glanced at my cheek, winced, and said "ouch."

"You should have seen it last night. This is an improvement." I was beginning to feel better despite myself. I would have liked to tell him about my Cliff-Mr. Pendling-North problem, and I would have if he'd been alone. But I wasn't quite comfortable doing it with Julie there, and she didn't appear to be going anywhere.

"See you later," I said. "Have a good day…both of you."

I left the door to my classroom wide open as I prepared for my morning classes, a clear sign that I was available to students. Billy stuck his head in to say good morning, and a couple of girls from my first-hour class came early, but I saw nothing of Cliff.

All day I waited for the other shoe to drop; it didn't. I

wouldn't have been surprised to find Cliff absent eighth hour, but there he was, rushing to his seat right on the bell, just in time to avoid collecting another tardy. He had another black eye. I wondered why he kept getting in fights. I could only assume he was as antagonistic toward other kids as he was to adults.

Cliff never mentioned the makeup work that he had demanded to do the previous day. He took the quiz on that day's assignment and managed to stay awake for all fifty minutes of the class. As he left, he dropped something on my desk before walking out with Rick and Jack.

I didn't even want to open the envelope. I suspected it would be a note from his father, repeating the demands and complaints he had made on the phone. I was wrong. It was from Mrs. Pendling, and it was one of the strangest letters I had ever received from a parent.

Mrs. Jackson, it began. *Perhaps you are not aware of our family's standing in this community. We are high profile and high responsibility. People look up to us as role models. Those responsibilities can be extremely time-consuming. Occasionally, because of this, details can fall through the cracks. That is apparently what happened with Cliff's makeup work...*

Role models. Give me a break. Out of patience with the entire Pendling family, I didn't bother to read the rest of it. I tore the page into two pieces, and those pieces into two pieces, and I kept going until the note was confetti. Then I threw it into the garbage can.

It had been a strange day, to say the least. Another unsettling day in a school year full of them.

————

With grades due the next afternoon, I got to work as soon as I had eaten a quick dinner. I went through my day period by period, averaging and recording grades. It was late by the time I got to Cliff's class. I carefully added his scores, including zeroes on the work he had not turned in. When I finished my long division, his grade came to 59.4 percent.

"Oh, please, let this be wrong," I murmured to Marm, who was sleeping on the table next to my grade book. I rechecked my math—once, then twice. But the results were the same. Cliff was failing by one tenth of one percent.

I went to write his F on my list of grades, but hesitated. He was so close to passing. While I was certain his parents would not be happy with a D–, they would be furious with an F. I could save myself a lot of hassle if I just gave him the higher grade. It wasn't so much that I would be giving him a break. I considered it giving myself one. On the other hand, I took pride in never having given a student a grade he or she hadn't earned.

I put the decision off while I finished the grades for the rest of Cliff's class and recorded them. Then, wanting to be done with the whole process, I recorded what he had earned, an F—but in pencil.

CHAPTER 23

October 29

I woke up the next morning second-guessing my decision. The first person I ran into at school was Bud. I motioned him over to the side of the hallway for a private word.

"Bud, have you ever given a kid a grade that he hadn't really earned? I mean, it's real close in this situation, and I'm having a hard time deciding what to do."

"Yeah, I have, um, *adjusted*"—he drew quotation marks in the air as he said the word—"a grade on occasion. Haven't you?"

"No, I never have. But I'm tempted to this time because doing it would make my life a lot easier."

"Would you be giving a higher or lower grade?"

"Oh, higher."

"Then do whatever will make your life easier, Andrea. No kid or parent is going to complain about a higher grade than they deserve, that's for sure."

"Thanks. You've helped me make up my mind." I marched back to my room and erased the F written in pencil next to Cliff's name. Then I used a pen to mark down a large, bold F. I didn't care what Bud said. I did what felt right to me.

I took a moment to congratulate myself about the mature decision I had made. Again, I had done the right thing despite the consequences, as with my decisions to strike and to try to clear Sarah. It was another Huck moment.

My burst of confidence lasted less than a minute. Susan walked into my room. "Are you finished with your grades?"

"Yes, I just marked down the last one."

"Great. Then you will have time to cover a class for me." It would have been nice to have been asked, not told, but that was Susan. "It seems that Mr. Antag has been lax about keeping up his grade book. Now, with grades due, he just decides to tell me he won't make the deadline unless he has the entire day off from teaching his classes. I could wring his worthless neck for this, but I have to get those grades out of him before I can kill him. So what do you say? Can you teach his ALS seventh hour? They're in the Huck Finn unit."

"I suppose." I was dog tired and my mouth was still tender from the dental work. The last thing I wanted was to teach an extra class. But I had already admitted my grades were finished, so what could I do? "Yeah, okay."

After dreading the extra duty all day, I got to Sadie's—I mean Antag's—room to find a film on Mark Twain threaded in the projector and ready to turn on. While I took attendance, an undercurrent of restlessness in the class disturbed me. I wondered how the long-term sub was really doing as an instructor. Then I started the movie and sat back at Sadie's desk to watch the film with the kids. If it looked worthwhile, I'd use it myself when my own classes got to the Huck Finn unit in two weeks.

Thinking I might want to take a few notes on the film, I looked for paper and pen. The desktop was bare, so I opened the top drawer. There were pens and pencils but nothing to write on. Then, way back in a corner, I felt a sheet of paper and pulled it out. In the dim light in the room, I could see that one side was blank. It would be fine for my purposes.

The film ran nearly all of the period. I only had time to rewind it before the bell rang and I had to get back for my eighth-hour class.

When I was cleaning off my desk at the end of the day, I came across my notes on the film. I wouldn't need them for more than a week, so I slipped the paper into my Huck folder where I would be able to find it.

I took my grades to the office and handed them to Brenda.

As I did, I saw her check off my name on a list. "Something new?"

"Yes. Like a lot of other things around here." I hoped she would elaborate, but she didn't. As I turned toward the door, Chrissie walked in with her grades.

I waited for her in the hall. "Do you have time to go out to the Post?" I asked. "I feel like it's been a long time between chats."

"Gosh, I wish I did, but I don't. Tonight's the last home game of the season, and the coaches—well, actually their wives—are putting on a team dinner. I have to run home to pick up my food and get back here to help set up. I'm so sorry, Andrea. Let's plan something for next week, okay?"

"Sure. I'd like that. Hey, do you need any help with the dinner? I happen to have time."

"Thanks, but I think I'm all set. But if you feel like coming to the game later, find me and sit with me."

"That might be fun," I said. "Maybe I'll see you later."

CHAPTER 24
October 29–31

It was perfect football weather, and a chance to spend some time with my best friend, even on the noisy bleachers, sounded good. I hurried home and fed Marm and myself. I put on slacks and a sweater, grabbed a light coat and a scarf, and was almost out the door when my phone rang. I stopped and went back to answer it on the slight chance that it might be Tom.

But it wasn't Tom. It was Mom, though her voice sounded so terrified that I might not have even recognized it except that she called me "Snoopy." Her fear was contagious.

"Mom, what is it?"

"It's your dad, honey." And she began to cry.

"Mom…Mom, tell me. What's wrong with Dad?"

"He's had a heart attack. At least, the doctor thinks that's what happened."

"Oh no. Is he going to be all right? Are you at the hospital?"

"Yes, honey. We're at St. Luke's. I'm praying that he'll be all right, but they haven't said much yet. They're still doing tests."

"When did it happen? And where? Oh my God." I was on the verge of hysteria too.

"We were at home, about to eat supper, when he started sweating and got sick to his stomach. Then he had tightness in his chest and had trouble breathing. I've never been so scared in my whole life. Somehow I got him into the car and drove here to the hospital." She paused. "He has to be okay, Andie. He just has to be."

"Yeah, Mom. He has to be. Listen. You hang in there. I'm going to leave right now. I'll be at the hospital in three hours."

"No, Andie. I don't want you to make the trip tonight. You're tired and upset. Wait and come in the morning."

"Mom, I'm leaving in ten minutes. I'll meet you at the hospital. What about Alan? Does he know?"

"I'm going to call him as soon as we hang up. But are you sure you're coming tonight? Now I'll have to worry about you and your father."

"I'll be fine, Mom. I can't just sit here all night wondering what's going on. Go ahead and call Alan now. I'll see you soon."

Marm, bless his heart, sensed that I was upset and stayed right by my side while I made hurried preparations to leave. I called my next-door neighbor but got no answer. So I scribbled a note saying I had to leave because of an emergency and asked her to feed Marm until I got back. I ran over and taped it to her front door and then went back and gave Marm a big hug and kiss goodbye. "Wish you could go with me, boy. But I think you'll be happier here. I'll come home as soon as I can."

I checked my wallet and found a ten-dollar bill, enough to fill my gas tank on the way out of town and have a few dollars left for anything else that came up. I jumped in my Beetle and was off.

I was ten miles down the road before I realized I should have told Chrissie where I was going and why. But she would already be at the school, and I would have had to go over and find her. I wanted to get on the road right away. Besides, if everything checked out with Dad, I could be home the next day, or Sunday at the latest. If things were worse....well, I would cross that bridge if and when I came to it.

I had made the trip home enough times that my car stayed on course with little effort from me. There was very little traffic on the two-lane highways of northern Illinois. I drove through long stretches of lonely cornfields broken up by occasional small, sleepy towns. A full harvest moon lit my way better than any street lights could have.

I turned the radio off to be alone with my thoughts. A collage of memories from my childhood kept me company. My father, young and healthy with his farmer's tan, holding four-year-old me on his lap as he drove our little Ford tractor down the long gravel driveway to our mailbox. Dad pitching in to help Mom and a neighbor pick, husk and prepare sweet corn for the freezer—fifty quarts of corn, one for each week until the next crop was ready. My parents welcoming a school bus full of second-graders from the nearest city for a tour of the farm. Dad working late into the night to finish harvest before the snows arrived.

Tears filled my eyes as I tried to picture him in a hospital bed, still trying to take care of Mom, worrying about me arriving late at night. He would hate frightening us. I knew the soybeans were harvested, but half the corn was still in the field. How would he get it in?

Impatiently, I told myself I was borrowing trouble, to use another of my grandmother's stock phrases. Maybe Dad's heart attack had been a light one, whatever that was. Maybe he would already be home when I got there in—I checked the clock—a little over two hours.

I got to LaSalle-Peru and jumped on the interstate heading west to Iowa. Traffic picked up a little, but it was still nothing to demand my full attention. My mind wandered back to the first time I drove home from Hancock in the fall of 1970. I barely recognized that Andrea who had just begun teaching.

Though I hadn't been aware of it while it was happening, I had grown up a lot. On my next birthday I'd be twenty-five, speeding toward the milestone of thirty. *Never trust anyone over thirty*, I murmured to myself. When had I stopped believing that?

Looking back, I saw that teaching has a way of maturing the teacher. I was positive that I had learned more than my students during that first year. And the current school year was shaping up to be another long, painful learning experience.

This has been a year of losses, I thought. Sadie was gone. The old Sarah was gone. And, at least until we worked things out, Tom was lost to me too. Suddenly, the night became darker when the moon slipped under a cloud bank. I didn't think I could bear another loss. Dad had to be all right. He just had to be.

The next thing I knew, I was crossing the Mississippi River. The hospital couldn't be more than fifteen minutes away. I took the exit that would be the most direct route and felt my stomach clench.

I had been out of contact with Mom for more than three hours. Anything could have happened to Dad during that time. I prayed nonstop as I drove into the large, nearly empty hospital parking lot.

———

It was almost eleven when I got to Dad's room. Mom was still there. I stood silently in the doorway for a moment, studying them both. Dad lay quietly in the hospital bed, his eyes closed. Mom was huddled under a blanket in a chair near his bed. They both looked so much older than the last time I had seen them three months earlier.

I tiptoed into the room. Mom, looking dazed, slowly stood up. I rushed to her and gave her a long hug. She trembled slightly but smiled a teary smile as she said, "Thank God you got here safely. I'm really glad you came tonight."

"I'm glad too, Snoopy." It was a weaker version, but definitely Dad's voice. I walked to his bed and hugged him a bit awkwardly as he lay there. That wasn't enough. I grabbed his hands and squeezed them; then I freed my right hand and rubbed his cheek.

"You okay, Daddy?"

"You betcha, daughter. Doc says I'll be good as new by Monday."

Mom smiled fondly at him. "Well, that's not quite what the doctor said, Andie. They've done some tests—an EKG, chest x-rays, blood work—and they haven't found anything very concerning. But he'll be here over the weekend so they can continue to monitor him. And then they will repeat the tests on Monday. He was lucky, but he's going to have to take better care of himself."

"Got to get the crops in…"

"Shhhh," she said. "We'll have time to figure that out when

you get home. The main thing is, you have to put your health first."

"Yeah, I will, honey."

Once my fear subsided, fatigue washed over me. I sank into the nearest chair and tried to stifle a yawn. He noticed and said, "It's time for you two girls to go home and get some rest. I'll be fine tonight."

We both hugged Dad, Mom kissed his cheek, and we left with promises to be back first thing in the morning. We both had cars at the hospital, so I followed Mom home.

I went upstairs to my childhood room and fell into bed. Snuggling under the covers, I expected to drift into sleep, but I must have been too tired to sleep. It sounded like Dad would be okay, but new worries replaced my older ones. How would the corn harvest get done? What if Dad tried to do it himself and overdid it? What were the chances that he would have another heart attack down the road?

And what about Mom? She wasn't getting any younger either. How long should I stay to help them out?

How long *could* I stay to help out? I hadn't even thought of calling Susan before leaving town. If I weren't going to be back by Monday, I'd have to write lesson plans and, what, dictate them to her over the phone?

And Chrissie. She knew I was thinking about coming to the football game and would have been worried when I didn't show up. She might have called to check on me, and there wouldn't have been an answer. It was way too late to call her, but I would first thing in the morning.

———

I tossed and turned until seven and then got up feeling no more rested than when I had gone to bed. Yawning, I stumbled downstairs to the kitchen, where the family's only phone hung on the wall. I heard Mom stirring upstairs.

"Mom," I called from the bottom of the stairs, "can I call Chrissie?" Long-distance phone calls were not cheap, and my folks tried to limit them.

"Sure, honey," she answered. "How'd you sleep?"

"Fine," I lied. "I'll just give her a call to let her know where I am."

I was reaching for the phone when it rang. My *hello* was met with silence.

"Andrea? Is that you?"

"Tom? What are you—how did you know I'm here?"

"I didn't know," he said. "Why didn't you tell someone you were leaving for the weekend? When you didn't show up at the game last night, Chrissie got worried and called me. This isn't like you. What's going on?"

"It's Dad," I said quietly.

"Oh, no," he said, picking up on my tone. "What's wrong with your father? Is that why you took off?"

"Tommy, he's in the hospital and might have had a heart attack. They think he's going to be okay, though," I added quickly. "I realize I should have let Chrissie know, but when I got the call, she was already at the game. I didn't want to take time to drive over there and find her. I didn't think…I wasn't really thinking at all. I just knew I had to get here as fast as I could. And I was going to call Chrissie just now. In fact, if you'd called a minute later, you would have found the line busy."

An uncomfortable pause meant we had run out of conversation. The last time we had been together was in his office when he was so furious with me. I think we both realized how much we needed to talk—really talk things through—and how impossible that would be on a long-distance phone call.

Finally, I said, "I have to go. But would you call Chrissie and tell her what's going on, please?"

"Sure, of course I will."

"Thanks for tracking me down, Tommy."

"'Course I would, Andie. I'll check in with you again soon."

The warmth in his voice lingered with me after I hung up. The day suddenly looked brighter.

———

For the rest of the weekend, I was torn between staying and leaving. Dad looked better when Mom and I got to the hospital. But she became more exhausted and stressed as the day went on. I didn't see how I could leave them.

Yet there couldn't have been worse week for me to miss school. Monday and Tuesday were regular days; then parent-teacher conferences were scheduled for Wednesday and Thursday. I had barely begun to prepare for conferences, counting on having the weekend plus two school days to do that. I wasn't sure if a teacher had ever missed conferences in the entire history of Hancock High. I sure didn't want to be the first.

But neither did I want to leave my parents in their current state. While I was trying to be the calm, reassuring presence that they needed, I felt the turmoil inside me growing.

My brother arrived at the hospital later that afternoon. A college junior, Alan had grown into a man since I had last seen him. He took a long look at both of our parents and assessed the situation without my having to say anything. We shared a glance and then excused ourselves to go find coffee.

As soon as we were out of earshot, we both spoke at once. "I'll stay to help," I said.

"I can be here—" he said.

We stopped, laughed, and simultaneously said, "No, I will."

We stopped again, and he held up a hand. "Andie, I'll stay. I didn't get here until now because I was finishing my last midterm.

You have to teach Monday, right? I can afford to miss a few days better than you can."

"Well, yeah, it would be less complicated if I were there. But I could stay too, if I come up with decent lesson plans."

"That's not necessary. I can handle this. The main thing, besides keeping both of them healthy, is getting the harvest finished, right?"

"Right."

"Let me make a few calls when we get home. I bet the neighbors will be happy to pitch in when they hear what's happened. I really think I can do this." I looked at my kid brother in awe and appreciation for the man he had become. I hugged him, thanked him, and almost waltzed back to Dad's room.

———

I had hoped against hope that everything would be back to normal with Tom when I got home, but that, of course, was unrealistic. Yes, when he had been worried about me, his anger had thawed. But once he stood in my kitchen on Sunday night, we both found precious little to say. I think we were both reluctant to begin an argument that could damage our fragile relationship.

One positive thing had come from our time apart, though. We had both recognized that we still cared deeply about each other. I held tightly onto that ray of hope.

CHAPTER 25

November 4

    With parent-teacher conferences looming, I hit the ground running. My hard work paid off, and, before I knew it, it was the last day of conferences. Chrissie, Bud, and I were sharing a pizza in the teachers lounge during our dinner break.

    "Did you both vote before school today?" Bud asked. "With all that's gone on this year, it's like the election was pushed into the background. But, man, I can't think of a more important one. At least, not that I've lived through."

    "Yeah, I voted," Chrissie said. "There should be a rule that conferences can't be held on Election Day, though. The last thing we needed is something to make this day even longer."

    "That's for sure," I said. "I gave McGovern a vote, and I hope it makes a difference. But in this Republican county I probably shouldn't expect much. Not to change the subject," I said, and then did just that. "But I sure wish the Pendlings had scheduled earlier than eight thirty. I've been dreading their conference all day long."

"Yeah," Bud said. "If they're anything like people say, they'll be a royal pain in the butt. Hang in there, girl. You can be plenty tough when you have to be. And if you need backup, remember I'm just around the corner."

Chrissie squeezed my hand. "It'll be over soon. Before you know it, we'll be having a beer at the Post. Bud, are you coming?"

"Yeah, I can handle being in the bar and drinking Coke. But thanks for asking."

Most parents keep their appointments, but I had a no-show in the time slot before the Pendlings. Rather than relaxing, I spent the time pacing. I wondered if Sadie had had any idea that Wayne Pendling would give her such a hard time last spring.

When I heard two sets of footsteps nearing my door, I took a deep breath and pasted a phony smile on my face. "Hello, Mr. and Mrs. Pendling."

The couple was dressed much more formally than any of my other parents had been. Apparently, she was trying to make them look the part of the distinguished citizens that she so desperately wanted them to be. He wore a business suit with a jacket that wouldn't close over his large stomach, making his skinny tie look ridiculous. She had on a bright red dress that hung to her calves. During a season when both miniskirts and maxi dresses were in style, hers was neither.

He harrumphed and she avoided any eye contact with me as they took the chairs I indicated. I had no small talk prepared and didn't need it.

Mr. Pendling slapped a report card down in front of me "What's this grade supposed to mean? This F can't be right." His wife nodded, glancing from him to me nervously.

"Unfortunately, it is not a mistake," I said, willing myself to appear calm. "The problem is, Cliff hasn't turned in several of his assignments. As you can see from his tests here, his grades are not high, but the marks are passing. It's the zeroes on the missing assignments that pulled down his average." I realized I was talking too much, explaining as if I were justifying myself. Cliff is the one in trouble here, not you, I reminded myself.

"But," Mrs. Pendling whined, "Cliff wanted to make up his work. He tried to, but you weren't here so he couldn't."

"I've already explained that situation to your husband. And that was just one hour of one day. He had more than ample opportunities to receive help and didn't come in. Then Mr. North gave him an extra day, and he didn't take advantage of that either."

My words silenced them both momentarily, though his angry eyes and clenched jaw were still shouting at me. "Then explain this." Mr. Pendling laid a copy of the course syllabus in front of me.

I must have looked as puzzled as I felt. "That's obviously the course outline for American Lit Survey. But what's your question?"

"Mrs. Jackson, I've paged through Cliff's book, actually skimmed some of it, and I must say I find several of these readings objectionable."

My mind was racing. What could he be referring to? It's not like I'd handed out *Huckleberry Finn* yet, which admittedly was banned in some schools. "What specifically are you referring to?"

"I don't remember the exact names of them, but there's one about witchcraft and another one threatening to send us all to hell. And how about that guy who's encouraging the kids to rebel against the government? There's enough of that hippie crap in the world today without you teaching it to our kids."

He took a breath and then went back on the attack. "Between the propaganda you make the kids read and the poor example you set for them when you walked out on them—"

Ignoring his criticism, I repeated my offer to work with Cliff outside of class. I even promised to give him another week to make up his work from first quarter.

"Then you will change this grade, Mrs. Jackson," he stated.

"No, I won't do that. But remember, it's only a progress

grade. When he makes up his work, it will all count in his final semester grade. That's the only one that will go on his permanent record."

It was like I had been speaking a foreign language. "So you are refusing to change this F to a passing grade?" Mr. Pendling demanded. "Well, we'll just see about that. This could end up costing you your job." He stood up and headed for the door, his wife trailing behind.

In their snit, they had forgotten Cliff's report card. It took everything in me not to wad it up and throw it out the door after them. Mr. Pendling huffed back in, grabbed it, and walked out without looking at me or uttering a word. When he hit the doorway, I said to his back, "And it's Miss Jackson, not Mrs."

Most likely, they were on their way to the principal's office to report me, but at that moment I just didn't care. One thing was for sure: I knew exactly how Sadie had felt the past spring. He could be formidable and intimidating when he was on a roll.

Could he even be capable of murder? I couldn't rule it out, based on what I'd experienced.

———

I pointed my Beetle northeast out of town and headed to the rural tavern that had been our favorite bar since coming to

Hancock. The Outpost's rustic old room was overflowing with noise, laughter, jukebox music, and smoke when I walked in. Chrissie, who was perched on a stool at the bar, waved me over. I passed a large table where the women were singing/shouting along with Carly Simon's "You're So Vain."

Chrissie shouted over the music, "I don't want to give up this stool because I'll never get it back in this crowd. If Rob ever has a sec between orders, I want to talk to him. Hey, you look kind of stressed. Anything wrong?"

"Well, yeah, I guess you could say that. My conference with the Pendlings…" I was still a bit shaky and not sure I was ready to go into details, especially with the crush of colleagues surrounding us. Besides, with the noise level in the room, it wasn't a good place for a serious discussion.

"Chrissie, I'm beat. I'm going to grab a beer and go sit at the English department table. Are you joining us?"

"Try to save me a seat by you, and I'll be over in a while. I want to hear about your conference with the parents from hell."

I caught Rob's eye and gestured for a mug of beer. He nodded and obliged me. "Let me get this one, Andrea."

"Thanks, Rob. I'll get you next time we're all out together."

I tried to relax as I slowly made my way toward the English table at the back of the room, where it was a bit quieter. It was a small group around the table. Chrissie was no longer in the department, Sadie was gone, and Sarah hadn't shown up. Julie had been at conferences but left right afterward, probably to be with her fiancé. Bud and Jennifer, our part-timer, sat side by side, as did Dan and Dee Dee, leaving Susan at the head of the table. I took one of the two empty chairs next to her.

"How did your evening go?" she asked.

"Um, pretty well. How about yours? And is Sarah coming?" I hoped by changing the subject I would distract her from asking any more about my conferences. Guess I'll have to tell her eventually, I thought, but I'm not ready to right now.

Susan said, "I was hoping you'd know something about Sarah. I haven't seen her all day. I'm not sure if she's coming, but I really think she would have been here by now. I must say, I'm still very concerned about her."

"Me too."

"But I'm worried about you too. I walked out of the building with George, and he mentioned that the Pendlings had gone to see him after their conference with you. Was there a problem?"

I exhaled slowly before answering. "Yeah, I think you could say that. They pretty much tore into me." I paused for a breath to calm my nerves. "They were mad about everything—Cliff's grade, the content of the course—"

"What do you mean the content? You haven't even gotten to *Huck Finn* yet, have you?"

"No. Let's see. They complained about the Puritan beliefs, witchcraft, and Emerson and Thoreau's philosophies. Though

I got the distinct impression that they hadn't actually read any of the material they were objecting to."

"That figures. Anything else?"

"Well, yes. They claimed I didn't give Cliff a fair opportunity to make up his work. You remember the day I had that horrible toothache and had to go to the dentist right after school? Well, that was the one and only time that Cliff wanted to make up work. But he made it sound like I had been unavailable all of these other times too, which—"

"—isn't true," Susan finished for me. "And I can guess the rest. They took their complaints to George, and he believed them, or pretended to because he doesn't have the backbone to stand up to them."

"Well, I haven't heard from him yet, but that sounds about right. Susan, what am I going to do?"

"You are going to finish that beer you pushed aside. Then you're going to have another one for good measure. You're going to unwind tonight, have a good time, and Monday you're going to meet with me after school. If you haven't heard from George by then, we'll let it drop. If you have, we're going straight to his office and raise holy hell."

Just then Chrissie slid onto the chair next to me, leaned over, and said, "Hi, Susan. Mind if I join you guys? I don't seem to have a department anymore."

"Of course, you're always welcome, Chrissie. We don't

get to see enough of you anymore." Susan was showing her mellow side that night.

"Since it appears everyone who's going to come is here, let's get down to the business of Conference Champ," she said to the group around the table. Bud raised an eyebrow, and I gave him a confused look. No one other than Sadie and Sarah had ever won Conference Champ since we'd been at HHS.

Susan? I mouthed across the table to Bud.

He shook his head and held up four fingers. He was right. Susan taught only four classes because of her release time for department chair duties. She had fewer students than the rest of us, so she wouldn't be the winner. I shrugged my shoulders, as did he.

"Obviously, we have a new winner tonight," Susan said.

I felt a tap on my shoulder and, turning, saw Harve behind me. Susan spotted him too.

"I need to talk to Andrea," he said.

"Later, Harve," Susan said. "We're in the middle of important department business at the moment, and I need her here for a few minutes." Harve had gone toe to toe with the school board and its lawyers during the strike and held his ground, but he backed right down from Susan. Like most people, he couldn't tell when she was asserting herself and when, like this time, she was displaying her dry humor.

"Meet me by the bar when you're done," he said to me. It was an order, not an invitation.

"Now, where were we?" Susan asked. "Oh, yes, our Conference Champ, with forty-one conferences is…Andrea! Congratulations on a job well done." Chrissie hugged me as everyone applauded. "Way to be, Andrea," Bud called from across the table, as "Saturday in the Park" threatened to drown him out.

Susan waved toward the bar, and a waitress dropped off a large pizza and pitcher of beer. "Finish off that drink and have another on us, Miss Champ." Everyone but me reached for their wallets. The Conference Champ never pays.

Without warning, a wave of nostalgia swept over me. I blinked back tears as I raised my glass and waited for the others to join me. "Here's to the real Conference Champs, Sadie and Sarah." I was talking loudly enough to be heard over the music, but just as I spoke, it had stopped between songs. Everyone in the bar heard me. Glasses were raised and clinked as the toast spread throughout the room. "Here's to Sadie and Sarah!"

With a scowl on his face, Harve came back to our table and parked himself right behind my chair again. I stood and said, "Sorry to keep you waiting."

"Yeah, that's okay." His tone clearly said it wasn't. "Look, I need a word with you. Come on."

I followed him to the only empty table in the room, a small one just inside the door. I thought I saw him stumble a little as he walked ahead of me. Surely he wasn't drunk, was he?

I was mystified as to why he wanted to talk to me privately. What couldn't wait until Monday? "Um, Andrea, am I right that you have Cliff Pendling in a class too?"

"Yes, I do. He's in my American Lit class, and I have to say, he really gives me a run for my money most days."

Harve spoke a few words, slurring them enough that I had to ask him to repeat them. He was drunk, or well on the way to it. "What I mean to say is, did his parents have a conference with you tonight?"

"Oh, yeah, they sure did," I said. "Did yours go as badly as mine did?"

"God, yes. I've never been so p…furious in my life. They had the nerve to accuse me of incompetence. Me! Blaming me for his F in woodshop. Do you know how hard it is to fail my class? You really have to work at it, but Cliff found a way, all right. And I'll tell you why. All he ever does is b.s. with his buddies. And would he ever come in after school to try to catch up? Hell, no. He can't be bothered. And you know what else?"

I was enjoying it. Misery loves company and all that.

"He had the nerve to tell his dad that he couldn't get his projects done because there weren't enough hammers to go around. Yeah, well, he's right that I don't have as many as I did at the beginning of the year. The four that disappeared during the strike never got replaced. But, here's the thing…I'm starting to think that Cliff could be the weasel that took them.

The other day I came up behind him when he was yapping instead of working and—"

At that moment, someone convinced a bartender to crank the music even louder, until "Happiest Girl in the Whole USA" practically deafened me. I couldn't make out what Harve was saying, and I refused to get any closer to him. I shook my head and gestured toward the jukebox, but Harve didn't get the message. I saw his lips move, but that was it.

"Wait," I shouted across the three feet separating us.

"Never mind. I've said enough. I wanted to know if I was the only teacher who had trouble with the Pendlings tonight, and it looks like I'm not." He stood up and made his way back to the bar.

I wanted to follow him, to ask what he meant about hammers missing from his room. Shortly after the strike, Susan had told me there was some minor vandalism to the shop and art rooms but that nothing was taken. So, if there were tools missing after all, had he reported that to the police—or even to Mr. North?

A light went on in my head. Sadie had been killed by an object that had never been found, something hammer-like. Was there any connection with Harve's missing hammers? I wanted to ask him all of those questions and more. But, even if I could, was he sober enough that I could trust what he said?

No, it wasn't the right time or place. I'd take the weekend

to get my thoughts in order and then look up Mr. Harve Linck first thing Monday morning.

I went back to the English table only to find everyone putting on their coats and saying their goodbyes. Bud took another look at his watch and hurried off. "Hey, Chrissie," I said when the others had left, "you think Bud has a late date? He's been checking his watch every five minutes since we got here."

"I noticed that too. I couldn't begin to guess. Is he going out with anyone right now?"

"Um, I'm not sure…"

"What? Do you know something?"

"We need to talk, but not here."

"Yeah, let's. Let's do that soon."

As soon as I was in my car, I turned on the radio. A lot had happened that night, but I had not forgotten that it was Election Day. As I pulled out of the parking lot, I heard the unwelcome news.

Nixon was defeating McGovern in a lopsided election that had already been decided. I turned off the radio. Great. Four more years.

CHAPTER 26

November 8

I was talking to Marm as I got dressed for work Monday morning. "So what do you think would help solve the mystery?" He cocked his head and gave me a long, slow blink. "You don't know either, do you, boy?" I bent down to scratch his head.

"Well, finding the murder weapon would be a huge help." Nothing like answering my own question.

What did we have? The hammers that had been taken from the shop and were unaccounted for. What else would fit the vague description of the murder weapon—a heavy, small-diameter object on the order of a hammer? Chrissie had mentioned a gavel, but the ones I had seen wouldn't be heavy or sturdy enough. Or maybe Sarah's missing school bell? It was a lot heavier than it looked. Well, a gun, I supposed. The butt end of a gun would be a similar size.

I tried to wrap my head around the idea of a gun inside a high school, but I couldn't do it. Yes, the tragedy at the Olympics had made it clear that there was no safe place in the world. Still, the whole idea of a gun at Hancock High was unimaginable.

So that left me with the missing hammers that Harve had mentioned at The Post. When I got to school, I walked out to the shop wing to find him, but his room was dark. I waited a few minutes before leaving for my own classroom. Halfway there, I ran into him.

"Harve, do you have a couple of minutes? I'd really like to finish our conversation from Thursday night, if you don't mind."

"Sorry, Andrea. That's not going to work right now. I have to get to my room."

"I could walk back there with you and we could talk along the way."

"No, no. Look, you might as well save yourself some time later and go right to the office. North just caught me and chewed me out, and I'm sure you're on his list too."

"Why? Is this related to the Pendlings?"

"Of course. They must have given him an earful before they left after conferences. I'd offer to go with you as your union rep, but I'm in it as deep as you are on this one."

"That's okay. It's only my third year, but I've already served some time in North's doghouse. I'm used to it."

All morning I waited for my summons to the office, but it never came. When I went to my mailbox at lunchtime, I found out why. North had a bigger problem to deal with.

Cliff Pending was missing. According to the memo sent to all of his teachers, he had not come to school that day. When neither of his parents phoned the office to excuse him, Brenda called his home. His mother reported that he had left at the usual time. Once she understood that he had never arrived at school, she called her husband, who called the police.

North's memo instructed anyone who had any knowledge about Cliff's whereabouts to contact the office immediately. For the time being, there would be no announcement made to the student body, in the hope that Cliff would turn up on his own.

Where could that kid be? I was almost looking forward to eighth hour. Knowing how much the kids liked to talk, maybe I would learn something about his whereabouts. And if I could contribute any useful information, maybe I could even get North and the Pendlings off my back.

It was a subdued group of juniors that made its way into my room. Rick and Jack were in their seats before the bell rang, textbooks open. The kids' quiet chatter stopped as soon as I walked from my desk to the front of the room.

I paused, waiting to see if anyone would mention Cliff.

When no one did, I followed my usual procedure on test days. "As you know, we're taking our test on the Realism unit today. Does anyone have any last-minute questions?"

"Yeah, I do." The muffled words came from Candy's gum-filled mouth. "How can we concentrate on a test when Cliff is missing? It's not fair for you to make us take a test today." I could almost imagine her as a future attorney saying, "I object, Your Honor."

Although most faces grinned at the thought of a postponement of the test, I also saw genuine concern mixed in. "I'm worried about Cliff too," I said. "To be honest, I was hoping that one of you might have some idea what happened or where he is." I let the words hang there. When no one responded, we as a group turned toward Rick and Jack.

"Why's everyone looking at me? I don't know anything," Rick said.

"Me either," Jack echoed.

I waited a moment, but no one volunteered anything at all. "In that case, please put away your books and clear everything off your desks." I handed out the test, and they went to work.

I walked around the room, watching them work. Some were flying through the pages, while others lingered thoughtfully over each question. I knew from my first-hour class that there would probably be a few who used the entire period while others would take only a half hour.

By my third year of teaching, I had found solutions to

many of the most common teaching problems. But I was still looking for a way to keep students who finish a test early from bothering those who take longer. Punishing those who work faster by giving them extra work felt unfair. Making an advanced assignment for them to start was only marginally successful, especially in the last class of the day.

Rick, the weaker student of the twins, gave an exaggerated shrug of his shoulders as he handed in his test after half an hour. Jack, on the other hand, was still writing answers to the essay questions. Rick killed time by tapping a pencil on his desk. Lois, who sat behind him, cleared her throat and frowned. She was often the last to finish a test. Taking the hint to quiet down, he began doodling on the desk. I shot him the stare, and he slowly turned the pencil on end and erased what he had drawn. Still, things were much easier than they would have been if Cliff had been there.

Finally, with about ten minutes left in class, Lois walked up and handed in her test. Immediately, conversations broke out around the room. While I alphabetized their papers, I kept my ears open to the chatter around the room. Once in a while I heard Cliff's name, but every time the speakers noticed me looking in their direction, their voices dropped. Rick and Jack glanced suspiciously at me as they talked to each other. Only Lois sat quietly, studying her assignment planner. More than three months into the school year, the poor girl still hadn't made a friend in my class.

When the bell rang and the kids streamed out the door, Lois lingered by my desk. "Listen, Lois. I'm sorry if you had trouble concentrating during the last part of the test. The room wasn't as quiet as it should have been—"

"Oh, no, Miss Jackson. That's okay. I can tune out distractions just fine. I have four younger brothers at home, you know."

"No, I didn't know." I smiled. "That sounds like good training for surviving in here."

"Oh, it is." She smiled back. You know, she's nice, I thought to myself. I don't see why the kids haven't taken to her.

"Miss Jackson, I don't want to intrude into anyone's business, but I know that Cliff is missing…" I nodded. "Well, I wasn't trying to eavesdrop, but I couldn't help overhearing Rick and Jack just now. They were talking about having lunch with Cliff today. They didn't say where, and they said something about him not wanting to be seen. Maybe I shouldn't be saying this, but I don't think it's right to let people worry about Cliff when there's nothing wrong."

"Are you sure, Lois? You couldn't have misunderstood?"

"No, Miss Jackson. I clearly heard them say—"

The intercom clicked on, and an announcement blared out at top volume. "Cliff Pendling's teachers, please report to the library immediately for a meeting. Cliff Pendling's teachers, go to the library."

Lois headed for the door and then turned around. "Um, Miss Jackson, if you tell anyone what I just said, do you have to use my name?"

I paused, not wanting to make a promise I couldn't keep. "Lois, I'll keep your name out of it if at all possible." It wasn't all that she was asking for, but it was the best I could do.

———

A few minutes later, I was at a table with Cliff's other teachers. North came in and took the last chair. He looks different, I realized—older. Susan may have been right when she said he had taken the brunt of the anger resulting from our strike. He had been the target of criticism from the parents, the faculty, and, if rumors were true, the school board.

He sounded resigned to dealing with yet another problem. "As you know, Cliff Pendling was not in school today. Of course, there is nothing particularly alarming about that. But his parents are so concerned that they have notified the police and filed a missing person report."

"Why would they do that so soon?" Harve asked. "And did the police do anything about it?"

North hated to be interrupted. All of us, including Harve, knew that. North ignored his question. "I am not at liberty to discuss the actions of the police, but an officer will soon be arriving who may be able to give us more information."

"Has anyone searched Cliff's locker?" asked Mary, who I assumed was his math teacher.

"Er...no. We weren't able to get permission from his parents to do that."

Harve jumped in. "What? They want us to find their kid, but they won't allow us to search his locker?"

North shrugged his shoulders. "That's right."

Then Tom walked through the door, and my heart leapt. He made fleeting eye contact with me as he walked to the table. North rose to pull up a chair, but Tom said, "That's okay. I'll stand. I won't be taking up much of your time, but I do need to fill you in on the situation."

Obviously, this was more than a kid skipping school. What in the world had Cliff gotten himself mixed up in?

"As you may know," Tom said, "a missing person report normally cannot be filed until the subject has been unaccounted for at least twenty-four hours. But there are extenuating circumstances in this case because the subject is a minor and because of the unsolved crime at this school. We are concerned about the boy's whereabouts and well-being."

Tom had our full attention. "Late last night Cliff walked into the police station and volunteered some information related to the Sadie Malcolm case. We are still in the process of checking it out, but there is concern that he would go missing so soon after doing that."

I was shocked, as was everyone else around the table. How had Cliff come by information about the murder? And why had he waited until last night to report it?

"That's why I'm here," Tom continued. "I'm interested in anything you may have heard Cliff say recently. Or anything his friends may have said today that could help us find him. Even if you think it isn't important." He paused and looked expectantly around the table.

No one spoke, so I did. "Um, Tom, I mean Officer Jefferson, I may know something, but it is something a student told me in strictest confidence. I glanced at North, hoping he would take the hint and offer us some privacy. When he didn't, Tom said, "Thank you, Miss Jackson. I will speak to you in private in a moment. But, first, has anyone else thought of anything that might be relevant?"

One by one, my colleagues shook their heads. "Then I ask you to give this more thought overnight. If you do come up with something, please call the station to pass it along. Thank you for your time."

North could have let it go at that, but he paraphrased what Tom had just said before dismissing us. As usual, he had to have the last word. The other teachers left, and North took a chair at the table with Tom and me. We both stared at him. Finally, Tom had to say, "Thank you, George. I'll talk with

Andrea for a few minutes, and then I'll be on my way." That gave him little choice but to leave.

"Man, oh man," Tom said as soon as North was out of the room. "What's with him?"

"He hasn't been the same since the strike. I'm not sure what his problem is, but he's managed to alienate just about everyone here."

"Hmmm. Now, what did you learn about Cliff's whereabouts?"

"First, I need your word that you won't use my student's name. She's a good kid, a shy girl who's trying to fit in at a new school. If the others find out she passed along something she overheard, the kids will ostracize her. They're very attuned to what they call "narking.""

He shook his head. "I can't promise that, Andie. Surely you know that."

"Then I have to respect her confidence." I started to rise from my chair.

"Wait a minute. If you know something that could help us find Cliff, you've got to tell me. It would be—"

"Well, I won't." Why had I made that promise to Lois? "Wait," I said when his frown deepened. "What if I told you what she said but not her name? Wouldn't that be just as good?"

"Yes and no. It's not crucial that I know her name at this

time. But if I need more information or she ends up having to testify, then I won't have any choice."

"Okay. If it comes to that, I'll talk to her and try to explain. She's really a good kid and reliable as the day is long."

"What did this anonymous good kid tell you?" he asked with a little smile.

"She overheard two of Cliff's closest friends say that they had seen him during lunchtime today. He is obviously still in Hancock. And they also said that Cliff didn't want to be seen, which I guess is obvious. Anyway, she didn't hear the rest of the conversation. So is that helpful?"

"Yeees, that could be. Thank you for your help, Miss Jackson."

"You're welcome, Officer Jefferson." I risked a smile that he returned.

He rose, pulled back my chair as I stood, and we walked out of the library together. Then he turned toward the front entrance of the building while I headed back to the office.

He called me *Andie*, I practically sang as I floated down the hall. Just once, but he had said it. I hated the nickname but loved the way he had used it. He does remember. He still cares. Maybe, just maybe…

I got to my car and was about to back out of my parking space when his squad car pulled up next to mine. I lowered my window.

"Wait, Andie. Look, um, let's try this one more time. We

just worked out a good compromise upstairs. I'm wondering if we might be able to do that with our personal differences as well."

"I'd sure like to try, Tommy. I really would."

"Good. I'll be calling you soon."

"Okay, great."

He drove off, and I sat in my car for a moment, thinking. Why couldn't we compromise more often? The strike was over. I was doing a better job of keeping my nose out of his police work. At least, as far as he knew I was.

———

At times like that I really missed Chrissie and our talks. But with the football season over, Rob would be getting home about the same time she did. She would cook a special dinner; they would have a glass of wine as they talked over their days. They would clean up the kitchen together and sit down at the same table to do their schoolwork together.

I was happy for her. I really was. But I wanted her to be available to go to The Grounds with me, to hash over Cliff's disappearance, to rejoice over my talk with Tom. Yes, I could call her, but I didn't want to interrupt their cozy evening together, and it wouldn't be the same anyway.

I was pulling out of the faculty lot onto the circle drive when I saw Bud come out the side door of the school. I caught his eye and waved. He smiled widely and threw me a peace sign. He had been spending more time working in his room after school. But he looked happy, and that's what was important.

As I headed down the East Street hill, a girl in a bright red jacket walking down the sidewalk caught my eye. That looks like Julie, I thought as I came up behind her. I pulled over and reached over to roll down the window on her side. "Hey, Julie. Need a ride?"

"Oh, hi, Andrea. Thanks, but I think I'll walk. It's so beautiful out that it's just good to be alive. You know what I mean? Thanks, though." I waved and pulled back into the street.

She sure was in a good mood. Just like Bud. And they were leaving school at the same time—again—an hour after classes ended. Since she was teaching one of his classes, it made sense that they would be working on lesson plans together. But I couldn't remember when planning had ever made me so happy that I had glowed like Julie did.

———

I must have nodded off while I was reading on the couch. When my phone rang a little before ten, I woke with a start. "Hey, Andrea, hope I'm not calling too late." It was Chrissie, and she sounded mad.

Before I could ask what was wrong, she began telling me. "Listen, I thought you should know this. Rob's working at The Post tonight, and he just called me during his break. It seems that Wayne Pendling is out there, has been for a couple of hours, and he's managed to get himself drunker than a skunk. And get this: he's telling anyone who'll listen that his son has run away and it's all the fault of his teachers."

"What? What? Where does that man get off? What exactly did Pendling say?"

"That while the parents were at school for conferences, Cliff took off. They got home and he was gone. And he said it was because of the unfair treatment of his teachers."

"Oh, gosh, and I'll bet the others believed him too, what with the way the town's opinion of us was trashed by the strike. Chrissie, did Rob say whether Pendling mentioned any of us by name?"

"Um, yeah, I'm afraid so."

"Oh, no. Me?"

"Yes. I'm sorry. And Harve too. That's why Rob called right away, so I could let you know. He's furious and I had to warn him to calm down so he doesn't lose his job. Not that I don't want him sticking up for you." She added quietly, "I'm sorry, Andrea. I just wanted you to know."

"Thanks, Chrissie. And please thank Rob for me too. And tell him I don't want him to get in trouble defending me. Did he think Pendling was drinking because he's frantic about his son?"

"No, that's the strange thing. Rob thought he didn't seem all that worried about his kid; he was just ranting about the teachers. And wouldn't you think he'd be out looking for Cliff, or home reassuring his wife, or checking with the police? Anything but going out and tying one on?"

"Yeah, now that you mention it, I would. The more I learn about him, the more I think the man's pure crazy. Anyway, thanks again for the call, Chrissie."

She apologized again, and I reassured her again.

I was wide awake and so furious I knew I wouldn't be getting back to sleep anytime soon. "How did things get so messed up?" I asked Marm. He didn't know, or didn't say, but he stayed right by my side to be sure I was all right.

What should I do? What could I do? Did I need to do anything? Should I even be worried about one disgruntled parent who spouts off when he's drunk? How many people heard him complaining about us anyway? And how many of those believed him?

I felt myself beginning to calm down. There were other parents, a lot more of them, who did believe I was a good teacher. Pendling was blaming Harve and me for Cliff running away, yet I wasn't even sure he was gone. Rick and Jack said that they had seen him at lunchtime when he was already supposed to have been missing.

So where exactly was Cliff? Had he run away, or was he still in Hancock? And did his father really believe he was gone, or did he know where his son was? But what would be the point in pretending he was missing? Clearly, I wasn't going to figure everything out that night.

There were too many missing pieces. I only hoped that if I could find them all and put the puzzle together, it would show what had really happened to Sadie. And I prayed it wouldn't come too late to get the old Sarah back.

CHAPTER 27
November 9

Something was up. I had no idea what, but the minute I walked in the school door, I sensed something ominous in the atmosphere. Curious, I went to my mailbox and sorted through a stack of papers until I found "An official memo from HHS administration." Might have known.

I was about to read it when I heard raised voices coming from North's office. He and Harve were standing on opposite sides of his desk, their faces inches apart, shouting at each other.

"Why wait till now?" North asked.

"I didn't notice it until now."

"How could you not notice the absence of four tools that your students would use every day?"

Harve spluttered an answer that I couldn't make out.

The memo informed us that during first hour, three police officers would be conducting an all-school locker search. I wondered if it was the administration's way of getting Cliff's locker searched without his parents' permission.

I caught up with Susan in the hall and asked, "What do you think of this locker search?"

"It makes me sad more than anything. It's too bad that we've gotten to a point where the powers that be have to violate our students' privacy in order to search the locker of one kid whose parents refuse to permit it. Even if it might help them find their son."

"Do you think that's what Harve and North are talking about in there?"

"Talking? You mean yelling, right?"

"Well, yes. I'm amazed that Harve would feel so strongly about the rights of a kid that he detests."

"I'm sure he would say it's the principle of the thing. No pun intended," she smiled a little. "But if it helps the police find a student who is missing…"

"Yeah, *if* he is missing," I muttered to myself.

"What?"

"Nothing. I hope they find something helpful in Cliff's locker."

She agreed, and we parted ways to go to our classrooms.

Shortly after first hour began, the intercom clicked on.

Through a couple bursts of static, Mr. North said, "Attention. May I have your attention, please.

"During this period, we will be conducting an all-school locker search. Members of the Hancock Police Department, assisted by the school administration, will open and search every locker in the school. Rest assured, your possessions will be safe. The search will begin immediately after this announcement. No students will be allowed in the halls until it is finished. Teachers, do not issue passes for anyone to leave your room until further notice."

"Why are they doing this?" one of my juniors asked. "They've never done it before. Was there a bomb threat or something?"

"No," I answered with studied calm. "I don't know of any kind of threat."

"Then why?" several voices replied.

"I'm not sure. But I do know that it was planned ahead of time, so it's not an emergency situation."

I was fortunate that there are no lockers lining the walls of my hallway, so we didn't hear or see the search going on. It wasn't that hard to get the kids involved in the lesson I had planned on Stephan Crane's "The Open Boat."

Near the end of the class, Mr. North came back on the speaker, announcing the end of the search. I couldn't wait to get to the office to see if the faculty had received any information. But, when I finally got free, my mailbox was empty and there was no news in the faculty lunchroom.

————

My eighth-hour class, of course, wanted to do nothing but gossip about the locker search.

"Did you hear what they found? I heard it was an ax."

"No, it was a switchblade."

"No, you're all wrong. It was a big stash of pot."

"Wait, wait." I had to step in. "You're just spreading rumors. As far as I know, the results of the locker search haven't been announced yet. In fact, they probably won't be at all." Their groans threatened to drown me out.

Jack tentatively raised his hand. "Yes, Jack?"

"Could you at least tell us if they found any clues about where Cliff is?" He looked so worried that I wondered if he really had spent time with his friend the previous day.

"I'm sorry, but I haven't heard anything at all, Jack. I'm worried about Cliff too."

All of the kids nodded in agreement, even Lois, the one he so often taunted. Rick was chewing his lower lip, apparently lost in thought.

"Okay," said one of the girls. "I want to say something, and this isn't a rumor because I saw it with my own eyes. I sit right by the door in my first-hour class. I looked out and saw a policeman carrying a plastic bag down the hall. There was something in it that looked kind of heavy from the way he was carrying it. Oh, yeah, and he had plastic gloves on."

"Yeah, I saw something too," said the boy behind her. "In fact, I think I know what was in the bag. I had gym, and it was almost time for the bell so we were lined up by the door. Well, I kind of leaned out the door to get a better look, and I saw a cop take some hammers out of a locker and put them in the bag."

Lois asked, "Whose locker were the hammers taken from? And could they be the ones missing from the shop?" No one answered.

For me, there was an even more crucial question: could one of them be the murder weapon?

In the silence that followed, I noticed Rick and Jack whispering urgently.

Lois wasn't finished. "Weren't you guys saying there weren't enough hammers in the woodshop to get your projects done?"

"That's right," Jerry said. "When classes started up again after the strike, Mr. Linck threw this big fit because some of his hammers were gone, stolen probably. He blamed us, and he said he wasn't going to replace them. That was up to whoever swiped them to bring them back. But, the thing is, there aren't enough for my class, and the last four guys to get there don't get one and can't do anything but sand stuff all period." It was the longest speech I had ever heard from him.

There was another silence as we all digested the information. Finally, I forced myself back into instructor mode and dragged them, ever so slowly, into student mode.

Near the end of the hour, I noticed Rick and Jack having a whispered argument. It was a shock seeing anything but a united front from those two. Perhaps Cliff's absence had changed the dynamic of their relationship. When the bell rang, Rick raced for the door as usual, but Jack took his time. I thought for a moment that he was going to stop to say something to me, but he didn't. Still, something had changed, and I couldn't help but wonder if it had anything to do with Cliff's whereabouts.

———

The tentative knock on my open classroom door was so soft I almost missed it. When I looked up, there was Billy. I smiled and motioned him in. "I haven't had a chance to talk to you in ages, Billy, and there's something I keep forgetting to ask you."

"What's that?"

"Do you clean Sarah's room?"

"Yeah, sure…"

"Good. Then you know the shelves in the back of her room where she keeps books that the kids can check out?"

He nodded.

"And on top of the bookcase she keeps the awards that she gets every five years? The ones shaped like old-fashioned school bells?"

"Yeah?"

"Well, one of them is missing, the one she got her twenty-fifth year of teaching. And I was wondering if you've seen it anywhere, maybe somewhere else in the building?"

"No…I don't think so, not off the top of my head. I'll keep an eye open for it. But Miss J., I came to tell you something really important."

He walked back to my door and closed and locked it. "I'm not supposed to be telling anyone this," he said, "but I just have to."

"You know I will keep anything we talk about confidential."

"Yeah," he said, drawing a deep breath. "It's about the locker search this morning. I was there when the cops did it. I mean, it was my job to go ahead of them and use the master key to open the lockers so they could do their thing. So I was close by when they found the hammers. 'Course I tried to act like I wasn't seeing and hearing nothing special, you know."

I nodded. "I've heard the locker was down by the gym, right?"

"Yeah, that's right. But here's what you can't tell anyone that I told you."

I nodded again.

"It was Cliff Pendling's locker."

"What? The hammers were in Cliff's locker? Are you sure it was his?"

"Yeah, it's his all right. He carved his initials in the door. You know how hard that makes my—" He shook his head and started again. "I was hoping those hammers might give the cops a clue—you know, help them find Cliff."

"Yes, and also the hammers, or at least one of them, might help the police solve Sadie's murder." Billy looked surprised as he realized I was right.

"Then it's a good thing that it happened, right?"

"I think it just might be."

CHAPTER 28

November 16

A week passed with no sign of Cliff. Every day I looked at his empty desk and wondered where he was and if he was safe.

And, as far as I knew, there had been no progress on the murder investigation either. But one important thing had happened. Tom and I had enjoyed a pleasant date, more like the old times, though we still weren't where I wanted us to be.

Things at school settled back into a new routine. I guess you could say life was as normal as one could expect during a school year that began with a strike and a murder.

The next week my ALS classes would be starting to read *Huckleberry Finn*, so it was time to start preparing. I pulled out my folder of materials, flipped through the sheets, and came across my notes on the film that I had shown in Sadie's class. I skimmed them, then turned the sheet over and saw someone else's handwriting. That was when I remembered taking the sheet of paper out of Sadie's desk drawer.

My mouth fell open when I looked at the unpunctuated block letters. What was this anyway?

It was addressed to "SM," and said:

YOU MADE A BIG MISTAKE WHEN YOU DID THAT YOU WILL LIVE TO REGRET IT OR MAYBE NOT ITS TO LATE TO MAKE IT RIGHT THE DAMAGE IS DONE AND YOU WILL PAY FOR YOUR ACTIONS

That was it. No signature, no date. It didn't even use Sadie's name, just her initials. But its ugly tone was ominous. What was the big mistake that she had made and would pay for? Crossing the picket line? Or something else?

At that point, I realized I shouldn't be handling the paper. But I had, twice. I hoped the police would be able to find fingerprints other than mine on it.

Remembering how they did it on *Adam-12*, I ran to my kitchen and grabbed two clean plastic bags. I used one as a makeshift glove, picked up the paper, and cautiously slid it into the other bag.

Then I knew exactly what I had to do. "Tom, it's me," I said into the phone. "I just found something, and it might be important. Can you come right over?"

"Whoa, slow down, Andie. What did you find? And where are you?"

I took a breath and started over. "I'm at home, prepping my *Huck Finn* unit. And I came across a sheet of paper that I found in Sadie's desk last month. And Tommy, it sounds like it could have been written by her killer."

He whistled. "Don't touch it. I'll be right over."

That's the question, I thought as I waited for him. What had I found? Who had written it and why? Could Harve have done it after she crossed the picket line? Or could the note be older than that? Maybe it was from Pendling, when they had argued about his son's failing grade last spring. Or could it have been from a random student disgruntled about some real or perceived slight?

And why hadn't Sadie told anyone? She had considered it worth keeping, though not in a secure place. I couldn't imagine finding a note like that and not taking it to someone. As a matter of fact, I had been on the receiving end of a similar note two years earlier, and I had taken it to Susan as fast as my frightened feet could carry me. After I showed her the threatening letter that had been pushed under my classroom door, we both had gone to North and to the police from there.

But not Sadie. She had, to all appearances, kept the ugly words to herself. She was a lot stronger than I had realized. "I wonder if she told Sarah," I said to Marm. "I'm going to find out tomorrow."

Tom brushed my cheek with a kiss when I let him in. But

otherwise he was all business. "That it?" he asked, as I handed over the plastic bag. "Now tell me the whole story, starting with when and where you found this."

So I did, with every tiny detail that I could remember.

Tom nodded occasionally but let me talk until I finished. "And that was when I called you just now. I haven't touched it since I figured out it might be important, but I'm afraid I handled it before that." I paused. "So does that mean I have to get fingerprinted?"

"It probably does. If there are prints from more than one person on the paper, like I'm almost sure there will be, we'll have to get your prints for the process of elimination. Just off the top of my head, I'd think there should be at least three different sets of prints, maybe four. Sadie's would be on it too, and, of course, the ones we really want, those of the writer. And do you think Mr. Antag would have handled it?"

"He could have. But do you have Sadie's on file?"

"They would be in the autopsy report. Well, let's start with finding out whether we can lift prints at all. I hope so. We could really use a break in this case."

I nodded. It was bad enough losing Sadie. It would be much worse to never know who killed her or why.

"And that reminds me." Tom was looking at me carefully. "Have you heard anything more about Cliff Pendling's whereabouts? I wish we had his prints and also his bl—"

Blood type, I silently finished for him.

"I didn't say anything," he said.

"No, you didn't."

"Well, I have to get back to the station. Thanks for the call, Andie. This might turn out to be helpful."

"Will you let me know what you find out about the prints?"

He frowned. I knew as soon as the words were out of my mouth that I had overstepped again.

"I didn't say that," I said.

"No, you didn't." He smiled over his shoulder on his way out the door.

———

My mind was racing. There was no way I would get to sleep for a while, so I decided I might as well grade papers.

I had finished my third-hour class's papers on *Great Expectations* and was halfway through my sixth-hour section when I came across an essay that sounded familiar. I went back to the first stack and pulled the paper.

When I laid them side by side, I saw they were nearly identical. And, on a second reading, I thought both sounded like they had been copied from another source. I jotted myself a reminder to hit the school library the next day to see if I could get to the bottom of the plagiarism.

CHAPTER 29

November 17

Sometime during the night, I decided there was a place I needed to see more than the library. I wanted another look at Sadie's classroom. And I wanted to do it before anyone else was around. It wasn't that I felt guilty, exactly. I just didn't want to have to answer any questions about what I was doing.

Getting in her room was no problem because all of the English classroom doors used the same key. I began my search with her desk. The top drawer, where I had found the note, held pens, pencils, paper clips, and other office supplies. No more papers, though. I quickly opened and scanned two other drawers without finding anything promising.

That left just the double drawer that held file folders. It looked like it was filled with materials for the units Sadie had been teaching at the time of the strike. I wondered how Antag was preparing if he wasn't using any of her materials. Had he been winging it the whole time?

I was about to give up when I found a loose sheet stuck between two folders. It was not like Sadie to leave anything unfiled, so I grabbed it and slipped it in my book bag.

I was on my way to her file cabinet when a shadow crossed the window in the door. Hurrying, I opened the top drawer but then shook my head. It was so crammed with folders that I couldn't even read the tabs identifying the contents. The other two drawers were the same. Sadie must have kept every scrap of paper she had used in her entire career. I would never be able to sort through it all.

I gave up and tiptoed out into the hall, checking that the door locked again behind me. It was time to see if Sarah could be of any help.

She was at her desk grading essays when I walked in. She looked up at me through weary eyes. She gave me a little smile, though. "Andrea. It's been a while since I've seen you. What brings you in so early today?"

"To be honest, you do, Sarah. I want to talk to you."

"How sweet of you to come checking on me, dear. I'm as well as can be expected, I guess."

"I'm glad to hear that. I've missed you. But I came for another purpose too." I took a deep breath and began. "Sarah, did Sadie ever mention receiving a threatening note?"

Her eyes widened. "Noooooo. Why do you ask?"

"Because I found one, by accident, in her desk drawer when I was covering one of Antag's classes. I have no idea how long it was in that drawer, and there's no signature, of course. I was just hoping she might have mentioned it to you."

"Why, no. I'm sure I would have remembered something like that. Do you think it could have been that horrible Mr. Pendling when they had the disagreement last spring?"

"That was one of my guesses. And I also thought about...I hate to say this, but Harve was really upset when she crossed the picket line."

"Oh, my, I can't imagine a teacher doing something like that."

"I sure don't want to think that either. That's why I was hoping you might be able to help me. Of course, like I told you, I'm not really investigating. I'll leave that to the police. Perhaps when they get the fingerprinting done they'll know who wrote it."

Sarah was an expert at hiding her emotions. Teachers have to do that so often that it becomes second nature. But I thought I might have seen a quick flash of fear in her eyes. "Of course," she murmured. "I'm sorry I can't help you, and as nice as it is to see you, I really ought to get back to work. It takes so long to grade essays when you have so many grammar mistakes to mark."

"I'll be on my way, then," I said, feeling like a student she had just dismissed.

It wasn't the first time I'd suspected that Sarah wasn't telling me everything she knew. I found it very hard to believe that Sadie wouldn't have confided in her about the note. I just didn't understand why Sarah wasn't more forthcoming, especially when finding the killer would remove any suspicion from her.

The minute I got into my room, I relocked the door behind me. I took out the sheet of paper from Sadie's desk and skimmed it. Then I took a slower, longer look.

It was a two-column list of dates and injuries. Items like black eyes, swollen lips, bruises, and scrapes, were listed by dates from September through May. It was definitely Sadie's handwriting, but there were no names on the paper. I tried to remember if such a list could apply to any of the novels we taught, but I came up empty. Again, I wasn't sure what I had found.

———

I didn't make it to the library until after school, the one time of the day that it is nearly deserted. I headed right to the 800s section in the stacks and was so intent on finding books about *Great Expectations* that I didn't notice someone walking up behind me. A timid tap on my shoulder nearly sent me through the ceiling.

"Sorry, Miss Jackson. I didn't mean to scare you." I turned and found myself face to face with Jack.

"That's okay, Jack. I didn't know there was anyone else here. That's all."

"Sorry. But I was wondering…if I could talk to you for a minute?"

"Sure. Want to go sit at a table?"

"No," he said just above a whisper. "I need to do it right here. I mean, if that's okay."

I began whispering too. "Sure, that's fine."

"Please don't tell anyone—no one at all—that I told you this." When I nodded, he continued, even more softly, "It's about Cliff."

"Do you know where he is?" I whispered back.

"No. Maybe. I mean, at first I knew he was still here in Hancock, kind of hiding out."

"But why would he do that? He scared his parents to death."

He glanced around to be sure no one was watching us. "I'm not sure." I found that hard to believe, but I didn't want to interrupt him.

Jack continued, "I haven't seen him for days now, and I'm real worried about him. So is Rick, but he says we shouldn't talk to teachers or cops, that Cliff will be mad if we do. And remember, you said—"

"That I wouldn't tell. And I won't, on one condition."

"But you promised," he said, frowning.

"My condition is that you tell me what you know. For starters, why did Cliff think he needed to disappear at all?"

"He...um. I think he wanted to get away from his folks for a while. He wouldn't say why. He's been more, uh, secretive, I guess you could say, lately. He talked about finding something during the strike, but he wouldn't ever say what. When Rick and I asked, he'd just tell us to shut up."

Jack looked around again. "After he'd been gone a couple days, I called his house and got his dad. He said that he didn't know where he was."

"Did you believe him? Mr. Pendling, I mean?"

"I...I don't know. I guess I do. But I don't think Cliff would leave town without telling me or Rick. I have the feeling he was scared of something. I just don't know who or what."

Jack didn't seem to know very much. I must have looked a bit impatient because he paused and then said, "Okay, I have to tell you something else. I might know where he is. He has an uncle that he likes in Milwaukee. It's just a guess. Remember, you said you wouldn't tell anyone."

"And, I won't. But you should. You should tell the police what you know, in case it might help them find Cliff. And tell them your hunch that he was afraid of something. Or someone."

Jack took a long pause. "I was hoping you wouldn't say that. Will I get in trouble?"

"I don't think you have anything to worry about. Is that why you haven't already gone to them?"

"Well, that and I don't want the other kids to think I'm a nark. I'd lose all of my friends, especially Cliff."

"Jack, what if I could work it out so that no one knows you talked with the police? I mean none of your classmates. I do think your parents should know and should go with you to the station. I can give you the name of the officer to ask for when you get there. He's a nice guy, very worried about finding Cliff and very good at keeping things confidential—"

"You mean your boyfriend?"

"How did…? No, not really a boyfriend. Just a friend." I tried not to sigh. "His name is Officer Jefferson, and I know he'll be on duty this evening. I want you to think this over very seriously. You might be doing Cliff a huge favor, you know. Wherever he is, he may need help."

"I hadn't thought of it that way. Okay," he said with a decisive nod, "I'll talk to my mom as soon as I get home. Thanks, Miss Jackson."

He started to leave but then turned back. Avoiding my glance, he said, "I know that some of us aren't the easiest kids to teach, especially Cliff, and Rick and me too. I'm sorry." He left without looking me in the eye.

I stared blankly at the books on the shelf in front of me.

Where in the world was Cliff? Was he in danger? Did his parents know about the hammers in Cliff's locker?

"Can I help you find something, Andrea?" I was so lost in thought that I hadn't heard Margaret approaching. "I don't want to rush you, but I was hoping to lock up a little early today. I have to get to a doctor's appointment. You know how hard it is to schedule them around the school day."

"Yes, I sure do, Margaret. I'm sorry I'm taking so long. Listen, could I check out all three of these books?"

"Sure."

Two minutes later I was on the way to my car, lugging my book bag, purse, and the library books. I swung by the station on my way home but missed Tom. I left him the paper I'd found in Sadie's room, safe in a sealed envelope, and headed home.

The phone was ringing when I walked in my door. I patted Marm while I listened to Tom apologize for having missed me and wanting information about the list. The problem was, I didn't have any.

When he sounded ready to end the call, I worked up my courage to ask about fingerprints on Sadie's threatening note. "Did you find any others than Sadie's and mine?"

After an interminable pause, he said, "No."

"No, none were found, or no, none were identified?"

"The latter," he answered and then ended the call.

At least he hadn't gotten mad at me...exactly. So, if I

understood correctly, there was one or more prints, but they didn't match anyone under suspicion in Sadie's death. Not Sarah, not Harve, not Pendling, not Dalby. Did that mean the note was unconnected to the murder? Or did it mean that the real murderer wasn't even a suspect?"

CHAPTER 30

November 18

I ran into Chrissie at the mailboxes the next morning and walked with her to her room. I had been sidetracked with other matters, but I hadn't forgotten my suspicions about Bud and Julie. There was no one else I trusted to discuss them with.

"You busy?" I asked as I followed her in her door.

"Kind of, but come in and talk to me while I collate these handouts I just ran off."

"Here, let me help."

"Un-uh. Not with that white blouse you're wearing. I don't want you to get purple smudges all over it."

"Thanks. I'll just watch you then. But here's what I want to know: Have you noticed Bud acting secretive recently? Well, for most of the school year, actually?"

"Yeah. But didn't we talk about that already? I hope he's not into drugs again. I really haven't seen any signs of it other than, like you said, he's being secretive sometimes."

"I agree it's probably not drugs. And I don't think it's liquor either. I think he's into the really strong stuff."

She stopped in her tracks. "Heroin?"

"No, no, not that. Love. I think Bud might be in love, Chrissie."

"Oooooooooh! Finally. Who is she? Wait. How did you find out about this?"

"Well, to be honest, I'm only guessing. But haven't you noticed Bud spending time with the student teacher? Quite a bit of time?"

"I guess so, but they have to talk since she's teaching one of his classes. Why? Do you think there's more than that going on? Besides, I thought she was engaged."

"Yeah, she is. All I know is, I keep running into them—in his room before and after school, in the halls. Even when we were picketing he stopped to talk with her more than once."

"I've barely had a chance to meet her. What's she like?"

"I don't know her all that well, but she seems like a sweet girl, kind of shy, quiet, and serious. I know that doesn't sound like someone who would run around on her fiancé, though."

"Yeah, and she sounds like a total opposite of Bud in terms

of personality. But of course, you know what they say about opposites…"

"Yeah, and I just thought of something else. Remember how important the morals clause was to Bud during the strike? I thought that was a philosophical thing, not something personal. But maybe he was already getting involved with Julie back then. Or wanting to."

"You could be right," Chrissie said slowly. "And, if you are, do you know how many rules that would break? He could get in so much trouble if he isn't careful. And what about her?"

"Well, I can't imagine they wouldn't both be in deep trouble. But I'm sure he would be considered the one most responsible. He could lose his job…or worse."

Chrissie stapled the last handout and looked ruefully at her purple hands. "Listen, I'd love to talk more, but I have to wash up and get things ready for my first-hour lab."

Bud remained on my mind as I went through the day. Could I be adding two and two and getting five? Would he really be reckless enough to be involved with a student teacher? Maybe I was getting carried away with my sleuthing. I hoped that was all it was.

My two plagiarists admitted their guilt when I showed them the passage I had found in one of the library books. After that, it was easy getting them to agree to my proposal. I would hold off calling their parents for a day so they could speak with them first. And they would write new papers on different topics, guaranteeing that every word would be their own.

As soon as my last kid left at the end of the day, I went to Bud's room. I wasn't ready to confront him about his personal life, but maybe I would talk around the subject for a while and see if he said anything revealing. It didn't matter, though. I hadn't been quick enough. His lights were out, the door locked. I was about to leave when I spotted a small note taped to the door.

The paper was folded in half and taped closed. Feeling only a smidgeon of guilt, I pried off the tape and read, "J, meet me at the place." I had no doubt who "J" was. And if I was reading the implications correctly, Bud and Julie might have a secret spot where they spent private time together. But where?

It was probably somewhere in the school, based on the late hours he was spending there. The thing was, it was such a large, sprawling building with a hodgepodge of hallways, nooks, and crannies that there had to be a lot of possible hiding places.

"Hey!" I whirled in the direction of the shout and came face to face with Bud. "What are you doing with that? That's not meant for you."

Sheepishly, I handed the note to him. "I'm sorry—"

"God, Andrea, what's wrong with you? Do you have to stick your nose in every damn thing?"

"Bud, I'm so sorry. I don't know what else to say. I just—"

"Save it. I don't want to hear it." I had seen him that angry maybe once or twice in three years, but his anger had never been directed at me before. I felt a tear trickle down my cheek.

He shook his head, crumpled the piece of paper, unlocked his door and went in, slamming it in my face. I opened my mouth to apologize again, paused, turned, and slowly walked back to my room. I sat down at my desk, lowered my head on my folded arms, and sobbed.

What was wrong with me? Why did I keep doing this? First with Tom. Now with Bud. Yes, I had an intense curiosity. I always had since I was a little kid. But in both cases I was snooping to try to protect someone. Yet, despite my good intentions, I had endangered both my relationship with Tom and my friendship with Bud. I didn't even want to imagine how empty my life would be without those two in it.

I raised my head, wiped my eyes, and ran my fingers through my hair. I wanted nothing more than to get home, where I'd try my hardest not to alienate the other man in my life, Marmalade.

———

I spent the evening spoiling Marm with massages and treats and lap time. It didn't take a psych degree to figure out that I was trying to compensate for my treatment of Bud. Finally, my cat had had enough and retreated under the bed. "Not you too," I sighed.

When the phone rang around eight, I leapt to grab it, hoping it was Bud calling to say he had overreacted and everything was forgiven. It wasn't; it was Chrissie, and she sounded worried.

"Andrea, I just had a call from Susan."

"Huh? She still trying to run your life even though you're not in the department anymore?" I stopped myself and took a breath. "I'm sorry. I shouldn't have said that. I had a bad day, and I'm just really bummed."

"What's wrong?"

"Oh, Chrissie, I keep messing things up, and I can't seem to stop myself. Listen, do you have a couple minutes?"

"Sure. Besides, I have something I want to tell you too. Rob's filling in at The Post tonight and I've already finished prepping for tomorrow, so I'm all yours. Hey, I have an idea. You want to run out to The Post for a beer? We haven't done that in ages."

I looked at the clock. Just after eight, and I too was ready for the next day.

"Sure."

———

It was quiet at The Outpost for a Thursday evening. It sounded like someone had put a pocket full of quarters in the jukebox and hit all of the buttons for Simon and Garfunkel. Chrissie and I took a table in a corner where we could talk privately. "What's wrong?" she asked, as "Sounds of Silence" played in the background.

I told her what had happened with Bud after school. After I finished, she said, "I think you're being too hard on yourself, Andrea. You had no idea you were looking at a private note until you had read it. Think about it. If you want to keep something secret, you don't tape it outside your door for anyone to come along and read. I don't care if it was folded over. Besides, it doesn't sound like Bud even gave you a chance to explain, right?"

"No, he didn't. And I apologized as sincerely as I could."

"I'm sure you did. But here's what I wanted to tell you, and it might be related. I ran into Julie in the copy room at lunch time, and—get this—she wasn't wearing her engagement ring."

"No way! But do you think she just took it off to run copies?"

"I'm not sure, but I do think you might be right about her and Bud. And if he's involved with her, of course he's nervous about being caught. Maybe he overreacted with you because he's feeling defensive. Man, he *should* be worried. I hate to think what her student teaching supervisor would say, or North."

"Yeah, maybe you're right. It's just that you and Bud and I have been through so much together. I hate to think I've screwed it up."

"I'm sure you haven't."

"Yeah, well…hey, I never asked you what Susan wanted."

"Oh, she's worried about Sarah again. Or maybe I should say still. Brenda called Susan to tell her that Sarah had just called in sick for tomorrow. I didn't realize how often she's done that this year. I guess Susan asked Brenda to let her know whenever Sarah calls in from now on."

"No! Well, she has been gone quite a bit since the strike. And especially considering she probably hadn't missed more than a couple days in the time we've been here. I'm sure it's partly stress."

"Yeah, I'm sure it is too. I don't think she's going to be even close to normal until they find out who's responsible for Sadie's death. I still can't imagine anyone honestly thinking she's involved with it, though."

I thought carefully before saying, "I want to tell you something, but you have to swear you'll keep it to yourself. Okay?"

"Sure."

"I'm really, really serious about keeping this just between us."

"I will. You know you can trust me."

"Yes, I do." I lowered my voice so it was nearly covered up by "Mrs. Robinson." Chrissie leaned closer to catch my words.

"There's an object missing from Sarah's room, one that could possibly be the murder weapon."

"What?" she said, much too loudly. "I'm sorry," she said returning to a whisper.

"You know those awards they give out to the vets for the years they've taught? Like fifteen years, twenty years, like that? They're shaped like old-fashioned school bells, except they aren't real bells. They are solid metal, so they're really heavy and don't make any sound."

"Yeah, I know what you mean, but I've never paid much attention to what they look like. I doubt I'll be around long enough to get one. One of Sarah's is missing? How do you know?"

"I was in her room, oh, I don't know, not too long after the strike, and she wasn't there. So I was wandering around while I waited for her. You know that bookshelf she has in back of her room, the one where she keeps books that the kids can check out?"

She nodded.

"Well, I was straightening the books out, and that's when I noticed a bell was missing from the top of the bookcase. There was one clean spot on the dusty shelf, and I looked, and the bells skipped from twenty to thirty years. The one for twenty-five years wasn't there."

"So...? But you said murder weapon. Do you think someone took that bell and used it to hit Sadie? I don't see why anyone would ever think of going into Sarah's room and taking one of her...oh, I think I see. No one probably would think of doing that, unless they were already in the room and knew the bells were there. But Sarah?"

"Shhhh." She had raised her voice again without realizing it. "No, I'm not saying it was Sarah. God, no. It's just something I noticed, and I can't explain it, and it bothers me that I can't. All I'm saying is that the paperweight is missing. And it's the right shape and heavy enough to fit the description of the murder weapon."

"Yeah, but don't you think every vet in the school has at least one or two of those bells? Are you sure that's the only one missing?"

"Yes, no...I mean yes, I'm sure there are a lot of them in the building, and no, I don't know if there are others missing. And I don't know what was used to kill Sadie. It's just a loose end, and I have trouble with loose ends."

Chrissie nodded and we both sat in silence until Rob came over from the bar. "Time to hit the road, ladies. I just punched out, and our first classes start in eight hours."

Chrissie and I groaned. We shared a hug, during which I whispered, "Don't worry," and we three walked out together.

There were still so many unanswered questions, but I was sure of one thing: I felt much better than I had a couple of hours earlier. Spending time with Chrissie always had that effect on me.

CHAPTER 31

November 19

Bud walked past my classroom after school the next day. He had his coat on and was alone, not in any particular hurry. But something about his demeanor told me not to interrupt him.

On an impulse, I quietly closed my door and followed him at a distance. Yes, I felt sneaky and silly, but in a way it was fun tailing him like a TV detective.

He passed the door that led to the parking lot and headed toward the main office. I expected him to turn in there, but he didn't. Maybe he was going to run off a ditto. But no, he didn't climb the stairs toward the copy room either. Where could he be going?

When he went down the stairs toward the cafeteria, he

really had me puzzled. I dropped a little farther behind so there was no chance he might hear my shoes on the stairs. Could he be walking around aimlessly to sort out his thoughts? That didn't seem like a Bud thing to do. But with Julie in the picture, all bets were off. Could he be going to meet her at their rendezvous place?

I should not be doing this, I told myself. I should just leave right now, before he or anyone else notices me. But I didn't.

The deeper we went into the building, the warmer it got. I unzipped my jacket, lifted my hair off my neck, and unbuttoned the top button of my blouse. The smell of chlorine became stronger and the air heavier as we neared the pool. My heels were too loud on the tile floor, so I slowed more to let Bud get farther ahead. Then he disappeared around another corner. I waited a few seconds, tiptoed up to it, and peeked around. He was gone. I stared into the half-dark, empty hall.

Guessing he had turned into the cafeteria, I did too. I stood still for a moment and stared into the room. It looked so different after hours, with only security lighting on and all the chairs stacked on the tables. Bud, though, was nowhere to be seen. Had he already left through the door on the opposite side of the room?

Then I saw it. There was another door on the wall nearest the pool. I had looked at it probably a hundred times without really noticing it. It hadn't registered in my mind as a door at all. I had never seen it open, never seen anyone come or go through it. I had no idea where it went, if anywhere. Could Bud have gone in there?

I looked around to be sure I was still alone; then I walked over and examined the dark brown metal door. It was closed, as always. I tried turning the metal doorknob, and, to my surprise, it moved. Why wasn't it locked? Maybe Bud had gone through it after all. Again, my better judgment told me to back away and leave. Again, my curiosity overruled my better judgment.

The door was as heavy as it looked. I pulled on the knob until it opened a crack. Taking a deep breath, I peeked in. I couldn't see anything, so I forced the door open farther and tiptoed in, waiting a moment for my eyes to adjust to the near darkness. There was no sign of anyone else in the room, so I flipped the light switch by the door. Nothing happened.

I blinked once, twice, waiting for my eyes to adjust. When they did, I was unable to believe what I was seeing. All I could think of was catacombs. A narrow passageway grew wider as it extended back into the darkness. Several openings that looked like tunnels split off from the right wall.

I left the door open a few inches to give myself some light and stepped farther into what I guessed was the school's mechanical room. The wall to my left, a tall concrete slab, must have been one of the sides of the pool.

Once I got farther in, there was no need to be quiet.

Any noise I made would be drowned out by a cacophony of machinery noises—probably coming from the boiler, pumps, fans, and other equipment I couldn't identify. The whole place smelled musty. This had to be the oldest part of the school building. It probably hadn't been aired out since it was built in 1921.

Ducking under two low-hanging pipes, I walked into the shadows as far as the first alcove and cautiously stepped in. It was so dark that I could barely make out shapes. A few feet in, I stumbled over what might have been a broken student desk and nearly fell to my knees. This is crazy, I thought, as I backed out into the main room.

At that moment, the machinery shuddered and went silent. I took one final look and decided to get out of there. But, before I could move, I spotted something that hadn't been there before. A weak, flickering light came from an alcove farther into the room. I closed my eyes, opened them again. The light was still there. I had not imagined it. Could it be a flashlight? A candle?

Was Bud back there? Was this where he and Julie had been coming?

I could think about that later. The important thing was to get out before whoever it was realized I was there. Cautiously, I backtracked toward the door and checked to be sure the cafeteria was still empty.

By the time I made it back to my classroom, my pounding

heart had returned to its normal rate. I sank down in the student desk nearest the door.

"Hi, Miss J. Oh, hey, I'm sorry," Billy said when I jumped from the desk and whirled around. "I thought you knew I was here. Where you been? I've already finished up and was just gonna lock up for you."

"Oh, I was looking for Chrissie in her room, but I guess I missed her."

For a moment, I considered telling him where I'd really been. He could probably give me more information about the room I had stumbled into. But I couldn't think of a way to explain it without revealing Bud's secret.

It wasn't until I was sitting in my car that the potential impact of what I had discovered sank in. Had I stumbled on a hiding place for a tryst? Were Bud and Julie really meeting there? Who knew what secrets might be hidden in that mysterious place.

———

My brain ran in interlocking circles all evening. I was so desperate to concentrate on something other than Bud and Julie that I sat down at the kitchen table to grade papers. "What am I doing?" I asked Marm. "It's Friday night. I'm not supposed to be doing this. This is something Sadie and Sarah do."

Finally, around ten, I pushed aside the stack of papers, walked around, and opened a Pepsi. Stretching out the kinks in my neck, I gathered my hair, pulled it up off my neck, and flipped it over my left shoulder. Something didn't feel right.

"Oh, no. It's gone," I wailed. I reached for my peace symbol necklace and felt only bare skin. I stood up and shook out my clothes. Nothing.

Starting to panic, I tried to remember the last time I had noticed it. But I wasn't sure. I never took it off, so it couldn't have been lost. I loved that necklace, what it stood for, all of the memories connected with it—everything about it.

I searched my house, moving frantically from room to room. I found nothing and ran out to the garage. I checked the car, everywhere—behind and underneath the seats, even the trunk—and again came up empty.

It was getting late, but I took a chance and called Chrissie anyway. She answered on the second ring.

"Chrissie," I said. "When was the last time you saw me with my peace symbol on?"

"What? I don't know. You always have it on. Why?"

"Because it's gone and I can't find it and it can't be lost but it might be and I was hoping you…"

"Whoa. Slow down. You're going so fast I can barely understand you. So you're saying your necklace is missing?"

I took a deep breath and held it for a couple of seconds. "Yes, and you know how much it means to me. I don't know when I lost it. The chain must have broken, and I was hoping you could help me narrow down when it happened."

"Well, let's see. I know you had it on at lunch. But I didn't see you after school. I wish I could be more help. It's probably somewhere in your classroom. That would be my guess. Either that or…did you check your car?"

"Yes. I practically tore my car apart and it's not there."

"Then you should go over to school tomorrow and take a good look in your room."

"Yeah, well, I can't wait that long. I'm going over right now."

"No, don't do that. It's late and the school's all locked up for the weekend, so nothing will happen to the necklace. It'll be much easier to find it in the daylight."

"I suppose you're right. Thanks, Chrissie. Sorry I called you so late."

"She may be right," I told Marm. "It's probably at school, in my room." But Billy had cleaned my room after school. I had seen him as he was finishing, and he would have given it to me if he had found it.

Then I remembered. I could have lost it when I followed Bud. In fact, I could have snagged it when I was unbuttoning my jacket. I was probably going to have to retrace my steps all the way down to the pool. If I didn't find it there, I'd search the mechanical room. But wouldn't I need a key to get in? I thought. Hey, does Bud have one? He must have, but I didn't.

I fought the urge to rush over to school. What good would it do? I couldn't get to the pool area anyway because the security gates were up on weekends. So I'd be better off waiting until Monday. And even then I'd have to make up some kind of story to explain to Billy why I needed to get into the room. As much as I hated the idea of waiting, my better judgment said that was what I should do.

I undressed and got into bed, but sleep had become impossible. I kept touching my throat, missing my necklace. I got up and paced, reached for the phone to call Tom, but put it down without dialing.

It was hopeless. I wasn't going to get any sleep until I found that necklace. I could just as well go over to school right away and look for it. Maybe I wouldn't be able to get to all the places I needed, but at least I could check my room and walk the halls until a gate stopped me. I got dressed again and found the flashlight that Dad had given me for emergencies. If this wasn't an emergency, I didn't know what would be.

CHAPTER 32
November 19

I expected to find the school parking lot empty late on a Friday night, but it wasn't. A car and a pickup were parked near the side door of the building. I didn't recognize either of them.

I fumbled in my bag to find my school keys and let myself in. The door closed, relocking behind me with an ominous click. I walked the dimly lit hallways to my classroom. There, I turned on the lights and searched the floor inch by inch. Nothing. No sign of my necklace. I would have to retrace the entire route I had taken following Bud.

It was slow going. I had to sweep the beam of my flashlight across the whole width of the hall to be sure I didn't overlook the necklace. Gradually, I made my way past Bud's room and around the corner toward the art room. There, something shiny caught my eye. I knelt and reached under a locker. My hand came out clutching a gum wrapper.

I turned the corner just past the art room and was stopped by a metal security gate. With little hope, I gave it a yank and was surprised when it parted a couple of inches. I pushed harder, and it slid open far enough for me to squeeze through. Some security.

I went down the stairs, keeping my eyes on the floor as I headed toward the cafeteria. Was it just my imagination, or was the flashlight growing dimmer? It could have been. I had never replaced the batteries. But I wasn't willing to announce my presence by turning on any overhead lights. I saw no more shiny objects, not even gum wrappers.

Faintly at first, then more distinctly, the smell of chlorine told me I was nearing the pool. This was where I had taken off my jacket and loosened the collar of my blouse that afternoon. I searched the floor even more carefully, thinking if I had broken the chain, this could be where it would have happened. But I found nothing.

When I was almost to the cafeteria, I heard a noise behind me. Was it footsteps? I froze, turned off the flashlight. Then I stepped inside the door and waited. I mentally counted to ten. When I heard nothing more, I forced myself to take some deep, calming breaths. Finally, I began slowly walking again but kept the light off. Everything was quiet. I told myself it had probably just been my imagination.

When I got to the door of the mechanical room, my hopes of finding the necklace faded. My search would be over if the door was locked—at least until I could get in on Monday.

I dropped to my hands and knees in front of the door and slowly examined the floor in the fading beam of my flashlight. Still nothing. Then I pressed my face to the tile floor and directed the beam under the door. But I couldn't see anything except dust. It was useless. I wasn't going to find it.

While rising to my feet, I lost my balance and leaned on the door before I could steady myself. Had it moved a fraction of an inch? I pulled, hard, and it slowly opened.

I ran my fingers over the latch, and they came away sticky. I realized it must have been taped open. Was that how Bud and Julie were able to get into their rendezvous place whenever they wanted?

The hinges creaked as I pulled the door farther open. I switched the flashlight back on and looked around the room. Discarded classroom furniture, scraps of lumber, and rusty cans of paint lay scattered around the narrow room. Pipes hung from the ceiling, sometimes so low that I had to duck to keep from hitting my head.

It was time to resume my search for the necklace. I slowly swept the beam of my flashlight across the dusty, rough plank floor. Nothing. As I worked my way farther into the room,

I came to the place where the first alcove opened off the right wall. I had stepped in there that afternoon, so I had to search it.

Tall, dusty, empty shelves lined one of walls. My light showed several sets of footprints in the dust on the floor. Someone else had been there, and fairly recently. I dropped to the floor to look under the shelves. My knees were beginning to ache when I finally noticed an object. I took a longer look. Yes, there was definitely something way back against the wall, but it didn't look like jewelry. I reached for it, and my hand touched a bundle wrapped in plastic. Could it be drugs?

I pulled it out and knew immediately that it wasn't. It felt like a tool inside the plastic. Maybe a worker had accidentally kicked it under the shelves. But why wrap it? When I moved the light closer, I saw a hammer inside the plastic bag.

"Oh my God," I whispered softly. The missing hammer. The murder weapon. But how did it get—?

The hinges of the door creaked and I froze. My heart began pounding. I flicked off the flashlight and pushed the hammer far back under the shelves. Staying on my hands and knees, I willed myself to steady my breathing.

Who would be coming at this hour of the night? I couldn't think of a reason for anyone to be there, except possibly a janitor. Then it hit me. Maybe the creaking wasn't the door opening wider. If a janitor came along and saw it open, his natural reaction would be to close and lock it.

But no, it was getting lighter in the alcove, not darker. A

dim light bobbed as the person carrying it walked toward me. My fear grew when I realized a janitor would not sneak around with a flashlight. Could it be Bud and Julie? No. They would make more noise, probably be talking to each other. This seemed to be one person.

Ever so slowly, I turned, still on my hands and knees. And I waited, shrinking into the smallest mass possible. Whoever it was came slowly around the corner. I could make out a shape but not a face. When he stopped two feet from me, I stopped breathing, paralyzed, waiting helplessly to be discovered.

But he hadn't noticed me. He bent down and was groping under the shelves, apparently reaching for the hammer. I couldn't let him take it, not if it was the murder weapon. He obviously knew where to look, but I hadn't replaced it where he expected it to be. He stooped lower to poke his flashlight under the shelf. For an instant, the light illuminated his face.

No, not his face. Her face. It was a woman.

"Mrs. Pendling."

The light swung crazily around the cramped room. "Who's there?" she hissed.

There was no point in hiding anymore. I spoke in my normal voice, hoping she wouldn't notice it shaking. "What are you doing with that hammer? I bet it's the one that killed Sadie, isn't it?"

"Mrs. Jackson. You. What are you doing here?"

"The hammer, Mrs. Pendling. The one you came here

looking for. It's the murder weapon, isn't it? What are you doing with it?"

"What murder weapon? Mind your own business. I can't believe it. Friday night, middle of the night, and you're here? Why?"

"I have a good reason for being here, not that it's any of your business. I'm looking for something I lost, something important to me."

"Uh-huh. And you think you just happened to lose it here? Come on. Hardly anyone even knows this place exists."

"You're right. But you know. Why is that? What are *you* doing here?"

I had seen the woman a few times., but she looked bigger and stronger than I remembered. She had to outweigh me by forty pounds. Her face twisted into a grimace of desperation and anger. I wanted to get away from her—far away.

I rose to my feet and said, as calmly as possible, "My necklace isn't here, so I'm going now."

"No, no you're not. I can't have you broadcasting your crazy ideas about some murder weapon. I don't know where you came up with that anyway."

"Let me get past. I'm leaving."

"Not so fast. Where's the hammer? I'm not leaving without it, and you're not getting out of here until I have it. Where'd you put it?"

Rather than answer, I dropped to the floor again and shot

my hand under the shelf. She did the same, letting go of her flashlight. It fell with its beam aimed across the room, not helping either of us. But I knew where the hammer was and pulled it out. I raised it with my arm cocked, not quite sure if I could use it to strike another human being.

"Let me pass," I said in the steadiest voice I could command. When she didn't move, I raised my voice and said it again. "Let me out of here."

She lunged toward me, going for the hammer, but I was quicker than she was. I stepped to the right and twisted it out of her reach. Again, she ran at me and managed to get a hand on the plastic. I wrenched it away from her and kicked wildly toward her. I got her in the shin. She roared at me, "Gimme that."

I feinted toward the right once more. When she tried to follow me, I kicked out my leg again and tripped her. She stumbled and went down hard on her knees, letting out a cry of pain.

I got past her, but not quite out of her reach. She was back on her feet and caught my hair, yanking my head back. Scared and furious and desperate, I swung my arm around with all my might and felt the hammer make contact with her body. She called out in pain but released my hair. I ran for the door. Groaning, she stumbled after me, but I was too fast for her. I heard a loud bang, followed by a string of swear words. I realized she must have forgotten to duck and hit her head on the pipes.

I bolted into the cafeteria and took off for the outside door. If I could make it to my car, I would be safe. I ran as hard as I could, never slowing down to look over my shoulder. All I wanted was to be in my Beetle, doors locked, driving down the hill away from the school.

But I had forgotten the security gate. When I got to it, I yanked it like I had before. It wouldn't open again. What was wrong? Maybe she had pulled the gate all the way closed on her way in and it had locked.

I had to do something—fast. I could hear her footsteps getting dangerously closer. I gave the lock a sharp whack with the hammer, and it opened. I squeezed through and slammed it shut again, hoping it would relock behind me.

Just get down the hall and around one more corner, I told myself as I gasped for breath. I heard the old gate groan when she tried to open it. I prayed it would hold just another minute. With an adrenaline surge, I flew around the last corner.

Oof. The next thing I knew, I was lying on top of someone on the floor, gulping in air. I had been going so fast when I hit him that we both fell in a tangled heap of limbs. But the wonderful, familiar smell of Tom's aftershave filled my nostrils. "Tommy?"

"Andie? What are you doing here in the middle of the night? What's going on?" He got to his feet and helped me up. "I'll explain everything. But, Tom, I know who killed Sadie. She just tried to hurt me too. It's Natalie Pendling, and she's right around the corner. Well, she was right behind me in the hall, but it seems she's gone now. And I think this is the murder weapon." I handed him the hammer still covered by a torn plastic bag.

He shook his head, apparently beyond words. He laid it carefully aside, walked a few feet away and spoke a few sentences into his walkie-talkie. Then he was back, smothering me in a bear hug. "Don't worry," he said into my hair. "I've alerted the others to cover the exits and to watch for her. And if she doesn't try to get out of the building, they'll come in and find her. You're staying here with me where you're safe."

"I'm so glad to see you," I whispered. "How did you know I was here and needed help?"

"Chrissie called me and said you might be here looking for something you lost. She was worried about you in the empty building this late at night. When you didn't answer my call, I'd thought I'd check it out, and then I saw your car outside. What were you looking for that was this important?"

"My peace symbol necklace. I'm afraid I've lost it, Tommy. I came looking for it and never did find it."

"Gosh, I'm sorry, honey. I know how much it means to

you. But coming here like this…what exactly happened in there?"

Walkie-talkies blared, and officers converged on us. Tom snapped back to his professional self. I already missed being in his arms.

Tom handed the plastic-wrapped weapon to the chief, who said, "I have a feeling I know what this is. Good work, Jefferson. We got her, by the way. Lewis picked her up in the parking lot."

"Thank you, sir, but Miss Jackson was the one who secured the weapon." I tried to shush him. I wanted Tom to get the credit.

"Do we know anything about the perp?" the chief asked. Tom nodded to me to answer.

"It's Mrs. Pendling, Cliff's mom," I said. "She came looking for the hammer, and I think it's the murder weapon, and, oh, it's a long story. She showed her true colors in that room—she's a mean, hateful woman, but why would she kill Sadie?"

The chief shook his head. "We'll get it all figured out. And I hope very soon. Miss Jackson, do you feel up to answering some questions?"

Sleep was the last thing on my mind, so I nodded my agreement. Besides, I wanted some answers too, lots of them.

Tom and I walked out of the building together and over to his squad car. We lingered in our own little world for a moment, arms wrapped around each other. I wished I could stop time and exist in the safety of his embrace forever.

But we had to get to the station. He didn't open the door to the back seat like I was expecting. He bent the rules and opened the passenger-side door. Then he made sure I was in and gently closed the door.

There was so much to say to each other that we said nothing at all. Tom had to be full of questions about what had happened inside the school, but he was silent. The trip down the hill to the police station went far too quickly. We hadn't been that in sync for months, not since sometime before the strike. I didn't want the moment to end.

But it did, of course, as soon as we walked into the station. The chief met us and told me that Tom would not be taking my statement because of his personal connection to the case. Instead, once again, Officer Bertrand would be conducting the interview. Tom nodded his agreement, and I left with the other officer.

It was hard to concentrate, as the impact of the past two hours began to take hold. At times, I had trouble keeping my emotions in check. "I remember what happened," I told Officer Bertrand, "but a lot of it doesn't make any sense. I mean, why would she want to kill Sadie? I know there was the incident with the failing grade, but to resort to murder…?"

"Don't try to figure it all out right now. Just concentrate

on answering my questions, and let us worry about the big picture."

And so he took me through all of the events, beginning with why I had decided to go to school late on a Friday night. I could tell he didn't understand the importance of my peace symbol necklace, so my motivation probably didn't make sense to him. I was relieved he didn't think to ask why I had been in the mechanical room in the first place. There was no way I was going to drag Bud and Julie into the situation.

Instead, he asked, "How did you get through the halls to the mechanical room? I saw the security gates were up."

"Yeah, I don't understand that either. I got to the gate, gave it a shove, and it just opened. It must not have been completely latched. I know it will sound lame, but the same thing happened with the door to the mechanical room. It might have been taped open, but I have no idea why."

"Did you see or hear anything to make you suspect you were not alone in the building?"

"Well, there were an empty car and truck in the parking lot, but I didn't see anyone. One time I thought I heard something in the pool area before I got to the door, but I assumed it was my imagination. The school is spooky when you're alone there at night. Well, it probably wouldn't be for you, but it is for me."

"Now take me through the sequence of events in the mechanical room."

"Okay. I was looking around for my necklace, and I was using my flashlight. I saw a space beneath the shelves, so I got down on my hands and knees for a better look…" I retold the story in all of the detail I could recall. He stopped me occasionally to clarify a point, but for the most part I talked while he took notes.

"…and then Tom—I mean Officer Jefferson—came along. I gave him the murder weapon and…that's it."

But I wasn't quite finished. "Now, officer, can I ask you a couple of questions?"

"No."

I ignored that and asked, "It must have been Natalie Pendling who hid the hammer in the mechanical room. But why was she there? Was she going to move it or get rid of it… or…you don't think she was covering up for her husband, do you?"

"No."

"No to which part?"

"No to answering any and all questions. I can't discuss the case with you at all. Period."

"You're going to try to lift fingerprints from the hammer, not the wrapping around it, right? Those should be the killer's. Right?"

He said nothing, just stared straight ahead.

"Right. I get it. You're not going to answer any questions."

CHAPTER 33
November 20–21

My weekend was filled with visits and phone calls from Tom, Chrissie, Bud, Susan, and other friends from school. I had a long call with Mom and Dad, who needed to be reassured over and over that I was all right. And I really was. I assured them that I would be coming home for Thanksgiving soon, so it was not necessary for them to make the six-hour round trip to check on me.

My time alone was welcome too. On Saturday morning, I picked up my well-worn paperback copy of *The Great Gatsby*. I had read it every summer since my senior year in high school, but, due to Chrissie's wedding and the looming strike, I hadn't gotten to it that year.

Big chunks of my weekend sped by as I lost myself in Gatsby's world in the brilliant prose of Fitzgerald. I came to the last page, looked up from the book, and whispered the final sentence from memory: *So we beat on, boats against the current, borne back ceaselessly into the past.* It was better therapy than any doctor could have prescribed.

———

Sunday afternoon I settled down to grade the papers I had brought home on Friday. It seemed like so much more than just two days had passed.

I was almost through grading a stack of tests when my doorbell rang, startling Marm, who was sound asleep on the table next to my left arm. I opened my back door to find Sarah. I motioned her in, and she was hugging me before she even had her coat off.

"Are you really all right, my dear? When I heard what happened…" She began crying softly. "I am so, so sorry. This never would have happened if I hadn't asked you to look into Sadie's death. And to think I almost was to blame for you being harmed too. It is just too much."

I gently pushed her away so I could ease her coat off. With one arm around her shoulders, I reached for a box of tissues and handed it to her. Then I led her to a chair at my kitchen table and put on the teakettle. Once Sarah had calmed down enough to listen, I reassured her the best I could.

"First of all, Sarah, I am fine. No injuries, not even any bumps or bruises. If Tom hadn't shown up when he did, it might have been a different story. But he did, so put your worries about me to rest."

I could feel her relaxing just a bit. "And, also, you are not to blame because I got myself into a dangerous situation. That had nothing to do with you or even Sadie. I was at school that night looking for something I had lost earlier in the day. It's the peace symbol necklace that I always wear."

"Oh dear, and I see you still don't have it back."

"No, I couldn't find it. I'm afraid it's gone for good. But don't you see? None of this is your fault."

"No, I guess maybe it isn't after all."

"Sarah, I'm almost positive that the hammer I found is the weapon the police have been looking for. As soon as they check the fingerprints that are on it, they will know who the real killer is and this nightmare will be over."

As she processed my words, her posture began to change. She sat up a little straighter, held her head a little higher. She took a deep breath, and a wisp of a smile crossed her lips.

As she closed my back door on her way out, I crossed my fingers, hoping she had turned the corner into a happier place.

———

I had to admit, though, that the solution might not be as clean and simple as I had led Sarah to believe. Was Natalie Pendling really the guilty party? Did she kill Sadie with that hammer? Why had she hidden it in the mechanical room, and why did she come back for it?

More importantly, why would she kill Sadie? Was it because Sadie gave her son an F? How could that be enough reason to take the life of another human being? If Natalie could do that, what kind of mother was she anyway? And what about her husband? Surely, he must have been involved from the beginning.

And then there was Cliff. Did he know who had killed Sadie? Was his disappearance related to the murder?

Lots of questions. No answers and no way to get them. I touched my neck, forgetting for a moment that the necklace was still missing. I was going to miss it for a very long time.

CHAPTER 34
November 22

Then it was Monday morning. I was still taking off my coat when Billy walked into my classroom. "Miss J., are you really okay? I was so worried about you."

Without answering, I walked over and hugged him, long and hard. When I released him and stepped back, I saw his beet-red face. He mumbled something, clearly embarrassed by the hug. "Hey, did you get—"

"Did I get what?"

"Nothing. It was…nothing." Before either of us could say anything more, he was paged over the intercom. "Thank you for everything," I said as he left. I would thank him again when he had more time.

My students insisted on interrupting every time I tried to

start a lesson. Why had I been at school late Friday night? What had happened? Why did Cliff's mom attack me? Was it true that she was in jail?

I answered all of the questions with a mostly honest "I don't know," and was evasive about my own part in the events. During fourth hour, I heard a cough outside my door and looked up to see Mr. North motioning me into the hall. "I need to talk to you before your last class of the day. Is this a good time?"

"No." What was with him? "I only have a minute and I then I have to get back to my kids."

"Well, I'll make it brief then. Cliff Pendling is back in school and will be in your eighth-hour class. I am speaking with all of his teachers about this. By the way, are you all right?"

"Yes."

"Do not discuss Cliff's absence or whereabouts. His father is threatening to sue the school—"

"His father? What about his mother? She's in jail, I hope. But wait. Why would Mr. Pendling try to sue us? None of this is our fault—"

"Precisely. Do not say anything or react in any way that could give him ammunition."

"But—"

"Miss J., can I go to the washroom?" asked a squeaky voice behind me.

"Huh? Um, yes, Duncan. Take the pass from my desk. I have to get back to class, Mr. North."

"Remember what I said," he tossed over his shoulder as he left.

———

I remembered it. But how would I accomplish it? I was dying to know where Cliff had been and why. I was sure his classmates would feel the same way. Still, it was a direct order from the principal.

The eighth-hour kids walked in, looking around expectantly. Obviously, the news was out that Cliff was back. The seats filled earlier than usual. Last in the room were Rick and Jack. But Cliff's seat remained empty when the bell rang. The kids looked as disappointed as I was. Where was he? Faces turned toward Rick and Jack, who stared back and shrugged.

I tried to act as if everything were normal. After all, Cliff hadn't been in class for three weeks. I taught the lesson I had planned. I caught myself glancing toward the door from time to time, wondering if Cliff would make a late entrance. But the final bell rang, and my room emptied with no sign of him.

I shrugged off my disappointment and sat down to grade some papers before going home. After a few minutes, I glanced up and saw Cliff in my doorway. He appeared a little worse for wear, a little thinner, a little more unkempt, with his swagger nowhere to be seen.

"Cliff, come in. I heard you were back. It's good to see you." He looked surprised to hear the words coming out of my mouth. I was surprised by them too. But I realized I meant them, mostly.

"Uh, thanks, Miss Jackson. Sorry I wasn't in class. I was tied up in the guidance office. My counselor said I had to, I mean should, talk to you. So here I am." He spoke simply, without a trace of the old Cliff attitude.

"What can I do for you?"

"I dunno. I guess I need to make up some stuff so I can try to still pass the semester."

"That sounds like a good idea. But Cliff, if you don't mind my asking, where were you? You've missed a lot of school."

"Yeah. Well, I had to get away from home for a while is all." He paused, clearly trying to decide whether to say more. I kept quiet, but he didn't elaborate.

"All right. Well, I'll get you a list of your missing work so you can get started on it."

"Hey, you're really not going to have me do all of that, are you?"

"Of course I am. The usual policy is two days to catch up for every day that you miss, so that would be—"

"Oh, no. No, that's going to take—"

"You should be finished just in time for the semester exam. Good thing we have a vacation in there."

Cliff shook his head, but in a more good-natured way than I would have expected.

"Here's a copy of *Huck Finn* so you can start reading," I said. It wasn't the best time to hand out a book that his father would almost certainly not approve of, given his complaints during conferences. But I had no intention of changing the course content just because one ignorant parent was making waves with North.

"Cliff, I'll have everything else you need tomorrow. Don't forget to take your book home."

He shook his head again, but I noticed his lips twitch. I thought he almost smiled on his way out.

———

"And it went better than I would have thought," I told Tom a couple of hours later. He had come over for pizza and beer, just like in the old days. "I mean, Cliff will never be my favorite student, or probably much of a student at all, but he was more cooperative than I expected. Maybe it was because there was no teenage audience there to perform for, but the chip was definitely gone from his shoulder."

"Great. But did he say anything about the hammers?"

I sighed. "No. All he would say was that he had run away because he wanted to get away from home for a few days. No, now that I think about it, he said he *had* to get away from home. I wish I could be more help, Tommy."

"That's okay, honey. Actually, the hammers we found in his

locker are kind of a secondary option for us anyway. We are thinking the important one is the one you recovered in the mechanical room. It's still being checked for fingerprints and blood types, but I hope it will lead us to the murderer."

"But Natalie had the hammer, so isn't it obvious?"

"Not quite. It's highly likely she's the one, but we need the prints."

"Right. But there's no way that Sarah is still in the mix, right?"

"Only if her fingerprints are on the hammer."

"How about Cliff? He isn't going to be in trouble, is he?"

"Only if one of the hammers found in his locker turns out to be the weapon we're looking for."

"What about Mr. Pendling? Wayne?"

"He's being questioned as we speak. So far we don't know if he was involved in the murder or, if not, how much he knew. Again, the fingerprints will be the key."

"Good. When do you expect the results?"

"Soon."

"But here's what I still haven't figured out: how did the hammer get to the mechanical room?"

The slightest frown had begun developing between Tom's eyebrows, and I knew I had pushed him farther than I should have. Out of habit, I reached for my necklace before I remembered it was gone. Tom noticed. He looked like he wanted to say something but he didn't.

"That's it for tonight," he said. "I've already talked more than I intended to. It seems you have this magical power over me…"

"Wait, Tommy. Do you realize what just happened?"

"Well, I thought you just hinted that you might consider distracting me with your magical powers."

"Of course there's that. But seriously, look. I think I figured something out. I almost pushed you too far, like I've done so many times. Then your frown tipped me off, and I backed down right away, and you backed down…and everything is all right between us. Right?"

"Right. Now about you wielding your magical powers…"

"There's nothing I would rather do right now."

———

After Tom left, I cleaned up the kitchen, gave Marm his bedtime snack, and got ready for bed. But sleep wouldn't come right away; I felt oddly deflated. I had survived a dangerous situation, found and protected the murder weapon, and helped the police capture Natalie. But it was frustrating not knowing why she had done it. I couldn't fill in the details, and that bugged me.

So I took a few mental steps back and tried again. The hammer had been in the mechanical room, but for how long? How would Natalie—if she was the one who had hidden it—even know about that place or have access to it?

I couldn't turn off my mind. I tossed and turned for a long time. Just when I had almost dozed off, I awoke with a start. The list I had found in Sadie's room. I'd forgotten to ask Tom if they'd learned anything from it.

CHAPTER 35
November 23

It was already dark when I pulled into my driveway. I didn't notice the man sitting on my back steps until I was within feet of him.

"Bud! You almost scared me to death. What are you doing here?"

"Sorry. I thought you saw me. I'm waiting for you… obviously. Can I come in and talk to you?"

"Of course. Come on in, but watch out. Don't trip over Marmalade."

He followed me in, bending down to scratch Marm on his head. He really liked Bud. "How about I order pizza?" I asked. "Sorry I'm not more of a cook."

"No, that's okay. I can't stay long. I just…there's something I've wanted to tell you. I should have a while back."

We sat on my couch with Marm between us, purring at his top volume. Bud drew a breath and said, "You know about Julie and me, right?"

"Yeah, I know that you've, um, gotten close. And I've noticed that she isn't wearing her ring anymore. I've wanted to talk to you about it, but I wasn't sure if I should. But, first, I want to apologize again for intercepting the note you left her on your door. That was totally wrong of me. I've felt terrible about it ever since. If I could relive that day, it would never happen."

He had been shaking his head *no* since I began my apology. "Andrea, that is all water over the dam. God knows I've made more than my share of mistakes, so I'm in no place to judge someone else who does. Forget about it, okay? I have."

"Thank you, Bud. I can't tell you how much better I feel having that off my chest. And about you and Julie: you know you can trust me with your secret, right?"

"Yeah, I wouldn't be here if I wasn't sure I could. It's not so much for me, but I'd hate to see her get in any trouble. Or to have people saying nasty things about her."

"I'm not going to lecture you about taking chances. I'm sure you're well aware of the stakes. And Bud, I support you if this is what you want. I hope you know that."

"I do, Andrea. But that's only part of what I came to say.

After what happened to you this weekend, there's something I thought you should know."

My phone began ringing, interrupting us at a bad time. "I'm going to let it ring. If it's important they'll call back."

"Okay. Obviously, this is just between us. You can't tell anyone. I mean anyone at all."

There have been times when I agreed to secrecy and later regretted my promise. This felt like it might turn out to be another of them. So I hesitated, but he sat waiting me out, his mouth set.

"Okay, I promise," I said reluctantly.

"Okay. Julie and I were in the mechanical room one time when Mrs. Pendling came in and checked on the hammer."

"What? And she didn't know you were there?"

"God, no. We were damn lucky about that too. We had a candle lit, and when I heard someone coming I quick blew it out. She walked right by us with a flashlight, and I got a look at her face. But she was in a hurry. All she did was pull the hammer out from under the shelf, look at it, and put it right back. She was in and out of there in less than a minute, and besides—"

My phone started ringing again. Bud looked at me, and I shook my head impatiently. Once it stopped, I picked up where we had left off. "If it was dark, how do you know she had the hammer?"

"As soon as she left, I pulled it out and looked at it. Wasn't too hard to guess what it was or why she needed to hide it."

"When was this? Shortly after the murder?"

"Yeah, probably the week after the strike. And I know. I should have taken it to the police. But how could I do that without explaining why I was there, and then Julie might have gotten dragged into it?"

"Well, yeah…but let me think. Then the hammer was most likely there the whole time. I'm not sure why she would check on it, though. And I still can't understand why she chose that place to hide—"

When the phone began ringing again, Bud stood and said, "You better answer it. Sounds like it might be important. I got to go anyway."

I nodded. The moment he walked out my door, I grabbed the phone.

"Andrea. I was about ready to give up on you." It was Susan. "We're going to have an emergency department meeting tomorrow afternoon."

"Oh, all right. I'll be there. Three thirty in your room, as usual?"

"No, it will start a little later. There's going to be an emergency faculty meeting for the entire staff right after classes end."

"What's—"

"George is resigning."

"Mr. North?"

"Of course, Mr. North."

"But why? And why not wait to announce it until closer to the end of the year?"

"Because he's leaving tomorrow."

"What? Why?"

She sighed loudly. "He doesn't want people to know this, so keep it to yourself. He's resigning because the board is ready to fire him. He wants it to look like a retirement."

"Wow! That's all I can say."

"Yes, but when you think about it, is it really so surprising? Look at all of the ways he's screwed up this year. Parents were all over the way he handled the strike, with his bringing in scabs from out of town and keeping school open without proper supervision of the kids. And now there's another issue. It's just coming out that he has changed more grades than just Sadie's."

"That's awful. Do you happen to know if he changed any of mine?"

"No, we won't know how many or whose grades for a while. The only way to check it is to compare our old gradebooks to student transcripts. It's a slow process that will go on for quite a while."

"Wow! North was even worse than I thought. I can't say I'm sorry to see him go. Hey, Susan, did you try to call earlier? Two times?"

"No, I'm working my way down the phone tree. If you had

any other calls, they weren't from me. Well, see you tomorrow, and remember the department meeting after the staff meeting."

I wanted to ask her why the English department had to meet if the resignation would be made in the faculty meeting. But Susan had already hung up, so I would have to wait to find out.

I stayed up a while longer even though I was having trouble keeping my eyes open. I kept hoping that whoever had called earlier would try again. But when I wanted the phone to ring, it refused. Finally, I gave up and went to bed.

And that was when the phone rang. "Andie Jackson, are you still up?" Tom asked.

"Sure," I mumbled, seeing if he would buy it. He didn't.

"Doesn't sound like it to me. But as long as I—"

"Wait, Tommy. Did you try to call me earlier this evening?"

"No, why?"

"Oh, it's nothing. This is going to sound crazy, but could it have been the Pendlings?"

"No, it wouldn't have been them. They used her one call to get their lawyer down here. Natalie's being charged with Sadie's murder."

"Wow! What about Wayne?"

"No, just her. But let's leave that for another time. I called to see if you'd be free for dinner tomorrow. I actually have a Friday off, and I thought we might go someplace nice. What do you say?"

"I say it sounds heavenly. Just let me know when I should be ready."

CHAPTER 36

November 24

The day was shaping up to be a busy one, so I jumped on it and got to school early. When I stopped in the office for my mail, Mr. North's office was dark and the door was closed. I wondered how he would spend the last day of a career that had covered more than thirty years, all at HHS. There was a memo in my mailbox announcing the faculty meeting after school, but it didn't say anything about the reason for it.

While I was getting organized for the day, a weariness settled over me. Maybe that was how it would feel to get old. Soon I would be halfway through my third year of teaching. It was already getting harder to recall the combination of exhilaration and terror that had gripped me my first year.

Yes, I had come a long way, but I also knew I had a long way to go before I would master the ins and outs of teaching. Sarah and Sadie and, yes, Susan, had all done it. I thought I should ask one of them how and when it finally happens.

"Hey, Miss J. You okay? You look like you're a million miles away," Billy said from my doorway.

"Sure, Billy. I'm all right. I was just thinking about Sarah. You know that the police have cleared her, right? Now that they have arrested Natalie, it's all over."

"Good. I'm really glad. But I was kinda worried about you, Miss J. I tried to call you twice last night, and there wasn't any answer."

"Oh, that was you?"

"Hey, how did you know someone called if you weren't home?"

I felt my face redden. "I was there, Billy, but I was in the middle of a really important conversation and had to let the phone ring. I'm sorry. I didn't mean to ignore you, it's just—"

"No, no, that's okay. It wasn't anything earthshaking. Remember how you asked me to keep my eyes open for one of Miss Malcom's school bells that was missing? Well, I found it."

"You did? Where was it?"

"In Mr. Antag's room."

"I wonder how it got there. Maybe Sadie had borrowed it, but I don't know why she would do that."

"Yeah, I don't know either. But he was using it as a door stop when he wanted his classroom door open."

"What? How dare he use her hard-earned award…"

Two short bursts of the bell interrupted me.

"Sorry, I gotta go, Miss J.," Billy said as he hurried out.

———

Finally, it was time for the faculty meeting. I walked into the library and came face to face with Harve. "Andrea, I haven't seen you in a while," he said. "Never had a chance to tell you congrats for putting the Pendlings in their place."

"Thanks, Harve. Honestly, I didn't see it coming. I mean, it wouldn't have surprised me to find out he was guilty, but her…?"

"Yeah. And now another surprise with North leaving during the school year. Not that I'm sorry to see him go."

I nodded as we both went off to find empty seats. I winced when I remembered that I had once thought Harve might be capable of hurting Sadie. I had misjudged him. After all, he had led us through a successful strike. He was okay.

Bud slid into a chair next to me and whispered, "With any luck, this is the last time we'll ever have to listen to this jag-off blab on and on." I nodded and grinned. There weren't any long faces in the room. In fact, the meeting had a celebratory feel to it.

"Are you going to miss him at all?" Chrissie whispered.

"Nope," I said.

"Hell, no," Bud added. "The way I see it, it's almost Thanksgiving, and this is one big thing to be thankful for."

"Where's Sarah?" I asked.

"She probably won't be here," Susan said. Bud caught my eye and raised his eyebrow. "When I called her last night, she said she had an appointment she's had scheduled a while and had to keep. I filled her in on what's happening here, and she is hoping to get back in time for our department meeting. Have you had a chance to talk with her lately? I think she's beginning to show signs of healing. I'm encouraged."

The doors to the library opened. I expected to see North come in, but he didn't. Instead, Ray Dalby limped in and, staring straight ahead, hobbled to the front of the room. Bud whispered, "What the hell…" but stopped when he realized the room had fallen into total silence.

Dalby's cold, penetrating glare demanded our attention. I could count on the fingers of one hand the people that I actually hated. He was at the top of the list.

North was still nowhere to be seen when Dalby began. "George North has applied for and received release from his contract. As of this morning, he is officially retired." That much we knew, but I could tell there was more coming.

A member of the negotiating team raised his hand, but Dalby ignored him. "George served this district for a good many years. Now he has chosen to move on. I will not be taking questions on this issue, either now or in the future." I still waited for the other shoe to drop.

"At this time, I will announce his replacement. The board has officially promoted and appointed as the new principal of Hancock High School…Susan Smith."

I couldn't help it. I gasped in surprise. And I wasn't the only one. Chrissie's eyes opened wide. Dan and Dee Dee broke off their whispered conversation. Bud swore under his breath.

"I'll turn this meeting over to Mrs. Smith at this time," Dalby said. We sat in silence as he limped to the door, again making eye contact with no one.

Looking a little flustered, Susan made her way to the spot just vacated by Dalby. She cleared her throat and said, "This all comes as a surprise to me too. It wasn't until late yesterday afternoon that I received the call from Mr. Dalby informing me that the board had voted to appoint me principal.

"To be honest, I'm still getting used to the idea. After we get back from Thanksgiving break, I will call another meeting to discuss specifics with you. I plan to make some changes that I think we all agree are needed. But I don't want to rush into anything. That's all for now, except that I need to meet briefly with the English department in my room."

Only the English teachers got up to leave. The others

seemed content to spend a little more time sitting and letting the changes sink in. As I stood to leave, Chrissie tugged on my sleeve and whispered, "Call me."

———

Our department moved through the hall in a group, but we were lost in our individual thoughts. Susan was principal? Our Susan? I didn't even know how I felt about that.

Sarah was waiting for us in Susan's room. We pulled student desks into a circle—a smaller circle. No Sadie. And soon no Susan—at least not in our department.

She looked tired. Becoming principal should have been a huge moment for Susan, whose career was her entire life. But at that moment, she looked like she was carrying the weight of the world.

"If I ever start to do anything dumb, remind me I do not want to be an administrator," Bud said quietly, while Susan walked over to the door to have a word with Brenda, now her secretary. The others in the circle heard Bud, smiled, and nodded.

"Okay, let's get started," Susan said as she joined us. "First of all, I apologize for not giving you my news when I made the calls last night. I was led to believe that it would not be announced until Monday because George would be running the meeting today so he could say his goodbyes. I'm not sure when or why things changed.

"That said, I'm sure you have a lot of questions, which I will answer. But first let me discuss the uppermost thing on my mind, leadership of this department. I think it's obvious that I cannot do justice to either job if I try to be both principal and department chair. So I will be relinquishing some of my department duties now and the rest of them when a new head is hired."

She paused to wipe a tear, and I caught my breath. That was not like Susan. "I've daydreamed about this moment. And if it ever came, I always envisioned Sadie and Sarah sharing the job as co-chairs. I know neither wanted to do it alone, but I think I could have convinced them to share the position, and I think the department would have done well with them in charge."

Everyone nodded, including Sarah who was fighting back tears.

"I still believe Sarah has earned the right to the position. And that's why I'm happy that she has agreed to help me with it during this transition. Now, I don't mean anything negative with what I'm going to say next. I don't think any of the rest of you are ready to, or interested in, fulfilling the responsibilities of the job. At least, not yet."

Again, we nodded in agreement.

"I think the best long-term option is to bring in someone new. On Monday the administration will begin a search for an experienced English teacher to take over my teaching duties as well as the department chairmanship. For now, Jennifer has agreed to go full time and pick up two of my classes. I'll continue teaching the other two, as well as being principal. This isn't ideal, but I didn't want to bring in another sub while we already have one shaky one. It's not fair to the kids or to you."

"Susan, are you sure you can handle all that?" Dan asked.

"It won't be easy, but I'll do my best. With any luck, it will just be until the beginning of second semester. Looking ahead to next year, I'm hoping to convince the board to hire Julie, who is doing an admirable job student teaching and will graduate in June. I wasn't able to convince Sarah to put off her retirement for one more year, but she has agreed to sub for us next year, so we will have the benefit of her experience in the department. Now are there any other questions at this time?"

We all just sat, pondering the future. Then I said, "I don't think it's that we don't have questions, Susan. I think we need time to sort out our thoughts to even know what to ask."

"Good point, Andrea. Let's call it a day and meet again next week."

Still stunned, each of us congratulated Susan on the way out. I meant it sincerely, convinced that she would be a good principal. Certainly, she would be a big improvement over North.

CHAPTER 37

November 24

I literally ran in my back door. It was later than I had realized, and I still had to call Chrissie and fill her in.

"Hey, you sound out of breath," she said.

"Yeah, I kind of am. I've been hurrying around, but I wanted to tell you about the meeting before I get ready for my date with Tom."

"What did Susan say? Who's going to take over the chairman position?"

"Someone with experience from the outside. I think that will be best. It should have been Sarah, but, considering what she's been through this year, there's no way she could handle it."

"Yeah, you're right. Listen, you can give me the rest of the scoop later. I didn't know you had a date with Tom, so I'm going to let you go get ready. And have a great time."

I changed from my work clothes to the new sweater and pleated skirt I had been saving for a special occasion. It looks good, I thought as I studied myself in the mirror. Only one thing would have made it better. The neckline of the sweater could have been designed specifically for my peace symbol necklace. But it was time I officially gave up hope of finding it.

I brushed out my hair, again promising myself I would never cut it short. It was too much of my personality, like the peace symbol had been. I had just put on my lip gloss when Tom let himself in the back door. "I'm here," I practically sang out. "I'm ready. Where are we going? I'm starved. You won't believe what all happened today."

"Whoa. Slow down, Andie. First things first. He looked into my eyes and gave me a warm, wonderfully long kiss.

When we arrived at the Hancock Inn, the hostess led us to my favorite table, the one in the private nook by the wine cellar. We sipped cabernet while studying the menu.

We took our time over dinner, enjoying each other's company as well as the food. Tom listened with interest while I described the events of the day. "I think they should have made you department head," he said.

"Thank you for the vote of confidence, but I'm not nearly

ready for that. For one thing, Dan and Dee Dee both have several more years of experience than I do."

"Yeah, but I bet neither one wants the job."

"You're probably right. I don't think either could fit it into their schedules. Of course, it should have been Sarah and Sadie doing it together. But the way things worked out… No, I can see why the best permanent solution is to bring in someone new."

While we lingered over a shared slice of cheesecake, we fell into the familiar, teasing banter that I had missed so much the past few months. We talked books and movies and Thanksgiving plans. When I was so full I couldn't swallow another bite, I waited for him to ask for the check. But he didn't.

Instead, he looked me in the eyes and said, "You found the hammer in the mechanical room because Natalie stashed it there the day after the murder. She took it from the woodshop before the board meeting and concealed it in her purse."

"Then the hammers in Cliff's locker?"

"Unrelated. We had hoped they would be significant when we first found them, but they weren't. Cliff came to us shortly before he left town and told us he took them during the strike. He said he took them because 'they were laying out begging to be swiped,' as he put it. He hid them in his locker and they stayed there because he was afraid of getting in trouble when he turned them in."

"So that was all a dead end."

"Yes. But here's how the list of injuries that you found fits in. Sadie kept the list last school year when she had the older Pendling boy, Wayne Jr., in class. She was upset by the way he kept coming to school beaten up and decided to document it. It's just my guess, but she may have taken the issue to North."

I couldn't help interrupting. "And, of course, North didn't have the guts to do anything about it because he was afraid of alienating the parents. But they must have suspected Sadie knew…"

"Yes. In fact, Natalie claims Sadie threatened to come to us with her information. She confronted Natalie the afternoon of the murder. Remember, they were both in the school while the rest of you were outside.

"So that night, Natalie left the board meeting to find a washroom and spotted Sadie going into the lounge. After the meeting, she sent her husband and son home. They had come in separate cars, so that was no problem.

"She stayed behind until everyone left and then came across Sadie in the hall at the top of the stairs. She swears she just wanted to scare her to keep her quiet, but Sadie wouldn't back down, and she paid for it."

I picked up the story from there, watching the pieces fall together as I verbalized them. "And Mrs. Pendling was scabbing, and she had been supervising kids in the cafeteria and knew about the door to the mechanical room.

"After the fire alarm emptied the building that day, she could have hidden the hammer without anyone knowing. She got in either because the door hadn't latched or she had gotten hold of a master key. So Wayne Sr. really didn't have anything to do with the murder, except for beating up his kids, which is what caused the whole thing. And she was never fingerprinted because she wasn't a suspect."

"Right."

"But here's one thing I still don't know: where was Cliff during the time that he was missing?"

"With his uncle in Milwaukee for most of it. It sounds like he was fed up with his old man and took off. He caught the train into the city and then took the north line to Milwaukee. Actually, it was your student, Jack, who tipped us off about that possibility."

There was one more thing I had been wanting to get off my chest. "Tommy, Cliff had some minor injuries too, and I didn't report them. I guess I was afraid to say anything without more proof. But Sadie was so brave…"

He reached across the table and took my hand. "Don't blame yourself, Andie. It sounds like Wayne Jr. was the primary punching bag. From what you've told me, you didn't have nearly as much to go on as Sadie did."

"Yeah, I guess. I still feel bad, though. But why are you telling me all this? It's official police business. It's supposed to be strictly confidential."

Without waiting for his answer, I had another confession to make. "I know I haven't done a good job of showing you that you can trust me. I've continued poking around in the investigation even after telling you that I wouldn't. I'm so sorry. Now that Sarah is in the clear, I promise that I will retire from my sleuthing for good."

"Thank you for that, honey. And here's the other thing: now that our relationship is progressing, we have to be able to trust each other. In my job, I need to know that everything I tell you is confidential. And I do believe that I can trust you."

I heard every word that he said, but my mind kept going back to the first part. "Our relationship is progressing?"

In answer, he smiled and took two small velvet-covered boxes out of his pocket and set them on the table between us.

"Wha-what?"

He didn't answer. Instead he slid off his chair, lowered himself onto one knee, and said, "Andie Jackson, will you marry me?"

"Why are there two—? I mean, yes, Thomas Jefferson. Yes, Andie Jackson will marry you. I can't wait to marry you. But why two boxes?"

"Hmmm. Guess you'll have to open them and find out. This one first." He returned to his seat and pushed one of the identical boxes toward me.

My hands trembled a little as I picked up it up and slowly raised the lid. The ring was gorgeous. "I love it! May I try it on?"

"Of course, you can. It's yours, silly."

I slid on the sparkly diamond solitaire, and it fit perfectly. "How did you know my size?"

"I have my ways. Or should I say that Chrissie does?"

"Chrissie? I just talked to her and she didn't say a thing. So she knew? Just wait till I talk to her."

"Yeah, she knows. And so do your parents. I'm real glad you said yes, since I've already asked your dad for your hand."

"Oh my gosh. For once in my life, I don't know what to say. Well, wait. Yes, I do. What's in the other box? A different ring? I don't need two choices. I love this one. It's perfect."

"So the white gold is okay? I wasn't sure."

"Oh, yes, it's perfect. I never want to take it off. But the other box?"

"Guess you'll have to open that one too and find out."

I was mystified. As I raised the lid, a delicate silver chair began sliding out. I caught it and opened the box fully. There, on a shiny new chain, was my peace symbol.

"Oh, Tommy." My voice was thick with tears. "I didn't think I'd ever have this back. How did you get it?"

"That was Billy. He tried to call you last night to tell you that he'd found it, but you didn't answer. So then he called me, and I took care of having it put on a new chain."

I slid it over my head and adjusted it. I had been right. It was perfect with my sweater. "I'm never taking either of them off ever again. I love them, and I love you, Tommy. I really, really love you."

"Back at ya, Andie. Back at ya. Now where's your calendar? I don't know about you, but I'm not interested in a long engagement."

ACKNOWLEDGMENTS

I would like to thank the following people for their significant contributions to this novel:

- Kelly McNees, of Word Bird Editorial Services, for evaluation and copy editing of my manuscript

- Mark Lobo, of Indepth Graphics & Printing, for designing the covers and interior of this book

- Elizabeth Harmon for manuscript comments and suggestions

- Mike O'Brien (in memoriam) for sharing his memories of the Woodstock Teachers' Confederation strike

- Jim Pearson (in memoriam) for the use of his drawing of Woodstock High School

- Ron Bendis for an insider's tour of little known places in Woodstock High School

- Joe Accardi for sharing his knowledge of the music of 1972

- Olive Stolberg for advice on medical questions and for commenting on an early draft of this novel

Finally, I would like to thank my friends who kept encouraging me to finish this project. The book exists because you refused to let me give up.